BLOOD RAIN

A LOU THORNE THRILLER

KORY M. SHRUM

Copyright © 2023 by Kory M. Shrum
Cover design by Christian Bentulan
Editing by Toby Selwyn

ISBN: 978-1-949577-70-9

AN EXCLUSIVE OFFER FOR YOU

Connecting with my readers is the best part of my job as a writer. One way that I like to connect is by sending 2–3 newsletters a month with a subscribers-only giveaway, free stories from your favorite series, and personal updates (read: pictures of my dog).

When you first sign up for the mailing list, I send you at least three free stories right away. If free stories and exclusive give-aways sound like something you're interested in, please look for the special offer in the back of this book.

Happy reading,

Kory M. Shrum

DEDICATION

For Francis
(1953 – 2023)

*You will be remembered as a kind and adventurous man, who told
great stories. Thank you for raising an amazing woman.*

For Kimberly,
For being the amazing woman in question.

1

Louie Thorne leaned against the bar watching the two women sway on stage. Piper and Dani were singing Benatar's "Hit Me with Your Best Shot," loudly and off-key. Lou guessed that between the two of them, they'd drunk enough to bring down a grown elephant. They were celebrating the announcement of Dani's award. She was to be named Journalist of the Year by the city council.

She'd gotten the phone call that morning, and Piper, being the ever-dutiful girlfriend, had insisted they celebrate. They'd started with the cocktails before lunch and had yet to quit even though it was a Monday night and they both had work in the morning.

Lou had insisted they go to dinner, hoping that would sober them up. She had all but dragged them to The Praline Connection and got them through two courses of red beans and rice, juicy collards, and buttery cornbread. Once they finished the meal and regained a measure of their senses they'd wanted to wander across the street to the karaoke bar, where the drinking recommenced.

Now it was barely eight in the evening and Louie was wondering if she should take them home before they had a chance to really embarrass themselves.

Besides, Lou's feet were beginning to hurt.

One of the many *intensely* annoying things about being seven months pregnant was the way her body ached and protested in ways that it never had before. Lou had been shot, stabbed, cut, punched, kicked, tossed about in a rolling car—and yes, she would come away from those encounters bruised and sore, but she had never felt as physically *miserable* as she had for the past several months.

Her feet swelled. Her back cramped. Her breasts were always tender. She seemed to have a perpetual low-grade headache. Her irritation was a constant companion, an ever-present itch in the back of her mind.

She'd also begun doing something she'd never done in all of her adult life.

She cried. Hard and often. Which for some reason unknown to her made her feel all the more murderous.

"Are those girls your friends?"

Lou turned toward the voice and found a man at her elbow. He pointed his beer bottle at Piper and Dani, who were now rounding out the chorus for a second time. Piper's voice was beginning to crack at the edges. That was only marginally better than Dani, who seemed only to be breathing heavily into her mic.

"Yes." Lou gave the man a direct and unfriendly stare. "Why?"

"No reason." He held up his hands and backed away without further comment.

Lou supposed it was hard to see her pregnant belly in the dark bar. Usually if men noticed her stomach, they stayed clear of her. But with the low lights and her leather jacket, it was mostly hidden.

"No, one more, one more!" Dani whined as the MC tried to take the mic from her. "I want to sing *Whitney*."

At the same moment Lou decided it was *definitely* time to take her friends home, a sharp pull jerked her navel.

The intuitive hit came with a chord of panic, clear and bright.

Someone needed her.

You promised Konstantine you would be safe. It was her dead father's voice in her mind. *You can't run off into the night every time the alarm bell rings.*

I am being careful.

Lou closed her eyes, doing her best to listen to the darkness on the other side of the world. That's when she heard the little girl screaming.

Lou slipped through the darkness.

The New Orleans bar with its flickering lights fell away.

The balmy May evening was replaced by the chill of an early Italian morning.

The singing folded into hysterical tears. Lou had only just materialized onto firm ground when the child ran into her, colliding with her legs.

Lou caught her, staggering back a step.

There was only a moment to process the sight of the man raising a gun and pointing it at Louie's head before she bled through the dark again. If he'd managed to fire any shots, they must have only struck air.

Lou was still holding on to the girl when the villa formed around them.

Konstantine looked up. He was the picture of serenity, a paperback in one hand, a glass of red wine halfway to his lips. His chest bare above black silk pants, tattoos snaking up his arm.

He'd been reading by lamplight, no doubt waiting for Louie to come home.

But when he saw the two of them, he swore.

"*Dio mio*, are you hurt? Are you hurt!" He couldn't keep the fear out of his voice.

He put the wine and book down in a hurry, rising from the bed.

Lou was confused until she looked down and realized the child was covered in blood.

"It's not mine," she said, releasing the girl and taking a step back.

She began running her hands over the girl's body, looking for wounds. But there were no bullet holes, no puncture marks.

That meant the blood was someone else's.

The expression on Konstantine's face folded from fear to recognition. "*Stella? Stella, sei tu?*"

The sobbing girl turned on him. "*Zio Konstantino!*"

Konstantine opened his arms to envelop her, and she crumpled into his embrace.

"You know her?" Louie asked.

"This is Stefano's niece," he said. "Where did you find her?"

"I don't know," Louie said. "I just—I just went. I only had time to take her before the—There was a man."

Louie didn't know how much English the child knew and didn't want to say anything that might upset her more.

Killer. Murderer. Attacker—there were no easy choices.

The girl spoke in a flurry of Italian that Lou didn't understand. "*Sono tutti morti. Gli hanno sparato. Mamma. Papà. Filippo e Gianni.*"

"What happened?" Lou asked.

"Someone killed her family. She says they're all dead," Konstantine said. Lou didn't tell him that she knew enough Italian to recognize *morti*. "It is true? Did no one survive?"

"I didn't see anyone else."

Lou stretched that part of her mind out into the darkness again, searching for any spark of life or connection. *Are her parents alive? Siblings?*

She was met only with silence.

"I don't feel anything," she said. "I can go back."

"Not yet." Konstantine lifted his phone off the side table. After a short pause, into the phone he said, "*Ho bisogno che tu venga. Ora.*"

He ended the call. He held the crying child but was searching Louie's face. "Stefano is coming. We should try to clean her up before he arrives."

Louie understood his rationale but thought it was pointless. Stefano, Konstantine's second-in-command, was no stranger to bloodshed, and the moment he saw his niece there would be no mistaking why Lou had fetched her at all. Putting her in a clean dress or a pretty bow wasn't going to change that.

The only person that might feel better for the efforts was the girl herself, and for Lou, that was enough.

Lou had just finished brushing Stella's wet hair when Stefano walked into the living room fifteen minutes later, his eyes still puffy from sleep, the scent of cigarette smoke hanging about him.

"What's the emergency?" he asked with an air of irritation.

Even though Lou had wiped the blood from her hands and cheeks, his eyes still doubled in size when he saw her brushing Stella's hair.

"*Stella! Santa Madonna! Che è successo?*"

The girl burst into tears again. When Stefano shook her shoulders, Louie pulled her away from him.

"Stop it," Louie said.

"What's happened? *Che cazzo e' successo??*" he demanded.

Louie stood between them. She didn't think Stefano

would hurt the girl, but she also didn't need someone yelling at her after the night she'd had.

"She was the only one alive."

It was impossible for her to follow the flood of Italian that flowed between Konstantine and Stefano. They spoke so quickly and with such passionate fury, Lou wasn't sure where half the words ended and the next began.

Instead, she gathered up the girl and took her to the sofa. She placed one of the pillows under her head and pulled the blanket over her.

She rubbed the girl's back while the tears fell.

"*Riposa. Dormi ora*," Lou said softly. She wasn't great at Italian, but she knew she had enough for this.

Though Lou didn't know how she could fall asleep with Stefano screaming as he was. "I want the fucker *dead*! Whoever it is, I want him fucking—"

"Do you have to do this here? Right now?" Louie nodded toward the girl. "She's been through enough."

"I need to go back. I need to know if my sister lives. If my nephews live."

"I told you—" Louie began.

Stefano bit his fist before shaking it at her. "I need to see them!"

"I'll take you."

"*Amore*—" Konstantine began.

"I'll be careful," Louie said. She knew what his objections would be even before he spoke them. She'd tolerated his pleas for stealth and prudence for months now. They'd been endless since she'd confessed she was pregnant with his child.

"And if Stefano does something stupid, I'll leave him behind," she added.

Stefano waved her words away. "*Andiamo*. Andiamo."

Konstantine took Louie's place on the sofa beside Stella. "Don't let anyone see you."

Louie kissed him, a chaste brushing of the lips. "We won't be gone long."

Stefano pulled the gun from the waistband of his pants, checked that it was loaded and ready, and then reached for Louie's arm. No sooner had he grabbed her elbow did she pull them through the darkness.

The villa fell away. Konstantine's large, worried eyes and the girl's soft crying were replaced by a quiet so complete that it made Louie's stomach turn.

Still, she listened intently to her compass, scanning for danger.

Nothing moved.

Stefano released her, pointing his gun.

Lou stood where she was, still listening, her ears straining for the smallest shift in the atmosphere. The rustle of clothes. Footfall. Someone breathing.

She trusted her compass, but she also didn't want to get caught unawares like she had back in February, when that sick bastard John Gein had managed to take her.

But nothing moved.

Nothing here was alive.

That didn't stop Stefano from moving room to room, checking beds. She kept a polite distance but followed him like a phantom.

There were three bedrooms. In the one closest to the front door, they found the bodies of two boys, no more than four or five years old, so similar in their features that Lou wondered if they had been twins.

Her throat was tight as she pushed the blood-splattered hair back from their foreheads.

The bullet holes in their chests were far too large for bodies so small.

The bedroom at the end of the hall must have been Stella's. It had all the markings of a little girl's room. Pink walls. A desk covered with dolls and half-finished art projects. A backpack lying at the foot of the bed. Lou thought this must have been the room she'd entered earlier.

Had the gunfire woken her? Or had it been the screams of her parents? Her brothers? Had it been their blood on her when Lou discovered her?

Lou made a mental note to come back and gather her belongings. These toys and books. Pictures. Stella was only a little younger than Louie had been when she'd lost her father.

And just like that, Louie's throat was tightening again. Tears pricked her eyes.

God, she would be glad when this fucking pregnancy was over.

She found Stefano on his knees in the third bedroom.

A woman with two gunshot wounds to her chest lay dead in her bed. Her eyes were wide and unseeing, forever fixed on something above her. Blood soaked her clothes and trickled from the corner of her mouth. She couldn't have been more than thirty-five years old, close to Stefano's age.

The man beside her had half his face blown off, his brains thrown across the pillow, the wall, the lampshade.

Stefano kissed his sister's limp hand, tears running from the corners of his eyes.

Lou wasn't sure if he was praying or apologizing, only that Stefano spoke in whispered Italian, his voice quaking.

Looking over the bodies, Lou knew that their deaths had been quick.

Small mercies, she thought. But knew well enough not to say that aloud.

It didn't matter that Lou knew how cruel a killer could be. If the gunman had been so inclined, he could have dragged the children to their mother's feet before executing them before her eyes. They could have raped Stefano's sister, repeatedly, while her husband watched before slitting her throat.

There were a thousand insults and injuries they could have enacted if they'd wanted to send a message.

If there was a message here, Lou didn't see it.

She saw only the work of someone cold, exacting.

In a way, that's worse.

It was the ones who could kill without their emotions getting in the way that were usually the most dangerous.

Their focus was an advantage.

It had been a while since Lou had come across such a killer.

If this was gang violence, then the killer had been in the mafia game for a long time. Long enough to lose their sense of humanity.

She felt her own spine itch with anticipation. She would enjoy hurting a man like that.

It would be a good hunt, she thought.

The baby in her stomach turned, giving her a swift kick in the ribs. She'd been doing that a lot lately.

Lou placed a hand over her stretched skin.

I didn't say I would hunt him, she thought, half believing her unborn daughter could hear her thoughts. *I just think it would be fun.*

Lou lingered in the doorway, giving Stefano his space. She knew grief. There were no words, no shallow reassurances, that would make this situation better.

When her own parents had been executed by the Martinelli family, she'd heard many empty platitudes.

They're in a better place.

Time heals all wounds.

Everything is going to be okay.

Each condolence had been more infuriating than the last.

The only peace Lou had found had come after she'd avenged them.

No, Louie wouldn't offer empty words now.

Finally Stefano rose, wiping his nose on his sleeve. He looked to Lou with large wet eyes.

"I don't want to leave them here," he said. "I can't leave them like this."

"We don't have to," Lou said. "But we can't take them to the villa. Stella doesn't need to see that."

"We have an *impresa funebre*," Stefano said, pulling his cell phone from his pocket. "We will take them there. Let me— let me make a call."

Stefano pushed past her out into the hallway. Alone in the room, Lou went to the bedside, leaning over his sister's body for a better look.

I hope you died first.

The best-case scenario was that she went quickly and there hadn't been any time to even consider the fates of her children.

But if the boys had gone first—

Lou's chest clenched as cold anger simmered.

"They'll get what they deserve," she whispered. "That's a promise."

She was about to reach over and close the woman's eyes when she saw something in her hand. It was partially hidden by the blanket.

Lou pulled the sheet back and discovered the phone was open on a contact page, a bloody thumb still pressed to the screen.

It was Stefano's number.

Lou cleared the log and returned the phone to its home screen—a wallpaper showcasing the smiling family of five.

She was still looking at those bright smiles when Stefano came into the room again, his cheeks and nose red.

"They are ready for us. We can bring the bodies now."

Louie offered him the phone, watched him go through the call log and photos before giving an unsatisfied sigh.

I won't tell him, she decided.

Because Lou thought there were likely only two possible reasons for Stefano's number being on the screen.

Either she'd tried to call him for help before she was killed, or the killer had tried to make her and she'd refused—and now she was dead for it.

In either case, knowing such a thing would only torment Stefano. He didn't need to hear about her agony. Nor did he need to spend the rest of his life wondering if he'd just been quicker, maybe he could've saved their lives.

That was the kind of thought that could haunt someone. Consume the heart and the mind.

No, he didn't need that.

It was a pain that Louie knew all too well.

2

R obert King thanked the waitress as she refilled his coffee for the second time.

He's late.

Lifting the ceramic cup to his lips, he looked out the large glass window at the street for the hundredth time. His good friend Dick White, the lead investigator at their local precinct, was supposed to meet him twenty minutes ago. King had expected to wait, sure. He was early to appointments as a rule. But so was White.

He'd never been late before.

King was starting to wonder if he should cave and order the breakfast platter. Sitting here smelling fried potatoes and greasy bacon for half an hour was getting to him. His stomach rumbled.

King took out his phone, checked the time, and called White. It went straight to voice mail.

A pang of worry crept in.

It was alleviated eight minutes later when White's SUV pulled up to the curb. He didn't get out immediately and King wondered if maybe he was on a call.

If he had been, it wasn't a good one. White's brow was still creased as he crossed the street and slipped into the diner.

He spotted King easily and slid into the booth, taking the bench seat opposite him.

"I'm sorry I'm late," Dick said. He pulled a handkerchief from his pocket and began to dab his damp brow.

It was true that the temperature was creeping up. May was starting to feel less like spring and more like summer by the day. But King didn't think that the early-morning temperature could earn a man a damp brow.

"Is everything okay?" King asked. His nagging worry was morphing into real concern.

"No," White said, opening his briefcase. He'd half removed a file folder when the waitress appeared.

King didn't miss how quickly the folder disappeared back into the case again.

"What can I get you, honey?" the waitress asked, before popping her gum. "Coffee?"

"No, not today. Water. Just a glass of water."

When the woman looked affronted, no doubt doing the tip math in her head, King decided on the breakfast after all.

"I'll have the breakfast platter," he said. "Eggs sunny side up, rye toast, and house potatoes."

There. The tension in her face evened out.

"You sure you're not hungry?" King asked, returning his attention to White. "My treat."

White only shook his head, dabbing at his brow again.

The waitress seemed to sense something was up, too. "I'll get you that water, honey. And your breakfast will be right out."

As soon as she was gone, King whispered, "What's going on?"

"I have a problem. A huge problem, Robbie, and I need your help."

It wasn't that White was a proud man. They'd grown close in the years since King had moved to New Orleans. He'd been an adamant supporter of King as he'd adjusted to civilian life after decades with the DEA. He was the first to recommend King when the department needed an extra pair of hands with a case, and he'd always been an honest and straightforward man in their dealings.

But never in their years together had King seen him like this.

"Your kids okay?" King asked. "Your wife?"

"It's not the family. Thank God for that, but if I don't solve this, I'm likely to lock them in the house for the next twenty years. Or hell, move them out of NOLA altogether."

Solve this.

"Just tell me what we're dealing with," King said, returning his coffee mug to its saucer. "You know I'll help you however I can."

"Before I tell you—"

The waitress came back with the water.

"Anything else?" she asked.

"No, thank you." Dick took the glass and drank half of it in one go.

The waitress raised a brow. "I'll bring you the pitcher, honey."

"Thank you." King forced a strained smile. The silence buzzed between them until they were alone again.

White looked around the diner one more time before leaning forward and saying, "I was late because I spent twenty minutes driving around trying to spot my tail."

"A tail?" King kept his voice low, too, though the only other patrons in the diner were on the other side of the room and had arrived long before King himself, so it was unlikely that they were spies. "You think you have a tail? Why?"

White wiped his sweaty palms on his thighs. "I have something worse than a tail."

"Walk me through this," King said. "Start from the beginning."

Because King was confused. He didn't want the information piecemeal if he was to make sense of what Dick was saying.

"We have a bomber. Here in New Orleans," White said. He tapped his index finger on the table for emphasis. "A bomber. In *this* city."

"If you've got a bomber then you need to call the FBI," King said. "Or hell, Homeland Security."

Because while there were C-IED courses from the Office of Bombing Prevention, neither he nor White had been trained for bombs and King knew it.

"NTAS overtook Homeland Security's responsibility in that area, but I can't get either to take me seriously," White said.

King leaned back in the booth. "What do you mean?"

"Both agencies asked me what evidence I had, and when I turned it over, there was silence. Two *months* of silence."

"What evidence did you give them?"

"The letters. The bomber sent three letters. Creepy shit. Well, *four* now. But they don't care. They won't even return my calls."

King wasn't sure that a few letters would be enough to get the FBI or Homeland Security to move on a situation. But he also wasn't clear on why White was so convinced he had a bomber on his hands. He didn't want to cast doubt on the man's professional opinion, especially not when he was clearly very agitated.

"And you think this guy is following you around? Stalking you? That the tail and the bomber are the same person?"

"Yes," White said. "And the bastard has my cell number."

"What does he say?" King asked.

The waitress came and put King's breakfast platter on the table. After accepting a bottle of hot sauce and the pitcher of water for White, he thanked her.

"Sure thing, sugar. Holler if you need anything else."

White watched her leave before saying, "Nothing. He just breathes into the phone. Calls me night and day and *breathes*."

"How many calls are we talking about here?"

"Every other day or two for the last two weeks."

Hell. No wonder White was losing his mind.

"Have you tried to trace the call?" he asked.

"Blocked number, and he doesn't stay on long enough to be traced."

King poured hot sauce on the eggs. Piper crossed his mind while he did it, considering she was the one who taught him to eat this way.

"What do the letters say?" King asked, returning the hot sauce to the table and grabbing his fork.

Dick reached for his briefcase and opened it under the table. After a moment of shuffling, he slid a manila folder across the table to King.

"These are only photocopies, of course," White said, casting a nervous look around the restaurant again. "I've got copies locked in my safe at home. The FBI kept the originals of the first two, but they never saw the third or fourth letters."

King opened the folder. The letters used to craft the message had been cut from magazines and arranged in a chaotic fashion.

No eye has seen, no ear has heard, and no mind has imagined what God has prepared.

King read the words again, aloud, and raised his brows. "Ominous."

"It's a partial Bible verse from 1 Corinthians," White said.

King had never liked religious fanatics. Cases where God was involved were always unpredictable. The perpetrators usually followed unspoken rules that didn't always align with logic or reason, and it took time to figure out what those rules and beliefs were. Time that investigators like King didn't usually have to waste.

"It's definitely weird, but it doesn't scream bomber," he said.

White motioned for him to turn the page. "Look at the next one."

King pulled out the next letter. There were no cutout letters on this page. Only faces.

King didn't recognize most of them on the first half of the page. Then he spotted two familiar faces near the center. Dzhokhar and Tamerlan Tsarnaev. The brothers responsible for the Boston Marathon bombing. And here was another familiar face, Cesar Altieri Sayoc Jr., the would-be bomber who sent twelve pipe bombs in the mail to a bunch of politicians—and oddly, one actor—a few years ago.

"They're all bombers," White said. "I had to look half of them up."

At the bottom of the page, beneath the faces, there was a typed quote.

"Nothing but courage can guide life," King read aloud.

"The quote's by some French guy from the seventeen hundreds," White said. "And that looks like it was written on a typewriter, right?"

It did. Though King wondered if it was by the same person. Why use cutout magazine letters and then go through the trouble of typing a quote?

For the third and fourth letters he—if it was a he—was back to the magazine cutouts.

Soon it will be our time together, Detective White. Be ready for me.

"Were you able to pull any prints?" King asked.

"None. I thought I might have had a partial on the envelope, but it was inconclusive. I still ran it three times."

"And the agencies did nothing?"

"Not a damn thing. I even went over to the FBI office near Leon, and they brushed me off. They said there wasn't enough to move an investigation forward and that I should let them know if I have anything *of substance*." White slammed his fist on the table. King's plate jumped.

"Substance! Like a fucking dead body?"

"I hear you." King held up a hand. "Keep your voice down."

"I'm sorry." White refilled his empty water glass from the pitcher. "I'm just frustrated. I feel like this guy is taunting me."

And it looks like it's working, King thought. Because it wasn't like White to lose his cool. Once White seemed to get himself under control, King said, "Tell me what you want me to do."

"I was only able to get one thing from the letter. The stationery. Did you notice?"

King looked at the pages again, holding them up to the light. "This is the stationery from your precinct."

"It sure as hell is." White looked more exhausted than King had ever seen him. "Which means the prime suspects are people from my own fucking department. It could be a cop who wrote those letters."

King's heart sank. "You think someone's gone rogue?"

"Our stationery comes from a local manufacturer. Pelican Paper. You could go speak to them and see if there's a possibility that someone else could get ahold of that stationery. The bomber might be working at the paper factory for all we know, but I doubt it. My gut says it's someone from the precinct."

If that was the truth, no wonder White was jumpy. Cops needed to trust their partners, their coworkers. They were the people who kept them safe in dangerous situations. No one could focus on the job if they also had one eye open for a possible knife in the back.

White pressed on. "I'm the target. Whoever has an issue, has an issue with *me*. And plenty of people at the precinct fit that description."

He counted off the reasons for his suspicions on his fingers. "Anyone in that building can get access to the stationery. Anyone in that building has access to my desk, which is where I find each letter, and anyone in that building can get my cell phone number if they ask reception. And many would know how to clean off prints."

King couldn't argue otherwise.

Did he believe that a cop could go rogue? Absolutely. King's own partner, Chaz Brasso, had tried to kill him. King had gotten too close to uncovering his dirty dealings with Senator Ryanson. If not for Louie's intervention, King would have one of Brasso's bullets in his head now.

Decades of partnership had meant nothing in the end.

But what if White was right? What if there was a bomber in New Orleans?

Then King had a different problem.

It was the fact that the last time King had faced a bomber, he'd almost died.

The Channing Incident.

Eleven officers went into a building to collect the perp, Montgomery Channing, only to have the building blown apart on top of them. King's body had been pinned beneath concrete bricks for days. With plaster dust on his lips, he'd lain in the dark, praying, thinking that it was the end. When the rescue team finally dug him out, King had thought he was dreaming.

He'd been the only one of the eleven officers who'd gone into the building to make it out alive.

White must have sensed his reservation. "I need your help on this, Robbie. Please. I can't trust my own people and I don't want anyone to get hurt. I need someone to help me figure this out."

King knew he should say no. He wasn't trained for this. He had no bomb squad experience. He was just one man. But he also hated to let down a friend who was so obviously at the end of his rope.

King looked at the letters again. At row after row of faces in the grid-shaped pattern. There had to be at least fifty pairs of eyes staring back at him. Maybe more.

"I'll help you," King said finally, though his instincts were ringing like an alarm bell inside him. "Don't worry. We'll figure this out."

3

Piper Genereux was face down on the desk, slipping in and out of sleep, when she heard the bell above the door ring at the Crescent City Detective Agency. Her head snapped up.

It was King, coming in with a bag of fresh beignets, the bag greasy from oil. He placed a to-go cup of coffee on the edge of her desk.

She rubbed her eyes. "What time is it?"

"Almost noon," he said. "I came through here an hour ago and you didn't even hear me."

"I'm sorry, boss," Piper said, slapping her cheeks. "We drank too much last night."

She took a sip of the coffee and choked.

"It's black," he said with a snort. "I thought it would help with the hangover."

"How did you know I have a hangover? I just now told you I'd been drinking."

"I used to be an alcoholic," he said, coming around his own desk and taking a seat. "You think I can't smell it on you?"

Fair enough.

You can't con a conman.

Wasn't that what her dad had used to say?

"I gotta ask. I'd be an irresponsible friend if I didn't," he said. "*Are* you an alcoholic? Because I know someone if you need to talk. And those twelve steps are pretty good."

"I am *not*," she said. "But I guess that's what a boozer would say."

"True."

"Last night was the first time I'd gotten drunk in ages," she said. "I only had one cocktail and it hit me hard."

These were half-truths. In reality it had been three glasses of wine and a cocktail that had sent her up onto the karaoke stage. But it was equally true that she didn't drink a fraction of the alcohol that she used to. In the past, she would have started pre-gaming with Henry at eight, before hitting the bars at eleven. They'd drink through the night before getting up early enough to open Melandra's shop with minimal side effects.

Now she *looked* at alcohol and she felt tipsy. She wasn't sure if that's what happened when you got *old*.

After all, she was twenty-seven now. Practically geriatric.

"Don't worry about me, boss," Piper said, stuffing a beignet into each cheek. "We were just celebrating Dani's big win."

"When is the award ceremony?" King asked, opening his laptop and powering it on.

"Friday. She's very excited."

"Good. She deserves the recognition. She's a great journalist."

Piper was sure her chest would have puffed with pride if it hadn't been for the migraine assaulting the back of her eyeballs. The beignets were helping her acidic stomach, at least.

Marginally.

King put a folder in her hands. She tried to knock the sugar off her fingers before taking it and was only partially successful. "What's this?"

"Our top-secret mission," he said, returning to his seat. "We aren't to speak to anyone about it. Do you understand?"

"Talk about what?" Piper asked, pushing the beignet bag to the side of her desk. She took another sip of coffee and grimaced again.

"Good. Those are your copies. Don't show them to anyone except Lou and Dani."

"Roger that. But, uh, what am I keeping secret exactly?"

"White thinks New Orleans has a bomber. This bomber might even be a cop at his precinct."

That was sobering. "Holy shit. A bomber cop? They would make a scary-good bomb, wouldn't they? With all that cop stuff in their head?"

"Not necessarily," King said hopefully. "It depends on their background."

Piper opened the folder and found four sheets of paper. She wasn't sure if it was the hangover or just her own ignorance about crazy people who want to blow things up, but what she saw inside didn't amount to much.

"What am I looking at?" she asked.

"Letters the bomber sent to White. It seems like he's fixated on him."

"Why?" Piper asked.

"I've got some theories. But none that I'm impressed with," King said, leaning back in his chair, his brow pinched in concentration.

"Let's hear them."

"Either it's an empty threat and someone is just screwing with White because of some unspoken grievance, or it's a legitimate threat."

"That's definitely the first question we have to answer," Piper said. "And?"

"I'm leaning toward legitimate threat because White is genuinely rattled. He's not a reactive guy. Plenty of people have threatened him in the past. Convicts, defendants. But there's something about this that's getting under his skin. Either he's withholding something that he doesn't want me to know or he's just acting out of instinct. Both cases merit the same response from us."

"Okay. Let's say we do have a *for-real* bomber on our hands. What exactly are we supposed to do about that?"

"If it's someone in the precinct, it's possible they might try to detonate a bomb just to tarnish his reputation. If it got out that White failed to stop a bomber that he knew about, he might be pressured to resign. That's the only motivation that remotely makes sense to me right now."

"Other possibilities?" Piper was pushing him to do the thinking because she sure as hell wasn't going to put two thoughts together right now.

"It's possible the bomber isn't affiliated with the precinct at all, but is someone who is hoping White assumes they are, based on the clues they're leaving. In that case we're dealing with misdirection."

"What's our first move then?"

"I want to check out the paper factory and see who has access to that stationery. I also want to see if we have anyone in the area with a history that might suggest *bombmaker*."

Piper snorted. And immediately regretted doing so. It felt like someone had taken an icepick to her face. Under her breath she began to promise all the gods and goddesses in the universe that she would never drink again if someone would just take the pain away.

"What was that?" King asked, interrupting her pleas. "I didn't catch that."

"Nothing, just thinking aloud," she said. "What do you want me to do? Get you an appointment with the manufacturer? I bet Dani can get us a good list of people with the right kind of criminal history."

King was nodding as if he'd already thought of this. "Yeah, it's a good place to start. I'm hoping it's someone at the paper factory, to be honest. Because if it's someone at the precinct, it's going to get tricky."

Piper shoved another beignet into her mouth and sucked the sugar off her fingers. "What do you mean?"

"We'll have to figure out how to interview everyone without pissing them off. A chunk of our work comes from that precinct. If we treat them like criminals, they're not going to rush into our arms the next time they need help with a case. There's a risk we'll burn a bridge and hurt our agency if we don't handle it well."

Piper saw his point, secretly loving his use of *our* agency. "Maybe we can use something like Johnny and the Watering Hole."

King snorted. "That's for hostage situations. Not for interrogations."

Piper wasn't sure she saw much difference. But she could also admit she loved the idea of using their secret code during a case. Almost as much as hearing *our* agency. Even if it was only in the spirit of camaraderie that he said it.

She'd been itching to use the secret code ever since he'd taught it to her two months ago.

If either of them was in trouble but couldn't *say* they were in trouble, then they were supposed to use the code.

And Piper was convinced that using it in a case would be the most exciting moment of her life.

"I considered asking Lou to use her compass to find our suspect," King said.

Piper was pulled from her private-eye fantasies. "Nope. No way. Can't let you do that."

"Why not?"

Piper held up her hand. "We talked about this. We have to be careful about what we ask her for. Did you already forget about the rescue mission we had to launch back in February just to get her out of that freaking torture room?"

"We can ask her to do a little recon," King said. "A quick pop in and out. Maybe she can get us a face or a name. A picture."

"She's not invincible! She's hella pregnant and she's not faster than a bomb. What if you send her after this weirdo and there's a trip wire or something and *kaboom*."

Piper was still shaken by Lou's capture. Granted that sociopath had used Lou's one weakness against her—kids— but it still reminded Piper that her best friend in the world, bad ass as she might be, was *not* immortal.

Piper hadn't even seen the torture room itself, only the damage it had left on Louie's body.

That had been enough.

Man, what she wouldn't give to get her hands on that asshole Gein. She had a few torture ideas for that sicko.

"Look, I'd be an irresponsible aunt if I asked her to put my niecelette in danger for something we can *absolutely* one hundred percent figure out ourselves."

Piper stuffed another beignet in her cheeks.

King smiled at her. "Niecelette. That's cute. Lucy would've liked that."

"Of course it is."

King sat up. "Fine. We won't lean on Lou unless we need her. But that means we also have to be careful ourselves. We both know she'll be the first one to come after us if we get into trouble."

4

Lou watched Stefano collapse into the chair opposite Konstantine's desk, his sister's blood drying on his clothes. Konstantine's hands were folded as if in prayer in front of him. More than once, Louie saw him open his mouth as if he wanted to say something to Stefano, only to close it again.

There are no words, Louie thought. And Konstantine seemed to know this, too.

After all, his own mother had been shot before his eyes. There wasn't a person in this room who hadn't known grief and loss at the hands of gang violence.

Sensing that Stefano wanted to speak to Konstantine alone, Lou turned to go.

"*Amore mio*," Konstantine called.

"I'll be back," she promised, and closed the door behind her.

She wanted to check on the girl. That morning they'd entrusted Stella to the care of Matilda, the young woman who kept an eye on all the children who lived in the church.

Louie found her in the children's dormitory, curled on the cot, fresh tears staining her cheeks.

Matteo and Gabriella sat on the opposite bed, speaking to her softly in Italian.

Louie had been honest with them about what had happened to Stella's family. There was no need to protect these kids from the knowledge of what kind of monsters were in the world. They'd met the monsters firsthand—that was how they'd come to be in Konstantine's care to begin with.

Lou leaned against the doorway and watched them for a few minutes.

Despite their best efforts, Stella refused to get up from her little cot, no matter what toy, sweet, or adventure the children offered her.

"She is too sad," Matteo said, searching Louie's face with pleading eyes.

"Give her time," Louie said, placing a hand on his soft hair. "Just look after her until she feels better. She needs time."

"Yes. Okay, *Strega*."

Louie gave Gabriella's shoulder a squeeze and left the room.

Satisfied that Stella wasn't in any immediate danger, she'd walked through the cool halls of the Florentine church, her fingers trailing along the old stone walls. She paused in the cathedral and regarded the statue of Mary, arms open to receive her.

It was strange to walk about the church in this way, when she was so used to simply appearing where she wanted.

Sometimes it's nice to fill in the gaps, her aunt Lucy used to say, when she was still alive.

She mostly said it when Lou complained about walking, knowing full well they could simply travel by their own special means.

A pang of distress tugged at Louie's compass and she found herself following it to the courtyard outside of Konstantine's office. As soon as she reached his door, she knew it was their argument which had drawn her.

They were yelling.

Stefano's voice was loudest. "I ask you for nothing! Nothing, *fratello*. But my sister and her children are *dead* at the *impresa funebre* and—"

His voice cracked, faltering.

Lou went to the door and hesitated, wondering if she should open it or not.

"I have to know who is responsible. I *have* to know who killed them and if you will not send her—"

Her. They had to be talking about Louie.

Konstantine's voice rumbled in return, but it was too low for Louie to make out the response. She was certain only that it was some sort of refusal. Why else would Stefano be so angry?

Louie opened the door. The first thing that struck her was Konstantine's face.

His eyes were red and jaw tight.

Stefano's back was to her, so she could not see his face. But his shoulders shook.

"I'll go," she told them plainly.

"*Amore mio*, it's not safe."

"I won't be seen."

Konstantine came around the desk and placed a hand on her stomach. "We promised."

"I won't be seen," she said again. "I'll wait until it's dark. Night will be on my side. I'll be silent, and quick."

Of course Konstantine didn't believe her. "You won't take him to that lake of yours?"

"It's not my kill," she said. And it wasn't. The one who deserved to end that man's life was Stefano.

Stefano put his hands together as if in prayer. "*Strega*, I just need a name. Tell me who did this and I will end him. *Per favore*."

"What if he isn't alone?" Konstantine spoke to Stefano, his face still pinched with concern. "You can't face him alone, Stefano."

"Then I'll take others. Rocco. Carlo. Andrea." Stefano turned back to Louie. "But first I need to know who did this."

Konstantine wouldn't let go of her belly. She put a hand over his.

"I'll be careful," she told him. How many times in the last few months had she had to make that promise over and over again? It was like he couldn't hear it enough. Louie tried to be patient with him, but there was still a part of her that was more than a little insulted that he thought she wouldn't do everything she could to keep their daughter safe.

Finally he released her. "Please wait until it's dark."

Lou stepped away from him. "I will."

Stefano visibly relaxed. "Thank you, *Strega*."

"Don't thank me yet," she said. "I haven't delivered what you want."

"But you will," he said. "You will."

AFTER PASSING THE MORNING AT THE CHURCH, LOU returned to the villa. Konstantine had promised to go to the *impresa funebre* with Stefano to sort out the details of the entombment. Lou knew only that Stefano's family had a mausoleum somewhere on the west side of the city and that they would be moved there once the rest of his relatives were contacted and the arrangements were made.

Lou had left them to it, choosing instead to find a place to rest. She had never been a napper, but her pregnancy had changed that. Sometimes her feet were so swollen by the early afternoon that she found herself resting for the pure relief of being off them for an hour.

She'd already had to buy boots a size larger than usual, but at least she could still lace them herself. There was something delicious about sitting down and feeling the muscles along her spine release.

Almost as soon as Louie stretched long on their bed, she fell asleep.

She slept harder than she'd meant to and woke to darkness pressing itself against the windows of the balcony. Shadows had collected in the corners of the room, framing a patch of moonlight on the floor. A small gray form washed her paws on the foot of the bed.

Octavia, the British Blue, regarded Lou with accusatory eyes, as if it were Lou's fault that Konstantine wasn't home to give her the love she deserved.

He was her favorite, by far, but on rare occasions, she would lie next to Louie like this.

"He'll be home soon," Louie said, pushing herself to sitting. Her back protested and her face felt puffy with sleep. But she was up.

In the kitchen, she found a meal waiting for her.

Amatriciana with copious amounts of parmesan. A fish with a side of mixed vegetables.

He'd been home then, after the *impresa funebre*, but hadn't wanted to wake her.

Considerate.

Beside the pasta was a small box and a note.

"Use these," she read aloud. "Press the button on the side and it will record for up to one hour."

She opened the box and immediately recognized the glasses. They were the ones Konstantine had worn when they'd been trying to identify the two children who'd escaped Gein. When they'd refused to tell her who they were, she'd enlisted Konstantine's help. He'd used these same glasses to get the footage he needed to identify them.

She put the glasses back in the box just as the baby kicked her in the ribs. "It will be difficult to eat if you keep doing that."

Lou pressed a hand against her belly until the pain subsided.

Then she ate her fill of the pasta, half of the fish, and chased it all with half a bottle of water before changing into clean black clothes. She pulled her hair back from her face and secured it with an elastic. She decided on her twin Berettas, and though she intended to go unseen as she'd promised, she knew that things happened. It was better to have a gun should she find herself in a tight spot.

She could still pull guns from her shoulder holster as long as her breasts weren't feeling especially tender. The only difference she'd noted so far was a notably slower pull time from her hips. She suspected it was reaching across her abdomen that was slowing her down.

But it doesn't matter because I won't need them, she told herself. And yet here she was strapping a bulletproof vest across her chest. It wasn't her father's, which she considered her lucky charm. It was the Level IV piece of armor that Konstantine had bought her the day after finding out she was pregnant.

After strapping the vest into place, she was ready.

She took one last look around the dark villa, absorbing its silence in contrast to the city waking up around them. Then she went to the empty closet and shut herself up inside, her back pressed against the wall. The darkness was absolute.

She slipped the glasses onto her face and waited.

She forced herself to concentrate on her inner compass, tuning out the growing buzz of Florence.

Slowly, the rumble of passing cars and laughter died away,

and Lou caught the sound of something else. A tapping. What was the material? Plastic? She cocked her head as if this would make the sound stronger.

Where is he? she asked her compass. *The one who killed them—*

A face sharpened in her mind's eye and Lou reached up and pressed the button on the side of the glasses. A small light appeared on the inside of the frame, a counter ticking off the seconds as they passed.

Then the darkness swallowed her whole. The wall at her back fell away and she found herself in a room many degrees warmer.

A group of men sat around a table. All but one had dark hair slicked back from their faces. They wore dark t-shirts, their arms bare. The first thing Lou noticed were the matching tattoos.

Konstantine and the other Ravengers had ravens on their arms. In contrast, these men bore a wolf's head on the upper bicep, its mouth clamped around a chunk of bloody meat, suggesting a successful hunt.

She recognized this tattoo from her many years of hunting mafia.

The Celesti, she thought. The Naples crime family.

A man threw his cards on the table and swore. The opponent across the table from him gathered the pile of cash and pulled it toward him, laughing.

Lou tried to get steady footage of each man's face, turning her head slowly for the best angle.

But even as she did, she knew the one she was looking for wasn't among them. The eight men around the table were new to her. None of them had raised the gun at Stella the moment before Lou had carried her to safety.

Where are you? she thought. *Where the hell are you?*

Her compass insisted that the one she was looking for was

here. Right here. But she did not recognize any of these faces.
It tugged slightly to her right, but there was nothing there,
only more of the darkness she hid in.

Lou was tempted to slide along the wall and try for a
different angle. Maybe she would get better photos of some
of the faces. But she knew her stillness was giving her the
advantage. She could watch the small party from the dark
corner without them knowing she was so close.

Close enough to smell their mixture of cologne, after-
shave, and body odor.

Close enough to see the sweat forming on an upper brow.

Close enough to see a shaving nick on a check. Scars
across the knuckles.

Close enough to pull a gun and blow out their brains
before they ever knew what hit them.

Her skin itched with the possibility.

Not mine, she had to remind herself. *Not my kill.*

Something caught the corner of her eye. It was the
slightest of movements, and for a moment Louie hadn't been
sure she'd seen it at all.

But there it was again. A flash of something metal in darkness to her right.

At the same moment her compass pulled, snagging
through her navel.

"Smettila di dire stronzate, Modesto! La Strega non *esiste*."
The one who lost the game spoke with irritation.

"*La Strega*," the man folding his newfound wins into neat
stacks said. "*Una favola per bambini.*"

"*Lo penserai finché non ti ammazza,*" a low voice said.

A very *close* voice.

A man not three feet from her right shoulder stepped into
the light. No wonder the compass hadn't been clearer. She'd
practically been on top of him.

He's been waiting for me. Waiting in the dark, she thought.

Lou kept her GPS watch covered as she dropped a pin, marking the location of the killer. She did not need to see his face to know he was the one she was searching for. Her compass told her so. No sooner did she finish the task than the baby kicked Lou roughly in the ribs and a small grunt escaped her lips before she could stop herself.

The man turned, his eyes fixing on her in an instant.

It *was* the face she remembered from Stella's bedroom.

He wore the same cold expression as he lifted the gun for a second time, pointing it where she stood hidden.

Lou bled through the dark. The safety of her villa closet enveloped her. She ran a hand over the unmarred vest.

She stood breathless in the dark, holding her aching ribs. She struggled to slow her heartbeat.

"Jesus, kid," she said, touching her sore ribs. "You have terrible timing."

The closet door opened. Konstantine had a toothbrush tucked into one of his cheeks.

"*Amore mio?* What's happened?"

There were many things she could have said.

Your daughter is trying to murder me with her feet.

I was too close to him. I was careful and yet it was still too close.

Instead, she said, "Heartburn."

It was an easy lie. She couldn't admit how close she'd been to the killer, how long she'd stood in the dark beside him without knowing it.

Worse, if Konstantine found out that the killer knew about *her*, that he'd been waiting for *her*—no. Konstantine was already on edge with his hypervigilance. No need to scare him more.

Still, silently, Louie prayed that she wasn't the reason Stefano's family had been killed.

5

King knew something was wrong as soon as he spotted Beth sitting alone at the table.

She was fussing over the salt and pepper shakers, moving them from one side of the floral arrangement to the other, before smoothing her hand repeatedly over the white tablecloth.

After meeting White in the diner two days ago, he was starting to wonder if this was just the week for bad meals.

"Hey." He bent to place a kiss on her cheek before taking his seat.

"Robert," she said with a smile, though King thought that perhaps it was not as wide as it usually was.

Stop, he thought. *You don't always have to play the part of detective. It might not have anything to do with you.*

"Robert, I need to tell you something."

It absolutely has to do with you.

He took hold of his water glass. "I'm listening."

"I submitted my notice this morning. I'm retiring at the end of my term."

This wasn't shocking, given that like King, Beth was in her midsixties. She'd been floating the idea of retirement for a few months now.

"Congratulations," he said. "It was a good run. You should be proud."

She'd worked her way up from assistant DA to DA and had every right to feel accomplished.

"I am," she agreed, and this smile, at least, seemed genuine. And yet it was wilting at the corners. "But you and I both know I could've gone on as DA for another five years or so. There's a reason I decided to quit."

Don't be sick, his mind begged. He'd watched Lucy, the love of his life, wither away from cancer, and it was the hardest thing he'd ever had to do—to watch her go like that.

To *let* her go.

He didn't have the same love for Beth, but that didn't mean he wanted to repeat the experience.

"My son and his wife are pregnant. They've asked me to move to Orlando and help with the baby once it's born. You know childcare is a fortune, and they're both teachers. I've already started looking at condos."

There it was.

"Moving to Orlando was always your plan," he said.

She'd told him early in their relationship—if they could call what they had a relationship—that she planned to move to Orlando to be near her son as soon as her grandchildren arrived.

She visibly relaxed, reaching her hand across the table. "You're not upset?"

"Of course not." He took her hand and squeezed it. "Why did you think I'd be upset?"

"I don't know," she said. "We have a good thing going here."

He rubbed his thumb across her knuckles. "We do."

"And I was worried you might talk me out of going. You could do it, you know."

King wouldn't, of course. Not only because Beth had dreamed of these grandchildren for as long as he'd known her, but he wasn't the sort of person to stand in the way of someone else's ambitions.

Also, while he'd enjoyed his time with Beth, he had not been as enamored with her as he had been with Lucy. He did not care deeply enough for her to ask that she sacrifice a dream.

When Lucy had left him all those years ago, King had wanted to follow her. He wanted to uproot his life and promise her anything, *everything*, if it meant they could stay together. He'd let her go only out of respect for her wishes. The fact that they'd been able to reconnect in the last year of her life had felt like the second chance he'd always wanted, if short-lived.

He had none of that desperate longing with Beth. Maybe that was the kind of love that only came once in a man's life.

"Do you have a moving date?" King asked.

"June fifth. After the school year ends."

"We still have time," King said. "We can make the most of it."

"And that's it?" she said, her eyes showing a tinge of sadness. "*Finito?*"

He brought her hand up to his lips. He wasn't sure what she'd wanted him to say, only that clearly there *was* a desire for something more.

But King wasn't the sort of man who made empty promises. Orlando was over nine hours away. Saying that he would visit seemed out of reach—how often could he reasonably make such a trip?

He drew the line at asking Lou to drop him off for the occasional booty call, though he was sure she would do it.

No. It was best to break this off cleanly. Let Beth go. Let their time together come to its natural end.

And yet—why was she looking at him like that?

King did his best to carry the conversation throughout the meal. He was careful not to act any differently. He said the same sweet platitudes he always did while refilling her wine glass. Complimented her when the opportunity presented itself. He laughed at her jokes, kept his smile bright. But no matter his efforts, he felt he hadn't quite shaken off the cloud hanging over them.

Once King paid the check and they found themselves on the sidewalk outside the restaurant, his mind turned toward work again. To the problem White had dropped in his lap.

"Are you still coming over tomorrow night?" she asked.

"Of course I am," he said, and pulled her to him. "Beth, I meant it when I said we can make the most of the time we've got left."

"I'm just checking." She rested her head on his chest.

Holding her by the shoulders, he pulled her back and forced her to look at him.

"What is it?" he asked. "I'm not a mind reader. You'll have to tell me what you want. You've always been direct with me." *Very direct.* "Don't stop now."

"It's strange," she said. "I thought this would be easy. We both know I've always wanted to be in Orlando. I've carried this vision of raising my grandbabies in my head for so long that I've never questioned it for a minute. But what we've got here—well, that's nice too. It's nicer than I expected to find at my age."

King laughed. "Thanks. I'll take that as a compliment."

"Robert, you know it is."

"I know." He squeezed her again. "But once you're in

Orlando with that baby in your arms, you'll forget all about me."

She snorted. "I doubt that. You're quite the gentleman. I don't think you know how rare they are."

He was flattered, though he didn't believe her. Beth was a charming and beautiful woman. She'd have no problem finding a new partner if that was what she wanted.

She was putting on a brave face now, but King couldn't help but feel that he was disappointing her in some way.

He didn't know what she wanted.

A different reaction? Different words? Empty promises? For him to drop down on one knee and propose here and now?

Whatever it was, he wasn't delivering it.

He took her arm. "Let me walk you to your car."

"It's the opposite direction of your apartment."

"I don't care," he said, holding her close. "I'll walk you all the same."

And he did. Four blocks east and then to the third floor of the parking garage.

He kissed her one more time before holding open her car door. He offered one last wave as she pulled out of the parking space and rounded the corner out of sight.

He took his time walking home. With his hands in his pockets, he retraced his steps out of the parking garage, past the restaurant where he'd just had lunch, and west toward Melandra's Fortunes and Fixes.

As he walked through the French Quarter, the afternoon sun was at its worst. It felt like the back of his neck was blistering before the occult shop came into view. He was sweating even before he reached the horsehead post outside its door.

He spotted Melandra through the large glass windows.

She was bagging candles, books, and incense for a group of young women covered in Mardi Gras beads.

It wasn't Mardi Gras season. There were no parades, or king cake.

But that never stopped the tourists from buying the necklaces and wearing them by the dozen around their throats anyway.

One of the girls was petting Lady, their Belgian Malinois, and her wagging tail was slapping the side of Mel's long skirt.

King was smiling when Mel caught him looking through the glass.

His heart sputtered in his chest.

I'd better get out of this heat, he told himself, placing one hand on the warm metal post, his fingers resting between the ears of the horse's head, checking the bottom of one shoe, then the other.

One could never be too sure when walking the French Quarter streets. Everything from glitter to vomit could be picked up by one's shoes.

King walked up to the door of Fortunes and Fixes at the same moment that the women were leaving. He held the door for them, offering a polite smile as they filed out.

The air conditioning hit his hot skin like a blessing as he crossed the threshold.

He breathed an audible sigh of relief as the door swung closed behind him.

"Is it that bad out there?" Mel asked from behind the counter. "Your face is the color of a beet."

"It's getting there," he said. "Is it even possible this summer might be warmer than last?"

"You never can tell, Mr. King," she said, scribbling something on the notepad in front of her. King assumed it was notes on inventory.

Lady barked, looking up at Mel.

"*Ma grande.*" Mel placed a hand on her chest in mock surprise. "What? What is it? Is it that time already?"

She lifted her phone and checked the clock. "So it is. How could I forget? Mr. King, will you watch the store while I take Lady for a walk?"

"Of course." She didn't really need to ask him and they both knew it. He'd already relieved her of her post a handful of times this week, since both of her part-time girls were on summer vacations with their families.

Piper was supposed to cover several shifts next week as well, which she'd seemed very excited about when Mel had asked.

King would be disappointed when Piper took over after the end of the semester.

He liked having reasons to check on Mel during the day. Any reason at all to drop in unexpectedly just to see her face.

King leaned against the counter, watching Mel put the harness and leash around Lady's lithe form. Not that the dog needed it. She obeyed Mel as if she were God incarnate. But the city had its leash laws. Even so, most of the cops in the Quarter knew Mel and Lady. He doubted a single one of them would give her a citation even if they did see the dog off leash.

Cops in the Quarter.

King's mind turned again to White's bomber. To the feeling of plaster dust on his lips after a building came down on him. To the idea that maybe someone could put a bomb in a building, in *this* building, and bring it down on him and Mel.

His chest compressed unexpectedly.

"Your expression just turned very dark, Mr. King," she said, moving the leash from her left to right hand. "What are you thinking about?"

"I'll tell you later," he said. "Are we still on for tonight?"

"Of course," she said, the look of concern never leaving

her face. "But I'm tired of lasagna. How do you feel about hot wings?"

"I love hot wings. Bayou's Best?"

"You better believe it. And get me an extra cup of that dippin' sauce."

That would be easy enough. He had their menu on his fridge. "I'll pick them up and be at your place at seven."

"Sounds divine."

As Mel walked out into the hot afternoon with Lady at her side, King was struck by how much more excited he was for his evening with Mel than he'd been for his lunch with Beth.

It doesn't mean anything, he told himself. *She's my best friend. It just means I'm looking forward to spending time with my best friend.*

But if that was really all it was, then what about the dreams?

For the last month, King had been plagued by dreams of Mel. Not every night. He was grateful for that. If he'd had the dreams every night he would likely be out of his mind by now.

Still they came. Twice a week? Three nights?

And the dreams were always the same. They started with King and Mel together. Sometimes they were walking through the French Quarter. Sometimes they were on his sofa or hers, watching television and talking as they did most nights in real life.

No matter the initial scene, there was always a moment when the tone changed. Folding from friendly to sexually charged.

Sometimes it was the look she gave him that caused the shift.

Sometimes she would reach over and touch his arm, or

God help him, just above his knee. Whenever this happened, it was like his body came alive with fire.

The longing he felt was so intense that he often woke breathless and erect.

More than once, they'd gone so far as to sleep together in the dream. And the feel of Mel's curves under his hands was *so* crystal clear that he thought maybe he wasn't dreaming at all.

Maybe he was sleepwalking into Mel's bed at night.

"What's wrong with me?" he muttered to the empty store.

He loved her. Without question. She was one of the people he trusted most in this world. They'd almost died together more times than he could count. They'd cleaned blood off each other's faces, tended to each other's wounds.

They lived across the hall from each other, saw each other every day, and often ate together. If something troubled him, she was usually the one he turned to.

Hell, they shared a *dog*.

He would do anything for her.

But was he *in* love with her? In love enough that he would risk ruining their friendship in the simple pursuit of pleasure?

No.

Surely not.

Yet his uncertainty was beginning to feel more and more like a splinter in his mind.

King sank onto the stool behind the counter and watched the people walking past the large glass storefront.

"It doesn't matter," he said to no one. "Now's not the time for anything anyway."

Because he would never make a move while he was still seeing Beth. He'd never been the sort of man to sleep around, even if Beth had never asked him for exclusivity.

He knew dividing his attention between women didn't

make him good company. The only thing that divided his attention was work.

Still, he couldn't help but wonder if Mel was the reason King wasn't so sad about Beth's imminent departure.

Was there a part of himself, no matter how small, that was secretly *glad* Beth was leaving? Did *that* part of him believe that maybe, just *maybe*, her absence might open the way for something more with Mel?

King rubbed the back of his head as if this would clear away his obsessive thoughts.

"Pull yourself together. You're too old to act like this."

King reached out and adjusted the notepad and pen on the countertop, tidying the items before him as if they weren't already in order.

He busied himself with one fidgety task after another until the door opened and the chandelier moaned and flickered. Mel held the door open for the happy dog at her side.

"Anyone come in?" she asked, her face bright. The warm day and quick jaunt around the block had brought color to her dark cheeks.

"Nope," he said, finding he couldn't hold her gaze. "Just me. Here alone."

Why did he feel as if he'd been caught doing something?

I was only thinking. It's not like she can read my thoughts. And I'm never going to tell her about those dreams.

"Okie dokie." Mel's brow was arched. "Thanks for the break. I can take over now if you'd like to get back to the office."

"Sure. Piper's probably wondering where I am," he said, standing and scooting past her. He was doing his best to make sure no part of his body brushed hers. "Alrighty then. I'll see you in a few hours."

"Don't forget about my extra dipping sauce, Mr. King. If I

don't have enough sauce for my wings, it'll ruin my whole night."

"Wouldn't dream of it," he said.

Dreams.

And just like that he stepped out of the store, his ears warming, feeling as if her eyes were burning twin holes in his back.

6

Piper was spending entirely too much time on her outfit. She knew it. Dani knew it. And yet she couldn't find the will to stop herself. Events like this always made her self-conscious. It didn't help that tonight she was coming as the date of the person of honor. All eyes would be on Dani, but more than a few would also be wondering about the woman on her arm.

Given the fact that the whole night was about celebrating how amazing her girlfriend was, there was a part of Piper—a *huge* part—that felt like she'd better measure up. And that part of her was warring with the little voice that lived in her head for the sole purpose of convincing her that *measuring up* was never going to happen.

"Babe," Dani begged. She stood in the doorway of their bedroom, hooking a diamond earring through her ear. "You look amazing, but we *have* to go. I cannot make these people wait on me."

"Are these pants too tight? Are you sure they match the shoes?" Piper turned in front of the full-length mirror. She looked at herself from one angle, then another.

Dani took a steadying breath. Piper heard it even from where she stood. "Piper *Lynn*. I am only going to say this *one* time. You are literally the hottest you've *ever* been in your life. And when we get home after the ceremony, the first thing I'm going to do is tear those clothes off. But I'm going to need you to step away from the mirror and get in the car now. Right *now*."

"But—"

"*Now!*" Dani pulled her away from the mirror.

Piper took one final swipe at her hair before she was dragged from the room.

The car ride was no easier. Dani was a good driver and the traffic was light. Those weren't the problems. The problem was Piper's nerves were still escalating as they navigated away from the French Quarter into the Business District.

They were two blocks from the hotel when Dani reached out and put a hand on Piper's dancing leg. "No one would guess by looking at you that *I'm* the one who has to get up in front of everyone and give a speech tonight."

"I'm sorry. I'm not trying to take away from your moment," Piper said. And she wasn't. She didn't want to make this about her, but the feeling that she was going to embarrass Dani was consuming her, sending her anxiety into overdrive.

"You're not taking anything away from me," Dani said, and gave her knee a squeeze at the red light. "But you really have nothing to worry about. I'm going to walk up there, get my award, say my thank yous. Then it's dinner, a drink or two, and we're out the door. All you have to worry about is the small talk, and you're great at small talk. You talk to a bunch of strangers every single day."

Piper supposed that was true. The skill had been born out of her practice reading tarot cards in Jackson Square. Or perhaps it was running the register at Mel's shop for all those years. Even working as King's assistant investigator required a lot of people skills. Interviewing victims, witnesses, suspects. Coordinating with the police or DA's office. *All* the phone calls.

"I can small talk."

Piper couldn't deny she had a lot of practice talking to people she didn't know.

Dani turned on the blinker. "I promise, we'll be in and out."

"Don't say that," Piper said. "This is your night. We can stay as long as you want. I want you to enjoy it. You deserve to have every single person there tell you how amazing you are at *least* a hundred times each."

This earned her a sweet look from Dani, who put a hand to Piper's cheek in gratitude. Piper pressed a kiss into its palm.

Piper regretted her magnanimous offer to stay as long as she wanted almost as soon as they entered the hotel. It was one of the posh ones downtown with valet parking and everyone in suits and dresses. A woman with perfectly coiffed hair and a metal name tag led them through the lobby to the elevators.

"Your event is in our central ballroom on the tenth floor, and be sure to visit our newly renovated rooftop observation deck before you leave, Ms. Allendale, if you haven't already. The view of the Mississippi from there is just—" The woman punctuated her sentence with a chef's kiss.

They thanked her before the elevator doors closed.

"Ms. Allendale," Piper said. "They must do their home-work for these events if they know you by name."

"Actually, it's my parents that have quite a few business events here. I've met Darla before. Is it bad that I'm relieved they won't be here? My dad would've been fine but my mother, *god*. I'm lucky they'd already committed to the benefit in Atlanta."

Yes, please remind me how connected your family is before we walk into this social hell storm, Piper thought. Then, *No, don't be like that. This is her night. Stay positive. Be cool. And if I can't be cool, I can at least be a good girlfriend.*

"It's not bad. You're allowed to feel however you want, babe. And I'll tell you what's—" Piper mimicked the woman's chef's kiss. "You in that dress. Holy hell. You're sparkling in here."

There. Nailed it.

And Piper was being honest.

She wasn't sure if it was the elevator's soft lighting or the fact that the small space created instant intimacy between them, but Dani's curves were accentuated in that tight dress.

"Was your dress that lowcut when we left the house?" she asked.

Dani rolled her eyes. "Piper. Yes. I've had this dress on for the last hour. You would have noticed if you weren't so busy freaking out."

Piper took an involuntary step toward her. "And you smell so nice."

"Stop it." Blush rose to Dani's cheeks. "We can't do this here."

"The hell we can't," Piper said. "There's an emergency stop button. Where is it? It's with the other buttons, right?"

"Piper, stop! There are security cameras. I'm sure someone is watching us right now."

"If your parents do as much business here as you say, I'm sure good ol' Darla will look the other way."

Piper breathed into the side of Dani's neck before placing a soft kiss on the ridge of her collarbone. Then one after another up the side of her throat, until her lips were firm against the soft plane of bone behind Dani's ear.

Dani slid a hand into Piper's suit jacket and gripped her hip in response. It was a hungry gesture that Piper had gotten to know very well. "Piper, please. I'm begging——"

The elevator door slid open and they were no longer alone.

A tall woman in a stylish pantsuit and heels held a clutch on the other side of the door. Her ensemble screamed cosmopolitan. Piper saw her in the mirror opposite the door first and had to turn to face her directly.

Dani couldn't hide her surprise. "Izzy! I didn't know if you'd be here tonight."

Of course it was Dani's ex. Piper recognized her immediately given how much stalking she'd done of the woman on social media. How could she resist learning all she could about Dani's first girlfriend?

"I wouldn't miss your big night." Izabelle made no attempt to hide her gaze. She looked them both over. "But now I feel like I'm interrupting something."

A nervous laugh escaped Dani as she released Piper's hip. "Better you than someone else."

"They're looking for you. I was just coming down to call you. It's not like you to be late, but I see now why you were dragging your feet."

Izzy gave Piper a nod. "You must be Piper. I've heard about you."

Have you? Piper thought.

"Oh yes, sorry. Izzy, this is Piper. Piper, this is Izzy."

She tried to remember everything Dani had said about her ex.

Izzy and Dani had grown up together on the other side of Lake Pontchartrain and had gone to the same private schools all throughout middle and high school. They'd met riding horses, or some shit that rich girls do.

They'd officially dated from senior year through college,

breaking up because Izzy took a job at the biggest newspaper in New York City upon graduation. She'd wanted Dani to come with her, but Dani hadn't been ready to leave New Orleans behind.

That's what I told her anyway—as she explained it to Piper. Dani had wanted to break up for months before Izzy's move out of state but hadn't had the guts, afraid that it might ruin their friendship if they did.

"Izabelle." Piper extended her hand. "I thought you went back to New York."

"Not until Sunday." Izabelle took Piper's hand and gave it a firm squeeze. Too firm.

How cute. We'll be measuring our dicks next, Piper thought, keeping her smile bright despite the pain in her knuckles.

"I was in town for Meemaw's ninetieth birthday." Izzy turned her attention to Dani, finally releasing Piper's hand. "She missed you at the party."

"I know," Dani said. "I've been crushed by deadlines this week. Did she have a good time?"

They exited the elevator and followed Izzy toward the ballroom's large wooden doors at the end of the opulent hallway.

"She complained about us keeping her up past naptime, but yes, I think so. We let her have whiskey, and that always puts her in a good mood."

Piper pulled open the door.

"Thanks, baby," Dani said, and gave Piper's shoulder a squeeze before crossing the threshold.

"Baby," Izzy said under her breath. "That's adorable. How long have you two been dating again?"

"Two years," Piper said, letting Izzy cross the threshold despite a sudden strong desire to shut the door in her face.

"Two years *officially*," Dani corrected. "I was in love with her before that, but she wouldn't date me right away."

"How could you have possibly resisted? Ah yes, I remember now. Something about you being quite the player." Izzy pointed at a table near the front of the ballroom. "They've seated you over there. Just left of the stage."

Dani slapped Izzy's shoulder lightly. "I never said *player*. I said *popular*. That's totally different."

Izzy arched her brows again and put a hand over her heart. "My apologies. I've no idea how I could have confused the two."

Piper hoped that once they were at the table, the presence of others might tame Izzy's clear attempts to get a rise out of her.

And at first it did. There was the business of introductions, shaking hands, ordering their food. Piper wasn't thrilled that Dani sat between Izzy and herself. If it had been left up to Piper, she would have put her girlfriend on the *other* side, making sure Dani wasn't within reach of the pantsuit pirate.

But despite the irritation nipping at the back of her neck, Piper tried to play it cool. In a way she felt like she had this coming. Dani had had to endure the tyranny of Scarlett for months, when she'd turned obsessive.

Izzy's tone and insinuations paled compared to the lengths Piper's ex had been willing to go to to get Dani out of the picture.

Besides, Dani had assured Piper that while her friendship with Izabelle was important to her, there was nothing remotely romantic between them. And Piper trusted her.

Though watching Izabelle practically devour Dani with her eyes now made it clear that while Dani might be over her, Piper didn't think Izabelle was over Dani.

Not even a little bit.

"You look incredible tonight," Izzy said, her gaze heavy on Dani's face.

"Thank you," Dani said politely, and turned to smile at Piper. "Piper bought me this dress when the award was announced."

"You've improved it," Piper said. "It didn't look half as nice on the hanger."

Dani's smile only widened. "You're sweet."

Izzy's smile tightened at its corners.

Piper was certain then. Izabelle *definitely* still had romantic feelings for Dani, even if they were one-sided. Or maybe it was the power of the dress.

Piper herself couldn't look at Dani without noticing how it hugged each curve and drew the eye to the low neckline. Perhaps she could forgive Izabelle for being unable to control her gaze, if she didn't look ready to drag her girlfriend to the first dark corner she could find.

"Best purchase I've ever made," Piper concluded. Dani squeezed her leg under the table.

A microphone whined, sparking to life.

The MC's booming voice echoed across the ballroom. "First of all, I'd like to thank everyone for coming tonight. It's a very special night. Not just for *us*, our partners and local members of the Press Association, but also for our national chapter, which..."

Piper worked on her meal while the introduction waffled on.

"...and that's why tonight we're honoring one of the finest investigative journalists our city has ever seen."

"The *finest*," Izabelle parroted under her breath, so that Dani could hear her.

This earned another playful slap from Dani.

Piper repressed the urge to grab Dani's seat and slide her closer to Piper's side, away from Izzy.

"We can expect amazing things from this young woman. Last year she was named one of Forbes 30 Under 30, and this year we're honoring her contributions to the integrity of journalism here in the Big Easy. Ms. Daniella Allendale, will you please join me on the stage to accept your well-deserved Journalist of the Year Award?"

The room erupted in applause, and Piper clapped heartily along with everyone else.

Dani went up onto the stage, accepted the small plaque with one hand, and shook the MC's free hand with the other. They paused, smiled at the camera, and a flurry of flashing lights brightened the stage for what felt like a full minute.

Then the MC was handing off the microphone and Dani was standing on the stage looking at her.

"You'll be happy to know that my speech, like my writing, will be brief and to the point," Dani said with a bright smile. She waited until the laughter died away before adding, "I only want to take this moment to thank my team at *The Herald*. Your hard work is seen and greatly appreciated, and I couldn't do what I do without your trust in me. Thank you also to all the friendly faces here tonight." Dani met eyes with Izzy, who grinned like a cat. "Many of us have worked together in the last few years, and so it's fitting that you should share this moment with me. A win for one of us is a win for all of us. And I hope we can continue to fight for and champion the voices that are often overlooked and suppressed. Thank you for all that you do. Most importantly, I want to give a special thank you to Piper Genereux, who is here with me tonight. She is the best partner a woman could ever ask for. You have supported me in this and in all things, and I wouldn't have pursued half of these stories, dangerous as many of them were, if I hadn't had you at my side."

Lou is the one she should be thanking. She's the one who always shows up with a gun in the nick of time, she thought.

Dani's eyes found hers. "I love you, Piper."

Piper's face warmed.

"How nice," Izzy said, but Piper didn't miss the cold tone.

They clapped along with everyone else as Dani handed the microphone back to the MC and headed off the stage.

Izzy turned her attention back to her half-eaten chicken breast, but she didn't look very interested in finishing it.

You're disappointed because you're just a friendly face. I'm the best partner a woman could ever ask for, Piper thought pettily, indulging in her feeling of triumph.

She watched as Dani descended the stage and got caught in a crowd determined to intercept her on her way back to the table.

That left her with Izabelle.

I can be magnanimous, she thought, seeing the disappointment on Izzy's face.

"How's life in New York?" Piper asked.

"It's good. I love it there. The city is incredible. I'm sure Dani told you I wanted her to come with me, but she wasn't ready to leave. And now she's found you. It's a shame. She's wasted on this place. If you're really *so* supportive, you should tell her to take the job offer that Koch put on the table. It's the chance of a lifetime. I don't know why she would turn it down. A journalist with twice her qualifications would kill for that offer."

Piper froze, her last bite of steak halfway to her mouth. She hadn't heard anything about a job offer in New York. She couldn't say that now. She'd rather stick bamboo shoots under her nails than reveal to Izzy that Dani had never told her about it.

Izzy turned her water glass in the candlelight. "*God*, what I wouldn't do to have that woman in my office in NYC—there's no one like her. Surely you know that, as experienced as you are."

Piper chewed her steak slowly. *Is she making some kind of sex reference right now?*

"I'm aware," Piper said. She was unsure what else she could add without playing into Izabelle's suggestive tone.

Dani arrived at the table, her cheeks flushed. She immediately planted a kiss on Piper's cheek. "Hey. Sorry. Everyone wants to say hi."

"Don't apologize," Izzy said. "It's your night."

Piper didn't like hearing her words coming out of someone else's mouth.

"I need some fresh air," Dani said, still flushed. "Let's go up to the observation deck."

"You haven't eaten your dinner," Piper said, setting down her fork and knife.

"I'll take it home. Let's go find the bar." Dani reached for her.

Piper thought that maybe this was it. This was her chance to get away from the combative ex. But then Dani ruined it.

"Come with us, Izzy."

Izabelle didn't have to be asked twice. She'd grabbed her clutch off the table and made for the elevators before Piper had her napkin on her empty plate.

Good ol' Darla hadn't been exaggerating about the view from the observation deck.

It was gorgeous.

The breeze blowing off the water was perfect.

"God, it's so beautiful up here," Dani said. "Not too hot, not too cold."

"Do you want a drink?" Piper asked her. She wanted to beat Izzy to the punch. If that woman offered to get Dani a drink, Piper was going to lose it.

"I'll get it," Dani said. "They're serving over there."

She pointed at the bar at the end of the patio. Behind it, a woman in a tuxedo was rattling a shaker like a maraca.

"Do you still drink dirty martinis?" Dani asked Izzy.

"I do, but not tonight. Thank you."

"One Malibu coming up." Dani gave her arm a squeeze. "Be right back."

"How's Octavia?" Izzy asked.

"She's good," Piper answered, leaning against the guardrail.

"Oh, I thought you were allergic to cats. You guys don't live together?"

So you were digging. Piper should've guessed the question had a motive. She was dealing with a journalist, after all.

"We do. And I *am* allergic. Octavia lives with my best friend and her—" What was Konstantine? He'd recently been upgraded from mafia boyfriend to baby daddy. "Person. We see her all the time."

"It must've been very hard on Dani to give up her cat just to be with you," Izzy said. She wasn't even pretending to hide her accusatory tone, like Piper had thrown Octavia in a sack herself and tossed her into the Mississippi.

Dani was the one who'd wanted to give up the cat. It had been her mother who'd forced Octavia on her to begin with. Dani loved animals, but she thought their lives were too busy to give a pet the attention it deserved.

"It was Dani's choice," Piper said. "She wanted to live together."

And that was true. Of course, Piper had no desire to explain that to the ex. What could be gained by explaining that Dani had only moved in with her temporarily because her apartment had been blown up by the crazy woman who'd kidnapped her to provoke Lou out of hiding? Or that Dani's PTSD from being tortured by Dmitri Petrov was so intense during those early days that Dani had felt safer sleeping with Piper every night than being alone in a place of her own.

It was clear Dani hadn't told her any of that, and it didn't feel like knowledge that Izzy had earned.

"Are you saying you'd rather not live together?" Izzy's tone was hopeful. "I'm sure it would be easier to sleep around if—"

"I didn't say—"

Dani appeared at her arm. "Here's your drink. They didn't have pineapple juice so it's a Mai Tai. Closest rum cocktail she could make."

Piper took a sip. It was a shitty and probably overpriced cocktail. And she would die before she issued a single complaint in front of this interloper.

"Thanks, baby."

"You have goosebumps," Izzy said, reaching out to touch Dani's arm. "Are you cold?"

Piper repressed the urge to snap those fingers off. Instead, she shrugged out of her jacket and slid it around Dani's shoulders. "Here."

"Thank you." Dani leaned against her.

Izzy's face was unreadable.

I bet if she could push me off this roof and get away with it, she would.

"How did you two meet again?" Izzy asked, crossing her arms.

"Through work," Dani said.

"What is it that you do?" Izzy turned those cold eyes on Piper.

"I'm an assistant investigator at the Crescent City Detective Agency and I take classes in criminal justice."

"An investigative journalist and an investigator. What a match."

"We make a good team," Piper said.

Dani's smile brightened. "We do."

Izzy looked ready to gag. "What degree are you working on? At your age it's probably a master's? Or a PhD?"

Piper's guts twisted. "Nope. A bachelor's degree."

"Oh, did you study something else first? Law?"

"I considered law school," Piper said, which was true. "But no. This is my first degree."

"Ah. I see. Good for you." The condescending tone was thick enough to cut.

Piper made a conscious effort to unclench her teeth.

Dani nudged her encouragingly with an elbow. "And King thinks you'll qualify for the FBI soon. You'd be a very competitive candidate."

Izzy shifted her weight from one foot to the other. "You have plans on being an agent?"

"My mentor was a DEA agent for thirty years. He wants me to train at Quantico like he did. I'm not fully decided on what branch I want to pursue yet, but yes, I'm considering the FBI."

"I thought the FBI had a cut-off age," Izzy said. "Aren't you getting close? How old are you?"

"She's our age. Twenty-seven," Dani said, pulling Piper's jacket tighter around her shoulders.

"The cut-off age is thirty-six," Piper said.

"I'm sure King would pull strings even if you went over," Dani said, throwing back the rest of her cocktail.

Piper had barely drunk hers at all.

"It must be nice to have friends in high places," Izzy said. "They really can compensate for whatever a candidate *lacks*."

Piper wondered what would happen if she was the one who accidentally tipped Izabelle over the railing of the observation deck. Could she claim it was an accident? Or maybe she could work something out with Darla? Or were there too many security cameras up here?

Ah shit, there was one. And another.

"I'm ready to go." Dani wrapped herself around Piper's arm. "Can you take me home?"

Dani was looking at Piper with expectant eyes. She might actually be horny, but Piper also couldn't help but wonder if maybe she was trying to diffuse the tension. Surely she hadn't missed it. She was very good about picking up emotional undertones.

"I'd be happy to." Piper sat her gross cocktail on the nearest table.

"But you've only been here for like an hour," Izzy protested.

Dani turned to her. "We're still on for dinner, right? I'll see you then."

"Fine." Izabelle gave Dani a hug, holding on a bit too long, in Piper's opinion.

When she released her, she leaned into the deck's guardrail, her face the perfect mask of dissatisfaction. "Get some rest."

"She won't," Piper said, holding open the balcony door for Dani.

She couldn't resist. This woman had been intentionally testing her patience all night long.

Piper released the door so it could close shut behind them but not before she saw the flash of fury cross Izabelle's face.

Piper knew she was starting something, but she couldn't say she was the least bit sorry.

7

Konstantine sat at his desk, scrolling through the video Lou had captured using the glasses. He'd left the door open, and a cool breeze rolled across the courtyard, carrying the scent of roses into his office. Lou was stretched out in a chair, her feet propped up. It annoyed him, her very American tendency to put her shoes on furniture. But he would not complain. Her expression was dark, brooding, and he longed to know the cause.

Had something happened on her hunt? Had she seen something when encountering the killer? Or perhaps she was simply annoyed that her hunt hadn't ended in bloodshed yet again.

"She keeps kicking me," Lou said, pressing a hand into her ribs. "If I could reach into my chest and remove my ribcage, I would."

"She's a fighter," Konstantine said.

"You wouldn't look so happy about it if it were your guts serving as her punching bag," Lou said, turning those dark eyes on him.

"After this I will get you gelato," he promised.

"Gelato doesn't fix everything."

"Of course it does, *amore mio*."

Gelato meant more than the frozen treat. It now encompassed all of their afternoon routine: sex, a long nap, followed by actual gelato.

Konstantine could not remember the last time—if ever—he'd been this happy during his days.

His nights were another question. Ever since he'd learned of Lou's pregnancy, he'd had vivid flashbacks of the moment his mother was murdered.

Dreams of himself forced to his knees beside a grave that his father's enemies had dug for them, his mother beside him.

The gun pivoting toward his mother before it went off, cutting through her, her limp body falling back into the endless dark.

Only in his dream it was Lou who was shot, who was swallowed whole by the darkness. A darkness she went into but never returned from.

Or sometimes she held an infant, splattered in blood.

Each nightmare ended the same way, with him jerking awake, heart pounding and covered in sweat.

Now it seemed his days were slowly becoming more like his nights.

Whenever Konstantine thought of Stefano his fury burned inside him. It hurt to watch his friend suffer, knowing there was nothing Konstantine could do to eliminate that pain.

And he'd met Ilaria so many times in their lives. When they were children and as adults. She'd been a good, kind woman, and the sibling that Stefano had loved most because they were the closest in age, only eleven months apart.

Now she was dead along with two of her children. Killed by the bastard that Konstantine was working to identify on his computer screen.

"Well?" Lou said. "Who is he?"

"Modesto Detti," he said. He'd uncovered the killer's name not one minute before. And now, looking at his face on the screen, watching how he turned toward the darkness, had raised a gun at Louie—and his daughter—it summoned a cold rage from the base of his spine.

"He pointed a gun at you." Konstantine paused and rewound the footage for a third time.

"He didn't know what he was pointing at," Lou said without looking at him.

Konstantine tried to read her face but couldn't. Her eyes were closed, her head resting on the chair, her face pointed at the ceiling.

Konstantine wished the glasses had audio capabilities. He could see by the movement of their lips that they were speaking, but he wasn't sure what they were saying.

"Did you recognize any of the Italian?" he asked.

"No," she said, without opening her eyes. "They have a stronger accent."

"*Sì*, because they're from Naples. The Italian is different than what we speak here in Tuscany."

"Noted." Lou slipped her hands into her pockets. "I thought you were on good terms with the mafia in Naples."

"No one is on *good* terms with the Celesti." He rubbed the back of his head. "But we understand each other, Ettore and I. I reached out to him but he—"

Konstantine's phone buzzed on the desktop. He lifted it, seeing the text message flash on his screen. "This is him."

He read the text twice before speaking.

"Ettore says that Modesto isn't one of his anymore. He was exiled from the city for starting trouble."

Lou snorted. "Exiled. Why bother exiling him? Why not shoot him in the head?"

"Modesto is his wife's cousin. It was probably a courtesy."

Lou rolled her eyes, unimpressed. Konstantine stifled a laugh. "He is more afraid of his wife than Modesto. That's a good sign, *amore mio*. Maybe Modesto will be easy to kill."

"You don't know," Lou said. "Maybe his wife is a terror."

A shadow fell over them. Stefano stood in the doorway, blocking the sunlight from the courtyard.

"Tell me his name." He pulled a lighter from his pocket and lit the cigarette hanging between his lips.

Louie spoke before he could. "Your killer is Modesto Detti. He's related to Ettore Celesti's wife. He made some sort of trouble in Naples and was exiled."

"Will they be pissed if we kill him?" Stefano asked.

"I don't think so," Konstantine said. "Ettore said he would consider it a courtesy. If he's looking to conquer our territory so he can torment his brother-in-law, Ettore will be grateful we take care of his problem for him."

"Then I just need his face and his location." Stefano went to Konstantine's desk and turned the laptop toward him. He regarded the men on the screen. "Which one is he?"

"He's not playing cards," Lou said behind him, her eyes still closed, hands in her pockets.

Stefano looked at the video more closely, leaning toward the screen. "That one? The one who raised his gun at you?"

Konstantine felt his blood turn cold again. He would have to stop watching that part or his temper was going to get the better of him.

"It was a tempting invitation," Lou said, yawning. "But I saved him for you. You're welcome."

"Where is he?"

Konstantine checked the address Lou had sent him from her watch. He jotted it down on a scrap of paper before sliding it across the desk to Stefano. "He was here this morning."

Stefano took the address, read it before slipping it into his pocket. "I'm going now."

"Don't." Konstantine stood.

"*Vado, fratello.*" Stefano's jaw clenched. "That bastard isn't going to live another day."

"Then I'm going with you," Konstantine said.

"The hell you are," Lou said, finally opening her eyes.

"*Amore*—"

"I have walked away from thirty-seven kills, *thirty-seven*, since February. You can walk away just as well as I can."

"It isn't about that, *amore mio*. It is about protecting Stefano. He is my brother."

Not by blood, but he knew that Louie understood what he meant.

"You wouldn't let your friends fight alone," he insisted. "And I will not let mine go alone either."

"Then we go together," she said, standing. "You go and protect Stefano, and I'll go and protect you."

"No, *amore mio*. No, it's not safe."

Her jaw clenched, and the look she gave him could have stopped his heart. "If it's not safe for *us*, then it's not safe for *you*."

"We will be quick. We will be discreet. Be reasonable. I won't sacrifice—"

"*Sacrifice*," Lou interrupted him, her voice a low growl. She looked ready to pounce. "I let a woman die in the street two weeks ago. There was no way to save her without also taking a bullet and I *left her*, Konstantine. For the first time in my life, I walked away from someone who needed me. Don't talk to me about *sacrifice*."

"*Amore mio.*" How could Konstantine explain to her that the success of his underworld empire was secured only because of Stefano's loyalty to him? Stefano's own blood had paid for much of what he had. He couldn't let him down now, in his time of need.

If Modesto was vying for Konstantine's crown, if this attack was his attempt to provoke the Ravengers into battle, Konstantine couldn't let his friend go up against him and his people alone. They would be expecting him. They'd be expecting a fight. They would be *ready*.

"I can't abandon him," Konstantine said. It was a plea as much as the truth.

"Then go and die," Lou said coldly. "Die now. *Before* she's born. It will be better that she never knows you than loves you and loses you."

The words felt like a kick to the chest.

Regret flashed on Louie's face an instant after they passed her lips, but she didn't take them back.

She didn't apologize. She only turned away from him.

"It doesn't matter anyway," she said.

"It does," he said. He wanted to hold her. He wanted to kiss her and apologize. More than anything, he wanted to make her see why this mattered so much. He had to find a way to be there for all of them. Louie and their daughter. The children in the church. His people. Stefano.

He had to find a way to be strong for everyone.

"It doesn't," she said again, turning toward him. "He already left."

Lou pointed at the doorway. It stood empty, the soft light of the afternoon sun spilling across the office floor.

A breeze brushed the hair off Louie's shoulder.

She was right. Stefano was gone.

8

Lou hadn't meant to speak out of anger. It was true that she'd found it more difficult to hold her tongue since becoming pregnant. In some ways, she noticed herself becoming gentler, kinder with the people around her. In other ways, fiercer. When it came to the safety of the people she cared about, it seemed she couldn't accept even the smallest bit of carelessness.

And angry or not, she'd meant every word. A part of her *did* firmly believe that it would be better their daughter never know Konstantine at all than suffer the pain of his loss.

Yet the look in his eyes when she'd spoken the words—it was clear she'd hurt him. The way he'd looked away had felt like a punch to the gut. She found herself wishing she could take the words back.

She couldn't, so she tried to forget their argument as she walked the streets of Florence, enjoying the sunlight on her face.

That was another strange thing about her pregnancy. In the last month, she'd found herself longing for sunlight. For as long as she could remember, ever since she'd healed her relationship with her power, she'd craved darkness. She felt safest at night, when the shadows were on her side. She'd become nocturnal to better align herself with that strength.

But now, it was like she couldn't get enough light on her skin.

She'd developed the habit of wandering Florence's streets at high noon, her face turned skyward as if she were bathing in it.

More than once, she'd noticed the way her stomach warmed deliciously in this daily ritual. When their daughter had seemed determined to assault every internal organ that Lou had, Lou found that sunlight was the only thing that would calm her.

That was the driving force this morning behind Louie's decision to walk from the church back to their villa she shared with Konstantine on the Arno River. She could have simply stepped through the shadows in Konstantine's office and found herself home, but instead, she'd walked out the office door as if it were the most natural thing to do.

She'd made it only three blocks in the noonday sun before the baby gave one more stretch and went still inside her.

Am I growing a child or cat, she thought, amused.

It amazed her, the level of affection she had for the child she was carrying. She'd always been protective of children. She'd taken more than a few bullets in the name of saving them from darker fates.

When she thought of someone threatening *her* child, a fury so complete rose up inside her that she felt only a breath away from razing a city to the ground in a hell storm of fire and bullets—just at the *thought* that someone might want to harm her. It was enough to enrage her.

She tried to shake off these thoughts too, knowing she

would only infuriate herself again if she allowed her mind to go down that path.

Instead her mind turned back to Konstantine, to his face and that look of hurt in his deep green eyes.

She isn't the only one I have to keep safe.

Lou realized again, not for the first time, what a liability it was to bring this child into the world. Some decisions were proving harder than she'd expected. Once the baby was born it would only be harder.

She knew she'd always protect her child's life above her own. If it came down to her life or her daughter's—there was no question.

It was the same for Konstantine, if only because she didn't want her daughter to lose her father the way she had.

But other scenarios that her mind proposed weren't so simple.

What would she do, for example, if she had to choose between saving their daughter and Piper? Or between Dani and Piper?

She knew she'd choose her child, but that choice felt infinitely harder than the question of surrendering her own life.

And that's where he is now, Lou realized. Konstantine was trying to choose between his Piper—his closest tie—and the promise he'd made to their little family.

Lou had been furious that he would even suggest another choice, but now that she'd put a mile between them, she found she could be more honest with herself.

It would not have been an easy decision for her either.

Now Lou felt less confident that she wouldn't have put up a fight of her own had their roles been reversed.

What was the point in being this strong, this powerful, if they couldn't keep *all* of their people safe?

A cloud moved over the sun. Her daughter stirred, unhappy.

Lou placed a reassuring hand on her stomach as she crossed the piazza.

We can't keep going like this.

There has to be another way.

9

King spent the afternoon reviewing the initial case file that White had compiled for him. Most of it had been handed over on a thumb drive with only photocopies of the letters in the manila folder. Piper had torn open a bag of M&Ms, and they were spread across her desk as she looked from letter to letter.

"There is something really creepy about this," she said. She popped another chocolate into her mouth and lifted the letter to peer at it more closely. "Like who still gets magazines?"

"Doctors, lawyers, schools, offices, pretty much anyone with a waiting room. Hairstylists."

"Do you want me to run a check on any of that?"

"It's a waste of time," King said. "There's no way to run a background check on every office in the city. It's better to stay focused on White and work backward. The would-be bomber wants him. We just have to figure out why."

"Right, because whoever this guy—or girl—is, they really do seem pissed off at White."

King didn't bother to point out that it probably was a

man they were looking for. Statistically, bombers were usually men, with the exception of suicide bombers. He hoped they didn't have one of those on his hands, given that someone who was ready to die only cared about one thing—taking as many people with them as they could.

He paused in his scrolling to read White's notes. The sad truth was a great deal of it read like paranoid drivel. And that wasn't like White at all. Was he losing his edge? Going into the precinct every day, wondering if someone there wanted him dead—was it getting to him?

King hoped not. That kind of paranoia led to mistakes. Deadly ones.

"Since the paper manufacturer didn't turn up any leads, let's focus on the precinct," King said. *Because the sooner I can tell White that he's safe at the precinct, the less likely he'll be to accidentally put a bullet in someone.*

Piper grabbed another handful of candy off the desk. "We could also canvas the boards and socials to see if anyone is bitching about him."

King hated social media. Every time he found himself on it, he felt like his IQ dropped by at least thirty points. "I'll leave that to you. But given their penchant for magazine cutouts and stationery, I have a feeling they might be older. This feels very old school, doesn't it?"

This was the kind of thing he'd seen back in the nineties. Same for the quotes and the bit of typewriting. He couldn't remember the last time he'd encountered a threat delivered this way. And yet, even though it was old school, there was something young and immature about the letters. They felt like a sampler, a little bit of everything. Like maybe the would-be bomber hadn't decided on his style yet.

"Oh, and supermarkets!" Piper exclaimed as if she'd had a lightbulb moment. "Sometimes Dani buys a magazine on impulse in the checkout lane."

He waved this away. "Forget about the magazines."

Following that lead wouldn't get them anywhere. They were impossible to trace.

Their best bet was to find someone local who had a motive for hurting White.

The only problem was White. He'd been the lead detective at the French Quarter precinct for over a decade. His work, his testimonies, had put a lot of people away. A convict was a high possibility. But King was struggling to find a reason why they would come down to the precinct. Once someone was arrested, they tended to stay the hell away from the police and police stations as a rule.

Maybe a family member? Someone who felt like White had wronged the person they loved?

King pinched his eyes shut and rubbed the bridge of his nose. "Get some paper. I need you to make a list."

"On it." With a swipe of her hand, Piper shoved the papers and candy away and slapped a fresh legal pad on her desk. With a dramatic press of her thumb, she clicked her ballpoint pen twice. "Hit me, boss."

"Has anyone that White testified against been released from prison recently? It counts if White testified or built a case against them. Bonus if the court records show that the defendants made direct threats to White at the time. We also need a list of everyone who goes in and out of that precinct on a regular basis. And what about anyone who has ever made a threat to White or his family. We're looking for people with a history of arson, or violence. Or a history of mental illness."

He racked his brain. There were textbook motivations for bombers. Malice, mental illness, and—God, what was the other one?

He snapped his fingers. "Power disparity."

"Cool cool cool." Piper was nodding, tapping the pen against her chin. "What is that?"

"Someone who has less social standing than White. Fewer resources. Someone who likely feels directly threatened by him in some way. Or at least believes that White has a higher placement in their social hierarchy. That feeling usually increases a perp's desire to use something like a bomb. To level the playing field. If he truly felt like White's equal, he wouldn't feel the need to bring such heavy fire power."

She snorted.

When he raised his brow in question, Piper pointed the pen at him. "Oh, you didn't hear yourself, did you? *Level* the playing field?"

When King didn't smile, she rolled her eyes. "Ah, never mind. Forget the puns. Power disparity. Got it. What else?"

"Maybe the DA's office. They go into the precinct often enough."

Piper gave a fake gasp. "Your *girlfriend* is a suspect?"

Won't be my girlfriend for much longer, King thought. No sooner did he think it than Mel's face flashed in his mind.

"Okay, try not to look too happy about it," Piper said with a snort. "Seriously, if you're having some kind of handcuff fantasy right now, I don't want to know about it."

"I wasn't," he protested, and rubbed the back of his neck. It felt warm. "We should also get a list of groups that White is involved in outside of work. We can't write off the possibility that this is a personal connection who just went into the precinct as a calculated move to throw him off."

"Got it." She put the pen down and rotated her wrist. "Is that it?"

"You don't think it's enough?"

"Are you kidding me? Do you have any idea how many people can go into that building? You can walk in there off the street."

"Good point. I should clarify people who have access to

the offices on the second floor. To White's office in particular."

"Okay. But we're still looking at all the officers, janitors, or maintenance people. Tour groups. I think they've still got mentoring and shadowing programs for the high school kids too. Or at least they did when I was in high school. Are we really going to ask *everyone* if they're a bomber?"

"I don't plan to ask anyone if they're a bomber," he said. When Piper's face pinched in confusion, he added, "Like I said, I don't want to burn bridges with anyone if we can help it. I imagine all the cases the police and DA's office throw our way would dry up if it got out that old Robbie King was gunning for cops."

Piper shot him with a finger gun. "I can see how that would be a problem."

"We'll need to come up with a different story that can help us figure out who is pissed off at White and who has access to his office. We'll have to do the interviews ourselves and hope we catch something. There's no replacing gut instinct. Talking to someone usually gives me a good hit as to whether or not they've got something to hide."

"King, it's ninety degrees outside. Please tell me you don't want to walk all over this city interviewing everyone who has ever had a conversation with White."

"Not the whole city," he said with a mischievous smile. "At least not today."

KING SHOWED UP AT MEL'S DOOR WITH THE WINGS AND half a gallon of sweet tea ten minutes early. The fact that he had sweet tea in his possession showed how much he cared for Mel's happiness. He'd never drunk sweet tea in his life before moving to the South. In St. Louis, if he'd ordered tea, it came dark with a lemon—not a grain of sugar in sight. But down here, if he ordered unsweetened tea, it almost always came with a *you're not from around here, are you?*

Lady barked on the other side of the door.

"It's me," King called out, and the barking stopped. In its place King could hear a nose pressed to the crack beneath the door and the intense sniffing that followed.

He was still smiling when Melandra opened the door. She was already in her pajamas, her hair secured under its bonnet for the night.

"Don't look at me like that," she said, stepping aside so he could come in. "It's just you. I don't have to keep all that makeup and crap on when it's just you."

"No, you don't," he said with a little laugh. "It's just that I feel overdressed. Should I go put my pajamas on? Should we make it a pajama party?"

"No, I can't wait for you to change. I'm starving. I've been thinking about those wings all day."

Mel took the bag from him and started rummaging.

"You forgot my extra dippin' sauce."

"I did not," he said, and pulled two containers from his pockets. "How dare you doubt me."

She took them with a smile. "I stand corrected. My apologies, Mr. King. Let me get some glasses for the tea and I'll meet you on the sofa."

Meet you on the sofa, his mind echoed. He brushed this thought away even as it threatened to turn his mind in a new direction.

King took a seat, putting the food on the table. He opened and arranged the containers as Lady curled up in a ball at his feet. Her long tail thumped against his leg as he worked, and he had to resist the urge to reach out and give her rump a good scratch, lest he have to wash his hands again.

"Here you go, Mr. King," she said, handing him a clean glass and a plate.

"Thank you, Ms. Durand," he echoed. "Which episode is this?"

"Four or five, I think. Honestly, I've lost count. But definitely season three," Melandra said, adding a handful of wings to her plate.

King couldn't remember either. Once they'd finished the latest season, they'd decided to go back to the beginning and watch the ones they'd missed. King and Mel hadn't started their weekly *RuPaul's Drag Race* date until the show had already finished seven seasons, so there was plenty to catch up on. Now that they were watching reruns, they weren't confined to once a week. They could meet up whenever they liked.

Still, King found himself wondering what he would do if they ran out of episodes.

You'd find a new show to watch. Or maybe you'll have something more exciting to do together.

"Your face is getting red," she said. "Are the wings too spicy for you? I thought you were getting better with the spicy food."

"No, it's not the spice," King said.

"You sure? You *are* a white boy," she told him. "You're not built for this."

"It's not too spicy," he laughed. "I like spicy things."

She pressed his glass of tea into his hands. "Drink your tea. You're sweating."

He made the resolution not to think any other inappropriate thoughts about Mel. He was being ridiculous. They were best friends. He'd spent countless nights on this couch with her and he'd never acted this way before.

He was a grown man. He had to get himself under control. He *would* get himself under control.

But the mind rarely obeyed its master. And throughout the show, King found his mind kept wandering back to Mel.

To the look of her in his periphery. She felt like a splinter in his brain.

No, he thought. *We're just really close. I love her, but I'm not in love with her.*

But if that were true, what about the dreams? Those damn dreams that he kept having. They were polluting his mind, terrorizing his nights, and confusing his days.

It doesn't matter. Nothing is going to happen.

Because there was still Beth. There would be no exploration of feelings, no confessions of love, nothing. Not as long as he remained loyal to Beth—which he would be until her moving truck bound for Orlando pulled out of the parking lot on Prytania Street, the taillights disappearing in the distance.

In just a few short weeks, she'll be gone.

So soon.

"I want more ice," Melandra said, pausing the show. They were halfway through the episode already and King couldn't remember a single detail about it. Not what anyone had worn. Nothing about the competition or the dance numbers.

Where the hell is my head at?

"Well?" she asked. And he realized he'd missed a question. "Sorry?"

"I asked if you wanted more ice." She pointed at his glass. "Do you?"

He looked at the layer of condensation coating the outside of the glass and the one remaining cube hanging on for dear life. "Oh, yeah. Thanks."

She took his glass to the kitchen with hers. When she returned, she said, "You okay? You seem distracted tonight."

She'd noticed. *You'd better pull yourself together or you're going to have to explain yourself. And what will you say? "I keep thinking about this sex dream I've been having about you."*

"I'm okay," he lied, accepting the glass. When she arched a brow, he knew that he'd failed to sell this story. He positioned his drink on the coaster and said, "I saw Detective White again today. He thinks we've got a bomber in the city. It's a complicated case."

There, he thought triumphantly. *That was convincing enough.*

Mel's lips pressed together.

"We should pull some cards," she said. "Ask for clarity."

"Oh. No, no. It's okay," he said.

"A bomber is serious business, Mr. King. A lot of people could get hurt," Melandra said, her tone grave. But it was hard to take her too seriously in that festive bonnet. "What's the harm in asking for a little bit of guidance?"

None, he knew. And refusing her might prove more insulting than sitting through the reading itself. It had taken them a long time to get to this point. For years, Melandra had kept her beliefs to herself for fear that King would judge her. She knew him to be a rational guy with little belief in the afterlife, let alone things like fortune-telling.

At least that had been the case. King had to admit his beliefs had eroded since moving to New Orleans. This city could do that to a person.

The case they worked last September even brought King into contact with his first ghost. For that reason, he could admit, if only to himself, that he wasn't all too sure what he believed anymore.

Besides, he cared about Mel. They were friends if nothing else. He didn't want to hurt her feelings by calling her tarot readings bullshit.

It wasn't like the reading would change his investigative process. King would be as thorough in this investigation as he always was.

"Okay," he said. "Let's ask the cards."

With a smile, Mel rose from the sofa and went to the kitchen. "Gotta wash my hands first. I'm not touching these cards with wing sauce on my fingers."

She disappeared into her bedroom for a moment, leaving King on the sofa. With the door open, he could see her bed, the sheets turned down invitingly on one side.

His face was warm by the time she came out of the bedroom, closing the door behind her.

"Let's do this in the kitchen," Mel said. "I might only be fifty-nine, but my knees feel eighty years old. I won't be kneeling in front of the coffee table, that's for sure."

King took his sweet tea to the kitchen. The only problem with the table there was that King was too big for it. His long legs took up most of the space beneath. Anytime he moved, his knees brushed against Melandra's. He apologized three times only to be waved away each time.

"What should we ask first?" Melandra said.

King rubbed his temple, hoping his discomfort wasn't showing. "I guess it would be good to know if there is actually a bomber. Part of me is hoping that the letters are just empty threats and that no one will follow through on any of this."

Mel began shuffling the cards in her hands. King liked the sound of it, the cards sliding over one another.

"Is there a bomber?" she whispered under her breath. "Are they serious in their threat? They really gonna blow something up?"

King's lips quirked despite himself. He was failing to maintain his serious tone.

Mel pulled several cards, making a pile in front of her, until her hands hesitated. "That's it, I believe. Let's see what we've got."

She moved the stack over to one side of the table before gathering up the cards she'd drawn.

One by one she turned them over.

"A lot of swords," she said, frowning at the cards. "Three of Swords, Seven of Swords, Nine of Swords. Two of Swords. And the Five of Swords. Half the spread is swords alone."

"What does that mean?" he asked.

"A battle of wits," she said. "And sorrow. Misfortune."

"That doesn't sound good."

"A lot of anxiety," she said, tapping a card. "Jumping at shadows."

He found that he couldn't stop watching her lips as she spoke.

"I think that's Dick," he said. "I've never seen him like this."

"I think it's both of them," Melandra said, closing her eyes. Her hand moved from the Nine of Swords to the Seven of Swords. "Detective White stole something."

"Are you serious?" he asked, unable to hide his surprise.

"Maybe not in the legal sense, but that's part of the insult. This person feels—strongly feels—that Detective White has done him a disservice."

"*Him?*"

"I'm sensing masculine energy, but you're right. It might not be a man. Piper also reads as masculine energy sometimes."

"Men and possibly lesbians." That hardly narrowed King's suspect list.

Mel rolled her eyes. "Not all lesbians would have masculine energy."

"Okay. Can you tell me anything *else* about the person?" King asked.

"I think they're represented by the Page of Wands. And it's here with the Five of Pentacles."

King pursed his lips. "I don't know what that means."

"The Page of Wands is younger energy. Or it could simply mean that the person is in a weaker position than Detective White."

Power disparity. That was one of the things King was looking for.

"Pages are messengers, apprentices. The Page of Wands is hopeful, optimistic, full of big ideas and excitement to do the work and see growth. But because it's here beside the Five of Pentacles, it gives me the idea that he feels left out in the cold. He was supposed to be included in something but wasn't. Abandoned. He feels abandoned by White. I could ask if White really hurt him or if the insult is in his head. Sometimes the swords are about things in our minds."

Before King could agree, she'd already pulled two more cards. "Ten of Swords and the Devil. I hate to say it, but it looks like White really did betray him somehow. To what degree, I don't know."

That made King's stomach twist. "I guess it's probably beyond the scope of the cards to tell us what he did."

"*Specifically*, yes. But I can tell you that it looks like there was lying. Betrayal. And theft of some kind. That doesn't mean that Detective White or anybody else deserves to be *blown up*," she added. "But at least we know the insult isn't made up."

"So there really is a bomber? Are they planning an attack? Is it going to happen soon?"

She pulled two more cards. "The Chariot and the Eight of Wands."

She hesitated, then pulled another card.

"What? What is it?" When she didn't answer, he pressed her. "Don't leave me hanging, Mel."

"Both of these cards are about speed. At first glance I thought it was talking about the situation resolving quickly." She tapped the Justice card. "Resolution. Justice. Things coming into balance."

She rubbed her chin.

"But now I'm wondering if it's more specific than that. If we know it's a bomber, could we be talking about transportation? Because the Chariot can also be about travel. A car. A bus. A plane."

King felt the headache in the back of his head forming again.

Please don't let it be a plane, he thought. Not only because the body count would certainly be higher but also because a plane was so far out of King's jurisdiction there would be no way he could stop it. He didn't have the power to search airports or call planes out of the sky. At least with cars and buses he could make up stories and do searches on the ground. Maybe he could even bring in Lou when Piper wasn't looking.

"You have a look on your face," Mel said.

"I really hope it's not a plane or train, but I don't even like the idea of a car bomb," he admitted. "There were at least a thousand vehicle thefts in the city last month. Cars disappear and turn up all the time. It would be easy to take a car, arm it, and then leave it somewhere. That would make it a lot harder to track our guy down. I can see him detonating more than one bomb before we could catch him."

"Ask Louie for help," Melandra said.

"I might have to," he said. "Piper will be pissed. She says we can't put Lou in danger with a baby on the way."

"I'm sure Lou is smart enough to assess the risk for herself."

"Will we catch him?" King asked hopefully. "Or is that beyond the scope of the cards?"

At least here Mel had a smile for him. She tapped the Two of Swords. "Your intuition will keep you on track. Even if your eyes were closed, you'd find him. He's on your path."

She held up the card so King could see the woman with the blindfold snug across her eyes. "But—"

"But what?" He pushed the card away.

She placed a different card in his hand. It was the Nine of

Swords. The figure was in bed, crying, their face covered by their hands.

For a terrible moment, King thought she knew about the dreams. That somehow, just by looking at these cards, she'd uncovered his secret. His nights-long fantasizing revealed.

"This card says you're going to come up against your worst fear," she said. Her face was a mask of concern again.

His worst fear?

His worst fear was losing someone he loved, and that had already happened when he lost Lucy. Melandra seemed to understand his confusion.

"I think it's talking about your claustrophobia," she said. "That was a bomber too, wasn't it?"

He couldn't remember when he'd told her about the bomb. Was it after they were almost shot by Brasso? Or when the Russian mobsters had them captive? He knew it was the sort of thing that had come out late one night while they sat on his balcony, talking and watching the chaos of the Quarter unfold below.

In the intimacy of that darkness, he'd told her about what it had been like, lying in the rubble for days, wondering how long it would take him to die.

"It was a bomber," he affirmed. "The IED brought the whole building down on us. This better not be the part where you tell me I'm going to find myself in another collapsed building. Once in a lifetime was enough for me."

She put the card back on the table. "The thing about the Nine of Swords is it's about facing our anxiety and fear."

King didn't like the sound of this. He rubbed the back of his neck. "Wait, so how does it end? You said I'll find him, but you didn't say that we'd win and keep everyone safe."

"For someone who doesn't really believe in the cards, you sure are desperate for answers, Mr. King."

"It's bad news, huh?" he asked.

She laughed. "I didn't say that. The cards say it's not clear at this time. The Five of Swords is in the outcome position. The Five of Swords is the card of winning or defeat. You might win or you might be defeated. Or if you do *win*, it doesn't mean the battle won't have a high price."

"That's it? That's all the cards have got to tell me?" King was suddenly remembering why he never liked this tarot nonsense.

"No. That's not all. I haven't even mentioned the best card yet." She reached over and pulled the card from the top corner. She showed it to him. King's eyes fixed first on a girl falling from the sky, plummeting to the earth below.

"The Tower," Mel said.

"Looks cheerful," he said, unable to shake the unease growing inside.

"The Tower warns of chaos, upheaval. Or at best, a surprise," Mel said. "Something's going to happen that we don't expect."

10

Piper sat at the bistro table outside Big Mike's Muffulettas, watching the traffic roll by. Dani was ten minutes late for their lunch date, and that was adding to Piper's already mounting anxiety. If she was being honest with herself, her anxiety had been high ever since Izabelle made mention of the *amazing opportunity* that Dani had been offered in New York.

She'd thought about raising the subject with Dani more than once, but her courage had failed her each time the question found itself on the tip of her tongue.

Part of her believed—*hoped*—that Dani would have told her about the offer if she was seriously considering it, and the other part was convinced that Dani had already secretly packed a bag and was waiting for the right time to break the news.

Her phone pinged with a text. *Almost there. Five minutes. Can you order me the veggie muffuletta with salt and vinegar chips?*

Piper leapt up from the bistro table, grateful for something to do. Anything other than sitting with her thoughts until Dani arrived.

The air-conditioned sandwich shop was also a nice break from the heat building to its full strength in the early afternoon.

Piper put in their order, getting a Reuben for herself, before returning to their table with a plastic number and two bottles of water.

Piper spotted Dani's SUV as soon as it rounded the corner. She watched, her heart racing, as Dani parallel-parked across the street, sandwiching herself between two sedans.

She'd do just fine driving in the city, she thought. Then, *Stop it. You're making yourself crazy.*

Dani was smiling as she jogged across the street. Piper stood and Dani came up onto her toes to kiss her hello.

"Hey, baby," she said. "Oh good, you've got us in the shade."

"It hardly matters," Piper said. "It's still hot as hell."

"We could eat inside," Dani offered, sliding her purse off her shoulders.

"There aren't any seats." In truth, they could probably find two, but Piper was feeling too claustrophobic to sit indoors. "Aren't you always telling me fresh air is good for us?"

"You're right." Dani put her bag on an empty chair. "It is."

"Did you get hung up at work?" Piper ventured.

"Sort of," Dani said. "Izabelle came to see me."

Piper's stomach turned. "Oh yeah? I thought we were supposed to have dinner with her tomorrow night?"

Though Izabelle had changed her plans twice and Piper was beginning to hope against hope that maybe the dreaded ex would cancel altogether.

"She wanted to see *The Herald*. She came by and I showed her around."

Piper suppressed a bitter laugh. She wasn't the least bit convinced that Izabelle was interested in seeing *The Herald*'s office. She was probably envisioning some sort of clandestine affair on top of Dani's desk.

"What did she think?" Piper asked.

Dani rolled her eyes. "You know Izabelle. If it's not New York, it might as well be the backwoods of some desolate wasteland. I told her it's the twenty-first century. The world no longer revolves around New York. You can be an incredible journalist anywhere if you're willing to travel."

Piper's spirits lifted. "You don't want to live in New York?"

"I mean, I *would*, but I don't think it's the best city in the world like she does."

And just like that, Piper's spirits were dashed on a rocky shore. "You would? When?"

"I don't know. I might give it a try next year? I guess it depends on when you do your training in Quantico."

Piper had zero plans to do her training in Quantico within the next year. She still had so much to learn from King, her Spanish was shit, and she was only half convinced that she would pass the fitness test, even though she'd been doing her best to train with Bane at the boxing gym at least three times a week and run with Dani the other days.

She hadn't even fully decided if the FBI was the right move for her.

Given the way King talked about crooked cops and agents these days, Piper was wondering more and more if she should just stick with Louie and King. What they were doing mattered. Piper found meaning in it. If she worked with the FBI or the police, she would be fulfilling *their* agenda. The idea didn't appeal to her as much as following her own heart.

"Is this about the offer that Koch made?" Piper asked. She was surprised to find her voice was steady despite her tightening throat.

Dani was about to speak but the server appeared, coming through the front door of the shop with their plates. He placed the Reuben and chips in front of Piper and the veggie muffuletta in front of Dani.

"Can I get you ladies anything else?"

"No, thank you," Piper said with a tight smile. Once he'd gone, she turned her attention to Dani again. "Well?"

"I don't remember telling you about the offer," Dani said. And the look on her face was enough to make Piper feel nauseated.

"You didn't. Izabelle mentioned it during dinner at the awards ceremony."

She said a lot of things that night.

Piper had been able to let most of it go. Mostly because as soon as they'd gotten home, Piper and Dani had fallen into bed and had had incredible sex. It was hard to be mad at the jilted ex when Piper had the one thing she obviously wanted. The only shame was that Izzy had kept crossing her mind since, and if Piper could've figured out how to forget about her by now, she would have.

"She shouldn't have brought that up," Dani said, frowning at her plate.

"No, *you* should have," Piper countered. "I know we're just girlfriends—"

Dani's brows rose. "*Just* girlfriends?"

"—but shouldn't you have told me? Taking a job thirteen hundred miles away is a big deal," Piper said.

Piper knew the mileage because she'd looked it up.

"But I haven't taken it."

"Did you tell Izabelle that?" Piper pressed. "Because she seems pretty convinced that she can get you to New York like *tomorrow*."

Piper pushed her sandwich away.

"I'm half surprised she hasn't snuck into the apartment and packed you a bag. I've got the distinct feeling that you're not telling me things."

Dani put her half-eaten sandwich down and the look in her eyes confirmed Piper's suspicions.

"Because you're not telling me everything, are you?" Piper said.

"I was thinking about going to New York. For just a short trip. A few days. Tops."

"Where were you going to stay for these *few days*?" Piper squeezed her own knees under the table.

"Izabelle offered me her spare room, but if that makes you uncomfortable, I'll get a hotel."

That was a moot point and Piper knew it. If Dani was going to fuck her ex it didn't matter if she stayed at a hotel room or not. A bed was a bed. They could fuck in her hotel room just as well as in her apartment.

Hell, they could fuck anywhere.

"I was going to talk to you about it today. I didn't tell you because—"

"You didn't tell me because you weren't going to take me with you," Piper said plainly.

Dani didn't deny it. "You have a lot of cases, and your exams are next week. I figured you'd be busy."

"You figured but you didn't ask," Piper said. "Just say you don't want me to come."

"I admit I get tired of refereeing between the two of you, but it's not like I don't *want* you there."

At least Dani had the decency to look apologetic. "I'm sorry. I really was going to talk to you about it before we had dinner with her. I guess I was just dreading the conversation because I knew we were going to fight about it."

Maybe that was true, but Piper suspected Dani was also

afraid that Izzy would bring up the trip at dinner and that Piper might overreact if she didn't know in advance.

It felt more like damage control rather than consideration for Piper's feelings.

Piper rubbed her forehead. "Listen, Izabelle wants you to come to New York because she wants to get back together with you. She's hoping you like the city or the job enough to give her another shot. If you don't think she's going to put the moves on you, you're—"

She wanted to say *an idiot* but stopped herself. Dani wasn't an idiot. There was no need to call her names just because Piper wanted to wring Izabelle's neck.

"We're just friends. I don't see her that way at all," Dani insisted.

"She sees you *that* way."

"You don't know—" Dani began.

"I one *thousand* percent know," Piper said. "At the award dinner, she all but said she wanted to get back together with you."

"*No.* No way." Dani rolled her eyes. "I know she can be catty, but that's just Izabelle. She knows there's nothing there."

"I guess you're not going to believe me until her tongue is down your throat." Piper wasn't sure what else to say. She couldn't convince Dani that her ex was still in love with her if she was unwilling to see it. It was clear that she was clinging to the illusion that she could be friends with her as hard as Izabelle was clinging to the idea that she had a future with Dani.

It didn't help that Izabelle embodied everything that Piper was self-conscious about.

She had money. She was educated and accomplished.

Dani said she wanted Piper, that she didn't want Izabelle,

but Piper's mind was finding it difficult to accept that possibility when the math didn't add up.

Izabelle had more to offer. Period.

All Piper could do was be patient with the situation and try not to do anything that might make things implode.

Basically, the impossible.

"Hey." Dani scooted her chair closer to Piper's. She reached for Piper's hand, forcing it to stop incessantly rubbing her forehead. "Baby, look at me."

Piper met her gaze.

"It's true that Izabelle's editor, Kenneth Koch if you must know, offered me a good job. An amazing opportunity, actually. It pays well, it's a coveted position, with serious clout, and I wouldn't be doing grunt work. I'd just be focusing on the investigative stories I want. Two of Koch's teams have won Pulitzers. It's definitely attractive."

Piper looked at the sky, praying for composure.

Dani forced her to meet her eyes. "*But* I haven't said yes. I just said I'd come and take a look around. Have a couple business lunches. *Nothing* is decided. We don't even know where you'll be placed after you complete your twenty weeks at Quantico. Maybe you'll get placed in New York for all you know."

"*If* I complete it," Piper corrected. But Dani was right. King had said that the FBI could place her in any of the offices across the country, or even abroad, and that was one of the many reasons why Piper was hesitant to commit to that route.

Piper loved New Orleans. It was home. She wasn't sure she could ever be happy anywhere else because there was nowhere else like it.

"New York has more opportunity than NOLA does," Piper said. "You'll get noticed there. You deserve to be noticed."

"I'm already getting noticed." Dani tipped her head. "And I love this city as much as you do. I love *us*. I would *never* do anything to ruin that."

You say that now, Piper thought. *You might feel differently once Izabelle gets you alone.*

11

———

Relief washed over Louie the moment she stepped away from the old pine tree toward her lake. She stared at its placid patina. It must have rained hard in the last hour, because though the sky was a cloudy white, the ground was wet and fog hung in the air.

A dragonfly crisscrossed the surface before alighting, causing circular ripples to radiate toward the shore.

Louie wanted to take off her boots and walk into the water barefoot, but it was too troublesome. She simply removed her leather jacket and threw it over the low branch of a tree before walking off the embankment.

She touched the Berettas in their shoulder holsters to reassure herself they were still there.

Just in case.

She hadn't needed them the last few times she'd crossed over. But it was dangerous to make assumptions.

The water was cool against her warm skin. It soaked her pants, her shirt, and licked her bare arms. She was in to her waist when she took a deep breath and dove.

She waited in the dark, her eyes pinched closed. When

the twilight colors began to darken to blood red and the waters warmed, Louie kicked for the surface.

La Loon greeted her. A nightmare landscape that would make anyone except for Louie herself believe they'd crossed into Hell. The white mountains in the distance, hazy beneath the strange yellow sky. Twin moons hung above the jagged peaks, glowing in perpetual twilight.

The most horrific feature itself, the blood-red lake stretched in both directions. It went as far as the eye could see to the east, and to the west it stopped at a rough cliff face. Its shores were clotted with a black forest of short trees and heart-shaped leaves. The smell of sulfur was strong again today.

Then again, Louie felt that all scents were stronger now that she was pregnant. The doctor had assured her that it was a typical symptom and it would return to normal once her daughter was born. Lou paddled toward shore until it was shallow enough to stand. But she didn't leave the water entirely. Instead, she sat down as if soaking in a bath, everything below her shoulders still submerged.

Who needs prenatal vitamins when I can just soak in this, she thought.

They still weren't sure how these strange microbes were going to affect the baby, but Lou hoped they would only benefit her. After all, they were the reason Louie had healed from the brink of death countless times. Whatever it was in these waters, it could neutralize poison and speed healing. Louie wondered what else it could do that she simply hadn't discovered yet.

More than once she'd teased Konstantine with the idea of having a water birth in this lake.

Please, amore, *no. I beg you.*

It was clear that the notion of bringing his child into such a nightmarish landscape was too much for him to consider.

But she hadn't been able to help herself. It was too fun, tormenting him. Too easy a target, as far as their daughter was concerned.

It was true that he often deferred to her, wanting her to do what made her most comfortable, since it was her body that would bear the brunt of the trauma associated with childbirth. But he had standards and wishes all the same.

Because he loves her already, she thought. *And he loves me.*

Konstantine.

There was no point in brooding over her careless words now.

I'll apologize when I see him. Maybe.

The waters rippled and Louie looked up, half expecting to see the strange reptile-like orcas that hunted the deeper waters.

But it wasn't the orcas. It was one of Jabbers's brood. Its black serpentine body cut lazy waves in the water, diving out of sight before cresting again. There was something playful and otter-like about the way it moved. Seeing it made Louie wonder where its siblings were. Perhaps they were in the cave with Jabbers, which was where Lou always found her these days. But more and more often she was encountering the offspring in Blood Lake.

Lou knew the underwater caves must be connected to this larger body of water somehow.

The offspring crested suddenly, coming into the shallows and standing before Louie. Without thinking, she pulled her gun and pointed it at the creature.

She didn't want to hurt it. But she also was aware of the simple fact that these creatures were not as familiar with her as Jabbers was. She could trust Jabbers not to tear her open like a Christmas ham.

The beast made a strange clicking sound in its throat and moved closer. Its eyes were a deep orange, not the pus-colored shade of its mother's. The color variation made Louie think of hawks, and how some had paler eyes as young before they darkened with age.

And this creature had grown since Louie had last seen it, or perhaps it only looked longer because this was the first time encountering it in its full form out of the lake.

The body was still sleek and built for the water. It had none of the bulk that Jabbers had acquired over the years.

Not yet.

More clicks and a sound from deep in its throat that could be mistaken for a tiger's chuff. No, that wasn't quite right. But then again, what did Lou expect? There was nothing in her world, not a single bird or beast, that could be compared to the monster moving toward her.

It was ten feet from her now. Eight. Five. Four.

She asked herself if she was ready to pull the trigger and kill it at the slightest provocation of violence.

Or you can do what you did with Jabbers, she reminded herself.

There was once a time that she had not been friends with Jabbers either. The ring-shaped scar on her shoulder was her proof. The first time they'd met, Jabbers had fallen on her, sinking her rows of teeth into Louie's small shoulder, here on this very beach.

She'd been only ten at the time. And she'd likely only escaped with her life because the water had pulled her back through to her own world the moment Louie fell backward into it, trying to get away from the monster.

Her alliance with Jabbers had been conditioned over many years. She'd brought that creature hundreds of corpses to feast on. The way to the monster's heart had proved to be through her stomach.

This was different.

Louie hadn't brought a corpse to La Loon for months.

She'd walked away from every fight in order to keep the baby safe and had nothing to show for it.

Still the offspring was advancing, making those indecipherable sounds in its throat.

Lou raised the gun and thumbed off the safety. Her mind was already splitting, feeling as if she would betray Jabbers by killing one of her children, but at the same time, wondering if she could hide her crime by dragging its corpse out into the deeper part of the lake for the orca-like creatures to take care of its remains.

She'd just made her mind up when the beast pounced. But it didn't collide with Louie. It landed on the sandy shore and began to roll around on its back like a dog, its tongue lolling from the side of its mouth.

"Jesus," Louie swore, lowering the gun.

It kicked its legs, moving its torso up and down while obviously trying to scratch an itch.

With her exit no longer blocked, Louie eased deeper into the water. She would see Jabbers and the others next time.

Lou had made it out several feet before the beast sat up and looked around for her.

It caught sight of her just as she slipped below the surface.

Lou dove, hoping to make it through to the other side— back to her own world—before the creature caught up to her.

The last thing she saw before the waters softened from red to dull gray again was a sleek, serpentine form diving beneath the surface to join her.

On the shores of her own lake, in her own world, Lou waited for a long time, watching the calm gray waters, half expecting to see the creature rise from their depths.

But the waters remained still, the early evening quiet.

She had almost relaxed, leather jacket in hand, when a chord of fury echoed through her.

The frantic pull of someone in need. Without thinking,

she slipped through the shadows collecting beneath the tall pines.

When the world formed around her again, she was almost hit by a flying glass. She ducked out of its path at the last second. As she stood, she pulled her gun, thinking she'd walked into a fight.

But there was no target.

It was only Stefano in his living room, chest bare, hurling Italian curses at the air.

His chest was bleeding. Lou could see at least two wounds. A gash across his upper bicep which had bled a curtain of blood down his arm, and another gash in his side. This line was cleaner, which made Louie think it had been done by a blade rather than a bullet.

The wound on his arm though—

"You've been shot," she said simply.

He spun on her, his eyes red with his grief. "So my prayers still work."

His fury wasn't directed at her. Lou knew that. "What happened?"

"He was ready for us. I took four of his, and he took one of ours. But he got away, that piece of shit."

"You'll find him again," Louie said.

He loosed a bitter laugh. "Not without you, *Strega*."

He took another lowball glass off the bar and filled it. Lou wondered how many drinks he'd had already.

"Your arm is going to get infected."

He waved her off, muttering incomprehensible Italian at her before throwing back the drink. He smashed the empty glass back on the bar. Lou supposed she could be grateful that he'd decided not to send this one through the air too.

"I want to find him before he has a chance to regroup. He's organized. Methodical. The only way to overtake him is to surprise him. I can't do that without you. I need your help."

"I want to help you," she said. That was the truth.

It wasn't only because she respected his position as Konstantine's second-in-command. Or because she knew Stefano was the only one that cared as much for Konstantine's safety as she did. It was also the restlessness. For months it had been gnawing on her bones like a half-starved animal desperate for satiation.

She wanted to kill.

He got on his knees in front of her. "Then please. *Please*, help me."

He took her hand and pressed his forehead to it. There was nothing seductive or romantic about the motion. It was only a soulful plea from a man at the end of his rope.

"You know this feeling," he said, his voice cracking. "You *know* what I feel with him out there, walking the streets. *Non può essere. Dio mi aiuti, non può essere.*"

Louie did know that feeling. It had consumed her for fourteen years. Her grief, her hunger and desperation, all of it had half driven her out of her mind.

Louie didn't want Stefano to lose himself in it. She needed him here. Strong and steady at Konstantine's back.

"If I help you then we can't tell him. He'll be pissed," Louie said.

What a hypocrite I've become.

After yelling at Konstantine, speaking to him as she had, trying to force him to adhere to his half of the bargain that neither of them would put themselves in harm's way for the sake of their daughter—look where she was now.

Stefano swiped at his red nose. "That's what he said about you."

"Stefano, I'm here. I've come." Konstantine's voice rang

down the hallway, out of sight. "I have a plan for how we can corner him. We will move in two—"

His words dried up when he saw her, entering the living room with a bulletproof vest in one hand and a gun in the other.

He looked from Stefano on his knees to Louie.

What did he think of the scene? His second clutching her hand, the grief and desperation crumpling his face.

There was a moment when he looked as if he might try to hide the bulletproof vest and the gun behind his back. That told Louie all she needed to know. He had also planned to go into battle.

He'd also planned to keep secrets.

"At least we're both liars," she said.

 King stood on the steps outside the Royal Street precinct, waiting for White to arrive. Officers came and went through the large double doors of the sherbet-colored building. He took a sip of the hot coffee he'd bought at the bistro next door, while reading the latest missing persons poster stapled to the pole outside the precinct.

Marshall Trinidad
24 years old
5'9
Black
Tattoo on his left forearm of the cross and rosary entwined

After committing the young man's information to memory, King turned his attention to running through his cover story for the hundredth time.

He spotted Piper running up the sidewalk. One hand clutched the strap of her backpack. The other shielded her eyes from the bright sunlight. "Sorry. Perkins was getting cold feet on me. I had to strong-arm her."

"How'd it go?" King had sent her to interview a potential witness on the B&E case. The woman had been skittish from the start, and King had discovered, much to his delight, that Piper had a soft touch.

"Good. *Eventually.* She finally agreed to testify on the condition that I'd take her to and from the courthouse and sit with her during the trial. That's fine by me because it means I can pin her in place if she tries to run out on us like the witness from that aggravated assault case. I still can't believe he snuck out."

"They do that sometimes," King said.

"Unreliable! I hate flaky people."

"Good work, Genereux," he said, and gave her shoulder a squeeze. "How do you feel about this?"

He nodded at the precinct.

"I'm ready. Consider me your personal stenographer. I'll also make notes on the body language, which I'll have you know I'm pretty good at *thank you very much*." She adjusted her backpack on her shoulder.

"I'm sure you are." King had been continuously surprised by her insightfulness, and how easy it had become to trust her instincts.

Her eyes were fixed on his coffee cup. "Hey, can I get a coffee before we start?"

"Why not?" he said. White was late. She might as well. He pulled a ten-dollar bill from his pocket. "My treat."

"You don't have to."

"I do. You're on the clock," he said, and stuffed the bill into her hand. "Go on."

"Thanks." She disappeared under the awning. Ten minutes later, White's SUV rolled up to the curb and parked across the street.

King threw a wave as he crossed to him. "Dick."

"Robbie," he said. He checked his watch and frowned. "Sorry I'm late."

King would've said he was making a habit of it, but it seemed unfair to kick a man while he was down.

"Not a problem," King said. He saw Piper approaching with her coffee in his periphery. "Are you ready?"

White gave Piper a nod. "Morning, Genereux."

Piper blew on her coffee. "Morning, Detective. Let's do this."

The precinct itself was calm compared to the chaos of the Quarter outside its doors. They stopped at the desk and got visitors' badges that would allow them to enter the upper levels of the precinct building.

"I'm going to set you up in the Westside conference room," White said as King attached his badge to the front of his polo shirt. "I'll send people your way as I find them."

He handed King a list of names. King scanned through it and guessed there were at least sixty people.

"Just mark off who you spoke to as they come in," White said. "And we can do a second pass if you want."

Piper was looking at the list over his shoulder. She pressed her lips together and said nothing. She didn't have to. King knew what she was thinking. It was a long list. They were going to be here all day even if they kept the interviews short and to the point.

A few minutes later they were at the conference table. They took seats on one side and positioned empty chairs on the opposite side.

Piper opened her laptop and positioned a legal pad next to it. She pretended to crack her knuckles and stretch her hands.

"Bring it on. I'm ready."

Two female officers came through the door.

"Stick to the script," he whispered.

King thought it was unlikely that the bomber was a woman. But he couldn't rule out the possibility even though it was true that female bombers were usually terrorists or political assassins of some kind. They usually didn't blow themselves up when they had personal grievances. And from reading White's letters from the bomber, it definitely felt like the grievances were personal.

"Hello, Officers," King said, offering each his hand.

"Hey, King," the one with short-cropped hair said, clasping his hand as she did so. "What're you doing here today?"

"Someone has made a threat against this precinct and White asked me to help him run interviews. We're just gathering information at this stage. Nothing special. Trying to ascertain means and motive. Have either of you seen anything suspicious in this building? People who stand out? Anyone who might want to hurt you?"

They exchanged a look. "We were just talking about the message in the ladies' bathroom. Someone carved 'I'm gonna kill all you bitches' into the bathroom stall. That was charming."

The other officer rolled her eyes. "I don't think it's a serious threat. It's probably one of the kids fucking around."

Piper's hands were flying across the keys. King suppressed the urge to look at her or ask what the heck she was recording this early in the conversation.

"What kids are you referring to?" he asked.

"We've got two shadow programs that bring kids through here. We get about twelve to fifteen kids from the high school each year. They come in, they shadow one of us for a few weeks, and if they stand out, we can recommend them for a scholarship to UNO. It's cute. They get these little goodie bags with stuff from the precinct and temporary badges and uniforms."

"Because most of the kids are juniors?" Piper asked.

"That's right," the officer said. "Hey, haven't I seen you at The Wild Cat?"

"Probably," Piper said, flashing a polite smile. "My friend dances drag there."

"Do you have the impression that anyone would want to harm either of you?" King asked, hoping to redirect the conversation.

They shrugged. "Not really. No one likes cops these days. We see that all over social media, don't we? But no one's made any threats to my face."

"Yeah. People talk a lot of shit, but they rarely follow through with it," the other one said. "Are you sure it's legit?"

King would have agreed with them if not for White's visceral reaction to the situation and Mel's reading. He trusted their instincts as a rule, but for both of them to be in alignment like that gave him greater pause.

"Humor me," King said with his best smile. "Have you seen anyone in the building that stood out to you lately? Anyone who was up here on the second floor with the offices and shouldn't have been?"

They shook their head.

King noted their relaxed form, their casual manner. He didn't think that either of them was hiding anything. The one wasn't even pretending to hide her interest in Piper, openly checking her out across the table.

Piper wasn't even looking at her.

"If either of you do come across anything suspicious, please give me a call." He handed each of the officers a card.

"What about you?" the short-haired one asked Piper. "You got a number?"

Piper looked up and smiled. "No, sorry. I left my cards at home with my girlfriend."

The officer's smile broadened and she tipped her head. "Noted. Have a good day."

When they were alone, King nudged Piper's knee under the table with his own.

"You handled that well. Very professional."

Her cheeks reddened. "Thanks, boss."

The next batch of interviews were equally unhelpful. No one had seen anything and no one seemed particularly worried about a threat of attack. More than a few looked exhausted and overworked, but King didn't detect any resentment or suppressed rage.

By lunch they'd made their way through two-thirds of the list.

They took their break at the café next door, grabbing a table outside with a view of the precinct.

Once their sandwiches and salads arrived, they reviewed their notes, eating in silence.

Halfway through the meal, Piper plunged her straw into her iced coffee and gave it a shake.

"I gotta say," she said, "apart from the lady cop, no one was giving me any vibes."

"What do you mean?" he asked. "You think the flirting was just a distraction?"

Piper put a hand on her chest in mock horror. "Are you telling me people only flirt with me to hide their *crimes*?"

He laughed. "No. I'm just asking if you think it was a diversion."

"No, I think she was genuinely interested. I'm just saying apart from her, no one stood out today. No one seemed nervous. No one seemed guilty. No one looked particularly suspicious."

King had to agree. "I noticed that too."

He was starting to worry that they were turning over the wrong logs. Maybe he should go back to the drawing board. Maybe even look at the paper manufacturer more closely. There was the real possibility that in order to undermine White's sanity, the bomber simply planted the seed of distrust so that he would start to doubt his fellow officers. Maybe the stalker-bomber really was hoping that White would become paranoid enough to make a mistake and tarnish his reputation, if not ruin his career.

"Maybe they're not here today," Piper offered.

"We have the full list of all authorized officers, staff, and building personnel. If we get through the list, that's everyone."

"We have a full list for the people who can access the second *floor*," Piper said. "What if they just come into the building? There's no way to track that."

"White said he got the letters on his desk. His desk is on the second floor."

"Yeah, but if someone delivers them to the first-floor letter box then it's carried up by the postman. Anyone can stick a letter in the box."

King didn't like that possibility since it was a dead end. There would be no way to track their bad guy if anyone in New Orleans could walk into the precinct off the street and drop something into the letter box.

Piper's face lit up. "Let's put a camera in there. Hide it in White's office in case the bad guy delivers another letter."

"That's illegal. Even if he consented, I think the precinct would bar it," King said.

She pouted. "Dumb. Then what do we do?"

The hairs on the back of King's neck rose. He had the distinct feeling of being watched.

He scanned the street. He combed the throngs of tourists, street vendors, artists painting their wares on the curb. The busker with his guitar case open, playing a country-western rendition of a Tracy Chapman song. The other bistro patrons laughing over their lunch, the din of conversation colliding with the music.

No one stuck out.

"Boss? Earth to King?" Piper shook her iced coffee at him. "*Hello?*"

He blinked, looking away from the street. "Sorry. What?"

"I said, 'Then what do we do?' If the precinct turns out to be a dead end, what do we do next? If the call's *not* coming from inside the house?"

King's eyes swept over the crowds while he spoke. "Then it's back to the drawing board. We'll have to go back to Pelican Paper and ask better questions. And we might have to follow White around. He said someone was following him. Maybe if we tail White, we'll catch the guy. Get a good look at them. Or at least a plate number or make and model that we can use."

Piper sipped her coffee. "Okay. Cool. Dani is going to be in New York for a few days anyway. I'll drive the SUV and you've got the Buick. Two tails are better than one. *Ugh, god.* That reminds me—"

Piper checked the time on her phone.

"I've got dinner with that witch tonight."

King's stomach tightened as he locked eyes with a man in the distance. Tall. Face hidden under a red ball cap. The man turned away before King could get a good look at him.

"One second." King leapt up from the table.

He shouldered his way through the crowd, issuing his apologies as he hurried after the retreating form.

From the back he was slender, wearing a light windbreaker and white sneakers. Acid-washed jeans.

Turn around, King thought. *Turn around and let me get a good look at you.*

But instead of turning around, he turned a corner. And by the time King reached it, he had disappeared altogether. There wasn't a single red hat or windbreaker in the sea of faces pushing past him.

Whoever had been watching King was gone.

13

Piper had to refrain from rolling her eyes when she realized that dinner was going to be at Carre Augusta's. A chic, expensive place in the Garden District that served elegant French fare.

"Did Izabelle pick the place?" Piper asked as they walked beneath the gold awning toward the restaurant. "Is she too good for red beans and rice? Fried okra?"

The doorman in his pressed black suit opened the door for them, but before they reached it, Dani turned on her.

She tucked a curling strand behind her ear. "Listen, before we go in there—"

Oh no. Am I in trouble already?

"—I know that Izzy can be catty, but promise me you won't make it worse."

"You want me to just let her talk shit to me?" Piper slipped her hands into her pocket. "That's a big ask."

"If she talks shit, I will run interference. I promise. But can you please let me handle her?"

The doorman was still holding the door open.

"Fine. But if she crosses a line—"

"She won't," Dani promised. "I'll kick her under the table if I have to."

"And yet you still think she doesn't have feelings for you?" Piper gave her a skeptical look. "You think she's just this combative because—"

"She's protective," Dani said. "That's it."

"Okay." Piper pressed her lips together to stop herself from starting an argument here on the steps of the restaurant.

Besides, she was feeling bad for the doorman. He was still holding the door open without complaint. His arm had to be on fire.

"Thank you," Dani said, and went inside.

"Sorry," Piper whispered as she crossed the threshold after her.

"Good luck," he whispered back.

"Thanks." Piper snorted, feeling marginally vindicated.

The smile was still bright on her lips when their table came into view and Izabelle was at her seat looking like a million bucks with her plunging neckline, on-point makeup, and a glass of wine in hand.

Don't be petty. You promised. And you have the girl. You're the winner here.

"I already ordered a bottle of Veuve Clicquot La Grande Dame," she said. "Let me pour you a glass."

"Thanks." Dani slipped out of her dinner jacket and Piper laid it over the back of her chair.

"Have you guys eaten here before?" Izabelle asked.

Piper felt like this was a test. "No, we usually eat out of buckets with our hands."

Dani snorted before she could stop herself. To Izabelle she said, "She's joking. Yes, we have."

"You're so *funny*." Izabelle tipped the bottle, filling Dani's glass. "Is that a natural trait or something you've cultivated?"

Piper had the distinct impression that Izabelle didn't find her remotely amusing. "Natural."

"Then I'll have to be sure to keep Dani plenty entertained while she's in New York," Izabelle said.

In that moment, Piper was glad that Dani had warned her ahead of time about the visit. Izabelle was clearly searching for a sign of Piper's discomfort.

And I'll be damned if I give you the satisfaction.

"Your apartment is in Manhattan, right?" Piper said without hesitation. "Baby, you should go back to that vegan restaurant we ate at. What was it called? It was French for 'plants.'"

"Le Botaniste," Dani said, before taking a sip of her wine.

"Right. I bet you can walk there from Izzy's place. You liked their food."

Izabelle frowned. "When were you in New York?"

"Oh, we've been there a couple of times this past year." Piper didn't mention Lou. She was the reason why they were able to pop in and out of NYC for lunch whenever it suited them. It didn't matter. Her words hit their mark.

Izabelle looked genuinely disappointed.

She searched Dani's face. "Why were you in NYC?"

"For stories. They were quick trips," Dani said, burying her face in the menu.

"And your friends Evangeline and Teddy," Piper pressed. "Are you going to see them while you're there?"

Piper had never met these people in her life. She just wanted to prove to Izabelle that she would do the button-pushing *thank you very much*. She refused to let this woman know just how much she was getting under Piper's skin.

"I haven't told them I'm coming," Dani said. "I didn't know if we'd have time to see them. It's a bit of a haul for them to get into the city."

Now Izabelle was the one pretending to look at the menu.

Piper decided she could retract her claws. For the time being.

Dani must have been worried that Piper was going to take another shot at Izabelle because she began filling the conversation with random details of her trip. What airline she was flying in, when she would arrive, the restaurants they would go to—apart from Le Botaniste. Izabelle wanted to take her to the Museum of Modern Art and the New York City Ballet. Apparently, she had already bought them tickets.

"And I believe Koch wants to take you to Broadway," she added. "In addition to the lunch with the staff so you can meet everyone."

"That'll be nice," Dani said.

Will it? Piper thought, her confidence waning.

Don't beat yourself up. Of course she's happy to meet new people and network with other journalists. It doesn't mean she's fantasizing about moving to New York and starting a new life without you.

Izabelle must have sensed the slightest shift in her mood. Her gaze fixed on Piper. "It's a shame you can't join us. Dani says you have finals."

"And your cases," Dani added. "You can't leave King now with the—"

Piper nudged her under the table. She didn't want Dani to mention the bomber. Izabelle couldn't be trusted with sensitive information like that. Hell, Piper wouldn't trust her with a grocery list.

"No, I can't," Piper said, forcing a smile. "Even if I didn't have the finals, work is kinda crazy right now."

"Seems exciting," Izabelle said, leaning forward. "But don't worry, Piper. I'll take good care of our girl."

"You always do," Dani said, as the waiter arrived to take their orders.

Yes, Piper thought. *That's what I'm afraid of.*

14

T his Florentine cathedral reminded Lou of the cathedral in New Orleans, the one in Jackson Square. Stefano stood with his family several paces away, his head bowed low, hands clasped as the priest spoke in a somber tone.

Lou and Konstantine hung back, watching from a pew near the middle. Far enough away to give the family their space.

"There are so many people," Louie said. She suspected this might have been the largest funeral attendance she'd ever seen. Even considering her own parents' funerals, which had been a citywide day of mourning complete with twenty-one-gun salute.

"Funerals are a community event in Italy. And he has a large family," Konstantine said, his arm brushing hers. "He's the oldest of eight kids."

"*Eight.*" Lou cocked a brow. "What is it with you Catholics and breeding?"

Konstantine snorted. "That was the reason Stefano ended up with Padre Leo."

"Because of the breeding or the Catholicism?" Louie was joking and keeping her tone light because she knew speaking of Padre Leo could be a tender topic. The old priest was the closest thing to a father figure that Konstantine had known growing up. Losing him had not been easy.

"Stefano was like me. I went to Padre Leo because I didn't want my mother to prostitute for money. Stefano went because he didn't want his siblings to be beggars in the street. When their parents died, they moved in with their grandmother, who was kind, but she didn't have enough to feed all the children. Stefano began to work for Padre. He has been providing for them—all of them—ever since."

"He's a good brother," Louie said, watching as Stefano placed a hand on Stella's shoulder and gave it a squeeze.

"Yes, he's worked very hard. *Molto fedele.* He has a good family."

"Are you feeling nostalgic right now? Wishing I hadn't killed your father and brothers?"

Konstantine's lips quirked. "No. We both know I did not have a *good* family."

"You had a good mother." Louie couldn't count the villainous half sister in Venice as *good*.

"*Sì*," he said, a flash of pain crossing his face. "*Ho avuto una buona madre.*"

Louie didn't point out that he also had Stefano and Padre Leo. She wasn't sure if that mattered in the sense he was talking about. Had she had a good family? Her mother had never been kind, but Lou had loved her father with all her heart. And Aunt Lucy had given her the world.

I had a good family, she thought. *It wasn't as big as Stefano's, but it was good.*

She placed a hand on her stomach. *And you will have even more than I did.*

Not only would her daughter have Louie and Konstantine,

she would have Dani, Piper, King, and Melandra. She'd have all the children at the church to look out for her.

You will be loved.

Konstantine seemed to read her thoughts. He took her hand and brushed a kiss across her knuckles. "We will be a good family, too."

"As long as you're aware that I will *not* be having eight children. I don't care how Catholic you are."

"I will be happy with any number of children, *amore mio*."

She suspected it was the gravity of the day that was making him sweeter than usual. Surely he saw Stefano grieving and wondered if that would be him one day, standing over Louie in a box.

And there was still the matter of Modesto Detti. They hadn't sorted all the details of their second strike against him, only that they *would* move against him. They'd promised Stefano that much.

They just had to find a way to do it that kept all of them safe.

Konstantine had changed his tune as soon as he'd realized Lou was as committed to helping Stefano as he was. How easily he'd switched from *let's finish this before she finds out* to *let's plan this well and be cautious.*

Still, she felt like a hypocrite. She'd ignored countless calls, urgings from her compass during her pregnancy. Now she was going to run into fire? Were the earlier sacrifices really so easy to forget?

It wasn't that she hadn't tried to rationalize it.

It's different. Stefano is one of our own. Konstantine and I will be safer if we work together rather than take risks behind each other's backs.

Tell that to the people who you let die.

Each excuse seemed weaker than the last.

The truth was that Lou hadn't felt like herself in months.

She'd entered this bondage willingly. She'd chosen to abstain from hunting, to avoid danger at all costs, for the sake of the child growing inside her, but the price of that decision was wearing on her.

She could admit that to herself at least, if not to Konstantine.

"Do you forgive me?" Konstantine whispered.

Louie looked away from the funeral scene and searched his face. "For what?"

"For telling you I would not go to Stefano but I did. You saw me."

"You saw *me*," she said. "It's clear that neither of us have it in us to abandon the people we care about."

"You understand, don't you?" His face was so earnest.

She appreciated it. She never saw him display this level of vulnerability with anyone else. She had expected the opposite. That perhaps because Louie herself was emotionally hardened, Konstantine would feel the need to mask his own feelings. But he had only ever been open with her, and knowing how difficult that was struck a chord of tenderness in her.

"I understand," she said. "The more I think about it, the more I realize our original promise was never going to work anyway."

"What do you mean?"

"We said we wouldn't do anything to put ourselves in harm's way so that she"—Louie touched her stomach again—"would never lose us. But unless we plan to give all of this up, unless we plan to move everyone we love to a deserted island at the end of the world, we're going to break that promise sooner or later. Our lives are too dangerous."

He considered this. "We could. I know an island."

Louie snorted. "Even if we *could* give it up—"

Lou had zero confidence that she could bring herself to

stop hunting forever any more than Konstantine could walk away from the underworld he'd been a part of for so long. She was barely holding herself back now, after just a few months.

"What about the people we care about? King and Piper would have to give up investigating. Dani would have to stop chasing stories. No one could do anything that put themselves at risk because if they were in danger, just like Stefano is in danger, we know that we would intervene."

Lou had watched enough movies to know that even when the killer vowed to start a new life, to leave all the death and destruction behind them and start afresh, it was usually a matter of time before it came knocking again, and someone she loved would get hurt.

Konstantine's eyes remained fixed on the priest. "Then what do we do? If we cannot avoid the danger, the risks, what do we do?"

"We get stronger," she said. "We become harder to find. Harder to challenge. We learn from our mistakes."

"Our mistakes," he repeated. "Like with Ilaria. That shouldn't have happened."

This was the first time that Louie was hearing Stefano's sister's name.

"Modesto found her. How? We need to figure out what methods he used and eliminate them. No one should be able to find one of our people that way again."

"It wasn't online," he said. "I am very careful."

"Then if it's word of mouth, we eliminate the source," she said.

"We can't kill someone just for knowing something."

"We can. Are you telling me you wouldn't do worse for your kid?"

"Of course," he said.

"Both you and I have had to be ruthless in the past," she

said. "I'm saying that we can be ruthless for our daughter too. *Brutal.* More brutal than ever."

He didn't like it. Louie knew that. She'd walked into his church sanctuary more than once to find him covered in someone's blood, a tired look in his eyes.

"We will do everything we can to hide ourselves. To make the people we love untouchable. Then if something still happens, we will be brutal. Take no prisoners. Leave a crime scene so horrifying that the next person who considers challenging us will be too afraid to even think about it."

That was the level of ruthlessness Louie was prepared to execute. It was true that many of the gangsters in the underworld feared her purely because she could be anywhere at any time. She could emerge from the darkness into any room and take their lives.

Until now, it hadn't deterred the Modesto Dettis of the world.

Lou would have to change that. And if she was being honest, she was thrilled by the idea, the possibilities, of what she could do if she *really* tried to scare them.

Konstantine was looking at her. "Why are you smiling like that, *amore mio?*"

"No reason."

15

———

King knew he was dreaming the instant Melandra clasped the back of his neck. He couldn't in his rational mind accept that she would do such a thing to him in the real world. If he was awake, he would be the one to kiss her first. He was sure of it.

But here they were.

"Robert," she breathed.

"You never call me that," he said. *It's a dream. It's only a dream.*

Except that his heart was racing and the feel of her fingers in his hair were so real he could have believed it.

Wake up, he begged. *It's a dream, wake up.*

She placed a kiss on his throat. Then another. When her lips pressed to his collarbone, he felt like his body had come alive with electric fire.

Wake up!

His body jerked, pulling him to consciousness.

"Robert?"

His heart sputtered in his chest. He sat up and looked

around the dark bedroom. For a moment he thought he was still dreaming. That despite his best efforts to wake himself he'd simply moved from one level of unconsciousness to the next.

Then he recognized the floral chair in the corner. The standing mirror. The framed photograph on the dresser of Beth with her arms around her handsome son, pressing a kiss to his cheek. His smile bright.

"Robert, what is it?" Beth asked, stirring beside him. "Are you okay?"

Robert.

It hadn't been Melandra calling his name. It had been Beth.

He ran a hand down his face and realized two things at once. First of all, he was covered in sweat, and secondly, his erection was so hard it hurt.

"I'm okay," King said, holding the blanket across his lap.

"Are you sure?" she asked, her eyes liquid black in the dim room. "You called out."

Shit.

"What did I say?" He hoped it hadn't been Melandra's name.

"It wasn't clear," she said. "It was more of a sound than anything."

Beth moved toward him. King moved away, reflexively. He didn't want her to know he had an erection. It was very possible that she'd offer to relieve him of it, and while it was true that he'd welcome the offer any other time, it didn't feel appropriate now, given that it had been thoughts of another woman that had aroused him.

Her face pinched.

"I'm all sweaty," he said by way of explanation. "Let me rinse off."

"I don't care if you're sweaty," she said. "It's four in the morning."

He slid out of her bed before she could object. "I'll be quick."

He closed her bathroom door behind him and switched on the light.

In the mirror he saw a red-faced man with sweat beaded on his forehead, his eyes wide with fear.

What is wrong with you?

He turned on the cold water and climbed in before it could warm.

Under the assault of cold water, his erection left him, and the sweat was rinsed from his body. King dried himself with one of Beth's plush, oversized towels.

He put on clean boxers and climbed back into bed, thinking that she'd already dropped back into sleep.

"Are you having a hard time with it?" Beth asked just as his own eyelids had grown heavy.

King said nothing. She couldn't be talking about the dreams. How would she know about them?

"I'm having a hard time too," she said, placing a hand on his chest.

Definitely not talking about the dreams.

"I'm not too proud to say it, Robert," she said. "I've gone and fallen in love with you."

Shit.

"Beth—"

"Just let me finish," she said. She moved her warm hand to his cheek, turning his head so he had to look at her.

"Okay."

He couldn't meet her eyes. Instead, he looked at the gray dreadlocks spilling over her right shoulder and bare breast.

"I know that when I asked you out, I thought we would keep it casual. I know you aren't over the death of your wife."

I seem to be over it enough.

"But I've grown real fond of you. I love your company. And you're a good man. I didn't expect to care as much about you as I do, but here we are."

"I'm—"

She pressed a finger over his lips. "Don't you go and apologize to me. I'm trying to tell you what a lovely surprise you were. You were so good for me. That's nothing to be sorry for."

He would've thanked her if guilt hadn't been pulsing through him.

Yet I'm lying here thinking about another woman.

"I want you to consider what we might be for each other in the future. We've still got at least ten or twenty years left in this life, and I'd like it if we spent them together."

Is she proposing right now?

"That's a lot to think about," he said.

"But can you do that?" she asked. "Can you just think about it, seriously?"

"I can do that," he said, and pulled her close as dawn broke over the horizon. But he was fairly certain his answer would remain *no*.

There was another possibility. It was possible that King needed to leave the city. To have an excuse to get as far away from Melandra as he could so that he didn't ruin their friendship.

He wouldn't go to Orlando because he loved Beth.

But he might go to keep his friendship with Melandra intact, if he couldn't get his feelings under control.

"I'll think about it," he said, and kissed the top of her head. "I promise."

Beth's words were still echoing in his mind as King began his third attempt at tailing White the next day. He'd managed to talk Piper out of joining him, just in case Mel's hunch about a car bomb proved accurate.

Perhaps he was overthinking it. After all, the first and second attempts at following White's SUV through the city had resulted in nothing. It had brought old memories back of King's early days in the DEA, trailing dealers.

Piper had done a good job of holding down the fort in the office, making progress on their outstanding cases and working with the DA's office. But King had felt bad leaving the brunt of that work to her when he had nothing to show for it.

He was also beginning to wonder if his lack of results only proved his feeling that White was paranoid. But whenever he began to question whether there was a bomber at all, he remembered Mel spreading her tarot cards on her kitchen table.

Was he really going to doubt *both* of his closest friends just because he didn't have any evidence yet?

No.

That felt more like a failing on his part.

Acknowledging that his loyalty merited at least a little faith helped King to persevere through the banality of the task. He was almost ready to call it a day when he caught sight of something interesting.

A red sedan. A Honda.

It was a common car, but King was certain this was the third time he'd seen this exact one in his rearview mirror. What were the odds that every red Honda he'd seen today would have the same ding on the hood, just above the left headlight?

What was that from, he wondered. Hail?

He slowed, hoping that the car might slide past him and give King a chance to see its driver, maybe even write down a license plate number.

But the car never overtook him.

In fact, once King hung back so much as to make it ridiculous, the car swung off Canal Street onto a side street out of sight. King cursed the one-way system. It was impossible to go against the flow of traffic and chase after the vehicle.

But when he'd turned, King saw the driver's profile, if not the face. At a distance, it looked very much like the man in the red hat that he'd glimpsed in the Quarter when he and Piper had sat at the bistro table outside the precinct. He couldn't be one hundred percent sure, but he thought that maybe the guy was even wearing the same red hat.

Was it a coincidence?

With a sense of sinking disappointment, King pulled his cell phone out of the Buick's cupholder and called Piper.

"What's up, boss?"

"Can you comb our suspect list and see if someone drives a red Honda?"

"Car, truck, SUV?"

"Sedan," he said.

"You got it."

He considered the only other discerning feature—the ding in the hood—but decided against it. If someone had ambitions to be a bomber, they probably wouldn't report damage like that to the police. They'd avoid unwanted police attention at all costs.

"Just let me know if anyone tied to White or the precinct drives a red Honda."

"Sure thing, boss. I'll do it right after I drop Dani off at the airport."

That was right. She was heading to New York today.

King saw White switch on his blinker and get in the turn lane. He was heading back into the Quarter then, probably to the precinct. That meant that King's tailing efforts for the day were ending.

"When are you heading out?" he asked her.

"Fifteen minutes. If I miss you, I'll just leave my updates on your desk."

"Roger that," he said, replaying the vision of the Honda whipping out of sight, over and over in his mind.

16

Piper decided it was a certain level of hell dropping her girlfriend off at the airport with the full knowledge that she was running into the arms of some would-be interloper.

Yet here she was, setting Dani's suitcase on the sidewalk beside the drop-off lane with the airport doors behind her.

"Baby, you look like you're going to the gallows." Dani sighed, letting her messenger bag slide off her shoulder and hit the pavement at her feet. "I promise, it's going to be fine. Come here."

Piper stepped into her arms. "If she puts the moves on you, you better tell me."

"She won't," Dani said. "But of course. I'd never hide something like that from you. I would think that it goes without saying."

"She better hope she doesn't. Because if she does, *I've* got a friend with a lot of guns who can be in New York like *that*." Piper snapped her fingers for emphasis.

Dani was smiling, but it was tight at the edges.

She's getting tired of hearing this.

How many times had they had this conversation in the days leading up to Dani's flight?

Countless.

Whenever Piper's insecurities crept up on her and threatened to drive her crazy, she had found herself making some small remark before she could stop herself.

"Go on then," Piper said. "Have a great time without me. I know you can't wait to go."

"I can't wait to come back and tell you I *told* you so." Dani came up onto her toes to give Piper a kiss.

"I can't wait for you to come back," Piper countered, wrapping her arms around Dani's waist for a final hug. "Stay safe."

"Always." Dani stepped away, bending down to pick up her bag. "I'll text you when I land."

It'll take all my self-restraint not to be there when you land, Piper thought glumly. She'd thought about asking Louie to help her spy on Dani in New York no less than a million times. She'd imagined them sneaking around the shadows, always within a few feet of Dani and the interloper.

But Piper knew it would damage their relationship if she did. Dani needed to know that Piper trusted her. Dani had already demonstrated it several times over, and now it was Piper's turn, though it was proving a lot harder than Piper had expected.

It's Izzy I don't trust.

"Bye." Piper gave her a final sad little wave as Dani stepped through security and was gone.

A dark form appeared in Piper's periphery. She turned to find Louie beside her, her hands in the pockets of her leather jacket. Eyes covered by her mirrored shades.

"Hey, did you come to see Dani off? You just missed her." Though Piper wasn't sure why it mattered. Lou could go to New York whenever she wanted.

"You sent a distress call." Louie pushed her mirrored shades up onto her head. "I expected to find something more dangerous than airport security."

"Nothing is in danger except my delicate feelings. But just out of curiosity, on a scale of one to ten, how comfortable would you be killing my romantic adversary?"

Lou was unable to hide her amusement. "Define romantic adversary."

And just like that, Piper was unable to stop from telling Louie about all that had happened with Izabelle, every snide remark and innuendo since the award ceremony.

"I'm trying not to be a needy little bitch here. It's not a good look, I know. But I am a thousand percent certain she's trying to get my girl. We *have* to kill her."

"We didn't kill Scarlett," Louie said.

Piper dragged a hand down her face at the mention of her ex booty call turned stalker. "Maybe we should have?"

Lou reached out and put a hand on Piper's shoulder. She gave it a firm squeeze, bringing Piper's agitation and racing thoughts to an abrupt halt.

"Even if Izabelle is stupid enough to try something, she won't get very far. Dani will stop her." Lou's voice was firm, reassuring. "You know that."

Not if, deep down in her heart, Dani knows she deserves better than me.

"What if, like, Dani gets drunk and Izzy takes advantage of her?"

Lou cocked her head. "*Then* we will kill her."

Piper couldn't help but visibly brighten. "Really? Is it bad that I'm almost hoping she tries it?"

"Maybe. But I understand. Trust is hard." Lou's gaze was fixed on something in the distance. Piper couldn't help but wonder what Louie saw that she didn't. A thousand dangers, probably.

"It *really* is. *Why?* Wait. Who are you thinking of? The Italian stallion? Holy shit, does he have a hungry ex lurking? Because I will *ride* if you need me to. Not that you couldn't, like, wipe the floor with her on your own. But you know I've been boxing with Bane."

"There's no hungry ex."

"Right. And I guess you don't care about that stuff. I feel like the stallion is more likely to be the possessive one. Do you really *never* feel possessive? Don't you ever wanna choke someone out for—"

"I feel possessive of you."

"Oh." Piper's face burned. "Thank you."

"And Dani." Lou placed a hand on her stomach. "And this one."

Every ounce of feeling special melted away. "Okay. Not just me. Cool. I mean, of course you should feel protective of your kid. But protective and possessive isn't the same."

"It is for me."

Piper bit her lip. "Maybe it's that hunter part of your personality. Is it like being territorial?"

Lou shrugged.

Piper cast one last longing look at airport security, but Dani was nowhere to be seen. She was probably at her gate by now. "Despite what your instincts say, I'm not *dying*, but I could use some company. Do you wanna hang out? You can distract me with a bit of globe-hopping."

Lou slid her mirrored sunglasses back down over her eyes. "Where should we go first?"

Piper gave her a sheepish grin. "New York?"

LOU DID WHAT SHE COULD TO DISTRACT PIPER FROM HER anxieties. She didn't take her to New York, but they did spend their Friday night exploring the world. They ate ramen for dinner in Japan and played video games in an arcade. They watched the sunset over the Pacific Ocean in Costa Rica. They went to Henry's drag show at The Wild Cat.

Lou couldn't ask directly if this was helping without bringing Piper's attention back to the problem at hand. But she thought it was. The smile on Piper's face had only wilted once or twice—particularly at the beach—which had prompted Lou to bring her somewhere less contemplative and more distracting.

Now she was regretting it. Her feet hurt. The muscles along her spine ached. And the baby was awake again, serving swift kicks to Lou's vital organs.

I like that you're a fighter, she thought. *But I would like it more if you didn't fight me.*

Piper only laughed when Lou made a comment about her pulverized insides.

"It's karma," Piper shouted over the loudspeakers while sipping her rum cocktail. "All those butts you kicked. Now you're getting yours."

When Lou shot her a look, Piper held up her hands in surrender.

"I'm sure they deserved it more than you do. My mistake for insinuating otherwise."

Lou saw her first, cutting through the crowd, her eyes fixed on Piper. The woman had close-cropped hair, her gaze sharp.

Lou stepped forward between her and Piper without thinking.

The woman froze. "You must be the girlfriend."

Lou wasn't sure what to say to that.

Piper peeked around her, her face lighting with recognition. "Oh, it's you. Officer—"

"Sisk."

Piper snapped her fingers.

"Officer Sisk. Right." She turned to Lou. "This is my—"

"Girlfriend," Lou said.

Piper looked surprised. "Yeah. My girlfriend. My very pregnant, very protective girlfriend."

The officer extended her hand. "I didn't mean any disrespect."

I'm sure. Lou shook her hand, but she also believed that if the woman had simply thought they were friends, it would have left the door open for her to make her move. With her guts half pulverized, Lou wasn't in the mood.

"You're packing," the officer said.

"I am." Lou didn't feel compelled to open her leather jacket and show the twin Berettas.

Piper squeezed herself between the officer and Lou. "Uh, Officer Sisk, was there a reason you came over here?"

"I remembered something after our interview," she said. "You asked us if we saw anything suspicious in relation to Detective White."

Testimony aside, Lou was sure the woman just wanted an excuse to talk to Piper. She knew a hungry look when she saw one.

"Oh, what did you see?" Piper couldn't hide her enthusiasm. She put her drink on the bar and fished a small notebook out of her pocket. She opened it to a blank page and snatched a pen off the bar, forgotten on a signed credit card receipt.

"There was a guy hovering around White's Escalade a week ago. When I yelled, he ran off."

"Define 'guy,'" Piper said, scribbling.

"Tall. Thin. Black. Red hat. If I had to guess, he was in his late teens or early twenties."

Piper looked up and frowned. "That's young. Are you sure?"

"He hadn't filled out," the officer insisted. "Older guys get a bulk to them that younger guys just don't have."

"I'll take your word for it," Piper said. "You didn't report it?"

"Nope. I didn't see him do anything wrong. I didn't even see him touch the car."

"Did you try to speak to him or anything?"

The officer shook her head. "No. A bum on the street asked him for some change and he took off toward Jackson Square. That was it. That's the last I saw of him. I hadn't thought anything about it until tonight, when I thought I saw the same guy scoping another car on my way here. I was starting to wonder if we had a carjacker on our hands."

"You didn't talk to this one either?"

The officer's face pinched in irritation. "No, he was already walking away by the time I got to him."

"What kind of car was it?" Piper asked.

"An old beast of a sedan. A Century, maybe."

Piper snapped her notebook shut. "Thanks. I'll report it to the boss."

The officer looked ready to ask for more, but one glance at Lou and she seemed to think better of it.

"Good luck with your search," the officer said, and disappeared into the crowd.

Once she was out of earshot, Piper picked up her cocktail and put the pen back on the bar.

"Girlfriend, uh? You really are territorial."

"She didn't look like the kind of person to accept no for an answer."

Piper nodded. "I got that feeling, too. Thanks for stepping in. You're way scarier than me."

The officer looked over her shoulder and made eye contact with Lou again. Lou offered her a sinister smile. "Anytime."

17

King stopped at a Café du Monde for a large black coffee and a bag of beignets. He'd wanted to ask its owner, Suze, about her kid's recital, which was what she'd been excitedly waiting for all week. King knew this because she'd brought it up in conversation every time he'd come to the café. He listened as she proudly reported how well her son had done playing the trombone.

As he took his time walking through the Quarter, watching the buskers and artists try to tempt passing tourists into making a purchase, his mind lazily reviewed his objectives for the day.

It would be his last attempt trailing White. If he didn't turn up any promising leads, he would have to consider a different angle. His first possibility hadn't panned out. None of the officers at the precinct, nor the staff or janitors, not even the postal workers—no one had a red Honda that matched the description that King had given for White's possible tail.

He was beginning to believe that he'd made it up in his

mind. Or that simply the car had been traveling in the same direction coincidentally.

Nothing more.

He took another sip of his coffee from its paper to-go cup as the Buick came into view.

He stopped. For some reason unbeknownst to him, Mel's words popped into his head.

You're going to come up against your worst fear.

Those words raised the hairs on the back of his neck as he stared at his car, sitting there in the alley beside Fortunes and Fixes, half bathed in shadows.

What had Piper said that morning when he'd stopped by the agency? She'd run into the officer at The Wild Cat, and she'd said something about a carjacker scoping out a—that's right. *An old beast of a car. A Century, maybe.*

At this distance King could see how his own car looked like a Century.

What if someone had tampered with it last night? What if he hadn't been wrong about the tail at all?

King approached his car slowly. Part of his mind chided him, telling him he was being ridiculous. White's paranoia and desperation were rubbing off on him. He was putting scant details together as if they were substantial enough to form a picture.

He had to meet White at his place in ten minutes. There was no time to waste.

He pushed his doubts aside and marched toward the Buick determined not to think any more about it. He was only two feet from the car, reaching for the handle, when two things happened at once.

First a rough hand grabbed him, pulling him back.

He felt the drop and squeeze of one of Louie's slips and knew it had to be her, pulling him through the alley's shadows.

When the world reformed around him, it was in time to see his Buick launch itself ten feet in the air in a fiery explosion before hitting the pavement with a crash.

Flames spilled from the broken windows and windshield, black smoke billowing into the sky.

"Holy shit." He dropped his coffee.

He turned to find Louie still held his arm. She'd moved them deeper into the alley, several yards from the car.

"You," he said.

"I came without thinking," she said.

He ran a hand down his face, his mind still dilating. The panic and disbelief inside him had rendered him speechless.

"Robert! Robert! *Robert!*"

Mel was screaming his name until her voice was hoarse.

"She can't see us," King realized. "No one can see past the flames into the alley. Can you—"

Lou pulled them through the dark again and he found himself in a small room that smelled like cardboard boxes. She pushed open the door and King found he was in the storage closet inside Fortune and Fixes.

He could hear Lady barking like mad from Mel's apartment upstairs. This merited a distant acknowledgment at best. His eyes were fixed on Melandra. Through the large glass storefront, he could see her in the street.

She was still screaming.

King bolted past the shelves of incense and occult books and out into the street.

"I'm here," King said. "Mel, I'm here!"

She turned, her eyes wide with shock and horror. There was too much white in those eyes. She grabbed ahold of him so hard he winced. She squeezed as if she wanted to prove he wasn't a ghost.

"I saw you," she panted. "I saw you walk past the windows to the car. And the bang—oh god. Oh my *god.*"

"Shhh. Shhhh." He pulled himself free of her grip and enveloped her in his arms. "I'm okay. I'm okay. Lou was quick."

"Oh Jesus. Oh my sweet Jesus." He could feel her hammering heart against his chest.

"It's okay," he said, stroking her hair. "I'm okay."

Mel reached for Lou and embraced her. "Bless you. God bless you."

Lou surrendered to Melandra's affection. "I couldn't save the beignets or the coffee. Sorry about that."

King followed her gaze.

Half of his coffee was on his clothes. The bag of beignets had been tossed to the ground beside the blazing car. Those closest to it had turned black. The paper cup was nowhere to be seen, likely incinerated.

That could have been me. Burnt to a crisp.

"I need to go," Lou said, pulling away from Mel gently. "There are too many eyes."

King saw dozens of cell phones raised, recording what was left of his burning Buick.

King knew the media circus was just beginning.

"Hey." He turned to Lou. There were no words for what she'd just done for him, but he'd try anyway. "Thanks, kid. I owe you."

A fire truck wailed in the distance. The police would arrive just after and then the media would descend.

Lou gave him a small nod before disappearing back into Fortunes and Fixes.

She didn't come out again. King assumed she'd slipped back through the supply closet off to wherever she'd been before saving his life.

He was going to have to get her an extra-big baby gift.

It struck him again just how lucky he'd been.

Officers appeared, clearing the road just as the fire truck

pulled to a stop on the curb, a tight fit given the Quarter's narrow streets.

Someone grabbed ahold of him and squeezed. King looked down to see a blond head.

"I knew it was you! I had the worst feeling as soon as I saw the fire truck roll by. I heard the boom too. I thought it was a band or something."

"Bomb. Not a band." King gave Piper a pat on her back. "I'm okay."

Piper stepped back so she could look at the car. "Holy *shit*. Your Buick is dead."

She clasped her hands at the back of her head, her face a mask of disbelief.

"This means we definitely have a bomber, right? I mean, they blew up your *car*!"

"King."

He turned to find White running toward him.

King had to fight the urge to step in front of the car. As if he could block the burning vehicle from White's sight. He had no choice but to watch the man's anxieties escalate and play out in real time.

White grabbed him by the shoulders, gripping hard enough to hurt.

"I told you. I *told* you. He's real."

Melandra's face hardened. "Detective White, how dare you."

She pulled White's hands away. "He could've died. He could've died helping *you*, and all you care about is that you're *right*?"

White's expression sobered. "No, no of course not. I'm sorry, Robbie."

King held up his hands. "We're good."

The look Mel gave White remained reproachful. "Bomber

or no bomber, I'm going to need you to show more concern for your friends."

White rubbed the back of his head. "Of course. Absolutely. I wasn't thinking. I—I was just so desperate for proof. I felt crazy, you know."

"I do," King assured him. Because hadn't he been doubting his own thoughts as he'd been walking to this very car? He could hardly fault White for succumbing to his own.

"I'm just relieved to know it's real. I'm not making it up. He's real. The threat was real."

Over White's shoulders, King saw an unmarked car roll up to the curb. As soon as they stepped out, King knew he was looking at the feds.

You must've been close, he thought.

"Ah, shit," Piper said.

"It's about to get even realer," King said, watching the agents approach.

18

Konstantine's fingers were flying across the keyboard. Lou stood in front of his desk, waiting, but he couldn't bring himself to speak.

"You're pissed," she said.

"I'm not pissed," he said.

"You're a terrible liar."

He watched yet another shaky cell phone video taken two hours ago. The amateur videographer was zoomed in on King's blazing car, but not before filming a full three seconds of Louie standing in the street. He watched *again* as Melandra grabbed her and held her close.

She wouldn't have acted that way unless there had been danger, he thought darkly. *It must've been close, too close.*

And if there hadn't been danger, Lou wouldn't have left their dinner so abruptly, practically disappearing before his eyes.

He'd taken great pains to prepare that candlelit dinner for her. It was his apology for their misunderstanding over Stefano. The very idea that she could have left in the middle of it and never come home—

"I was only worried," he said. "You could have explained."

"If I had stopped to explain it to you, he'd be dead."

He closed the laptop. He would doctor the rest of the footage later. If he spent another minute looking at Lou beside the flaming car, he was going to set something on fire himself. This city, perhaps.

He came around the desk and sat on its edge in front of her.

"I want you to trust your instincts. *Sempre*," he said.

They had kept her alive this long. Apart from the misstep in February when the serial killer Gein had used a child to lure her, they'd never failed her.

"Lucky for you, I do," she said, and stepped forward. She leaned into him.

Her belly pressed into his torso. He placed a hand on top of it.

Lou looked down. "Why doesn't she ever kick you?"

"*Sa chi di noi la vizierà*," he said, grinning.

"What was that?"

He shook his head. "*Niente, amore mio.* I'm just glad you're okay."

"When does Stefano want to take on Modesto?"

"He wants to wait until the rest of the family leaves town. I think he's nervous about losing someone else to Detti. I've got security watching everyone, but it's difficult. They are a large group."

"When do they leave?"

"After the funeral."

"But we just saw the funeral," Lou said. "I thought it was over."

"In Italy a funeral is many days. People will come and say goodbye. Then she will be carried through the street by Stefano and his brothers and taken to the cemetery."

"I thought he was desperate to end this," she said. "That's

a lot of waiting for someone who was ready to tear the city apart a couple of days ago."

"Our promise to help him has calmed him. I think he feels that Detti cannot escape now."

"So we wait for the funeral rites to end, and we send the family on their way. Then what?" she asked.

"Then we will move against Modesto. Together. I am already working on the plan. We will rely on your talents, but I also have precautions to put in place."

"What precautions?"

"I will tell you when we get home, *amore mio*."

She placed a hand on his bicep, and the office fell away and the shadows of the bedroom swelled up in its place.

"We're home," she said.

"Cheater." He enjoyed the feel of her hands on him, always, even if she was forcing the conversation.

"Tell me why *you're* hesitating about Detti," she said.

Konstantine had encouraged Stefano's desire to send his family to safety and put his sister to rest properly. He was the one coming up with excuses and delaying their confrontation with the rogue, but he didn't want her to worry the way he was worrying.

He sat on the edge of their bed and began untying her boots. She didn't protest. Could she still undo her own laces? Yes. But it was admittedly more difficult as the belly grew larger. Soon it would be an impossibility.

"Konstantine," she said.

She will make me say it, he thought. *So be it. Better she know and be careful.*

"I think you are the real target." He cupped her calf with one hand and removed the boot.

She had one steadying hand on his shoulder, but he still saw her hesitation, even from this angle.

Was she keeping secrets of her own?

"What makes you think that?" she asked.

"I spoke to Vittoria. She confessed that Detti had contacted her, asking if she would support him should he move against me."

"That's bold," Lou said. "How did he know she wouldn't come running to you?"

"He didn't. She told me nothing of it until I called her." He cupped Lou's second calf as gently as the first, enjoying the feel of her in his hand.

"Perhaps Vittoria only confessed because she thought you knew something."

"Maybe," Konstantine said, removing his own shoes after releasing her.

"*Maybe* it's time I visit her again. It sounds like she needs a refresher on what I do to Martinellis."

"Her silence was a slight to me, not you," he said.

Konstantine knew this to be true. If Lou really was Detti's target, it seemed more likely that Vittoria saw an opportunity to get rid of *La Strega*.

"A slight to you is a slight to me," she said, pushing her fingers through his hair. He rolled his green eyes up to meets hers, relishing the tingles running down his spine. "She knows that."

He couldn't stop his eyes from fluttering closed. "*Amore mio*."

"My list is getting very long," Louie said, pushing him back onto the bed. "By the time our daughter is born, I'm going to have a thousand people to kill."

She straddled him. He grunted despite himself.

She looked down on him. "Am I too heavy?"

"You've always been heavy," he croaked.

She rolled to her side, giving him a chance to breathe. She placed her head in her cupped hand.

She didn't look offended, for which he was grateful.

"You haven't told me why you think I'm the target," she said. "What did Vittoria say?"

He turned toward her so their bodies were facing each other. He rested a hand on the curve of her hip.

He knew better than to lie to her now. He only hoped this would not prove to be an invitation for Lou to confront Detti before he was prepared for the fight.

"Detti is boasting that if he kills *La Strega*, he will be the new Master of Florence."

"That's what he wants? To replace you? Then why come for Stefano?"

"He wants to know if you are real or just a scary story." That was Konstantine's most solid theory anyway.

"Provoking your second is one way to find out. Either I'm real and I retaliate, or I'm not and it's you and Stefano who responds and he gets his chance to take over the Ravengers."

"Or maybe he really does believe that without Stefano I am weakened," Konstantine said.

He could tell by the look in her eye and the silence that followed that Lou didn't disagree.

So she does understand what he means to me, he thought.

He took hold of the end of her dark hair, rubbing it between his fingers. "Vittoria said he asked if you were real. If she'd seen you with her own eyes."

Konstantine knew that Vittoria had seen Lou with her own eyes. Louie had killed half her entourage and wrapped her hands around Vittoria's throat because she'd dared to strike little Matteo.

Konstantine had never forgiven her for that.

Thinking of it still angered him. Or at least until his guilt crowded out the anger. After all, it had been Konstantine who'd made that misstep, sending Matteo to her to begin with.

Lou arched a brow. "What did she tell him?"

"She *says* she told him to fuck around and find out."

Lou snorted. "You don't think she did?"

"Vittoria would not give a rival the advantage. Even if she did want to rid the world of us, it isn't in her best interests to help Modesto. What's to stop him from challenging her next, once he's taken Florence? At least with me, she has some measure of peace."

Vittoria might have genuine affection for Konstantine as her brother when it suited her, but for Lou there was something closer to hate. He heard it whenever Vittoria spoke of Louie.

"How are the kids?" she asked.

"*Bene, bene,*" he said, grateful for the subject change. "Though they miss Stella. I think Gabriella was hoping for another girl her age."

"Where's Stella now?"

"She's not a Florentine orphan, *amore mio*. She has a family. Stefano arranged for her to live with one of the aunts. The one with a daughter Stella's age. He will pay for her schooling, everything she needs, but it is better that she lives with her family."

"They have family too," she said, pushing her fingers through his hair again. "They have you. It's not like you're going to force them to become gangsters. I know you'll send them away to school and on to lives of their own when they're older. They're lucky to have you. She will be lucky to have you."

Konstantine did his best for the children who lived at the church. He did not fold them into the ways of the Ravengers the way Padre Leo had. The closest he'd come to that was his mistake with Matteo.

It filled his heart when he saw them playing games outside the cathedral, and he enjoyed the boisterous way they took their meals together. The way they ran the halls of the cathedral, and told stories behind the Virgin Mary.

He made sure they wanted for nothing.

And yet he couldn't shake the doubt forever present in the back of his mind. The doubt that told him he could never replace what they'd lost. He could never remove the dark marks from their hearts.

He bent and kissed her belly. "I hope you're right, *amore mio*."

"I'm always right. Are you saying I'm *not* right?"

He chuckled, his voice vibrating across her stomach. "*Mai*."

She pulled him up, forcing him to look at her. "Then we're going with my name?"

"Jack is not Italian. Jacopo is closest, and it is not the kind of name I imagine for our beautiful daughter."

"Jack is a fabulous name."

"She's going to Italian schools. She will have Italian friends, no? Do you want her to be made fun of?"

Lou rolled her eyes. "Tell me this amazing Italian name you've picked out."

"Lucia Katerina Elena," he said.

Lou's brows rose. "I'm sorry, is that all one name?"

"Lucia Katerina for your aunt. Elena for my mother."

Lou's heart skipped a beat. "I didn't know your mother's name was Elena."

"*Sì*. Maria Elena. Though everybody called her Elena." He searched her face. "Do you like it?"

"How is it spelled?"

He spelled it for her.

"I guess it works. She'd have our initials. 'L' for me. 'K' for you. But we can't have another Lucy. She'll have to go by something else."

"You Americans and your nicknames." He was pretending to be annoyed. "Do you really like it?"

"She can be Lucia Katerina Elena on paper. But can I still call her Jack?"

"*Amore!*"

He covered his face as if grief-stricken. Lou laughed despite herself.

"Cia, Elena, or maybe Rina. Or Jack."

A long string of incomprehensible Italian swearing followed from his lips until Lou pushed his arm away.

"What was that? I didn't catch any of that?"

"No nicknames. *Per favore. No.* She can be Lucia or Katerina. Or Elena."

"We'll see. Who knows what she'll be doodling all over her notebooks." She pulled him close so they were nose to nose. "Like I said, there's no replacing Lucy. Will that bother you? Calling her by your mother's name?"

Konstantine's heart swelled. He thought of his mother's gentle face, her sweet voice. The way he'd felt when she'd push his hair back from his face and whisper encouragements to him.

The way she'd smelled.

The way she'd made him feel safe.

"No, *amore mio*," he said, and brushed a kiss across Louie's knuckles. "It would make me very happy to call her by my mother's name."

"How about Elena Katerina—Jacopo."

"*Amore!*" He threw up his hands again. "Stop it, I beg you."

19

Piper leaned back in her desk chair and covered her ears. "Oh my god, they're still ringing even when I cover them. I think I'm damaged. When will the calls stop?"

"Maybe we should invest in ear plugs," King said before answering his own phone for the hundredth time.

Like King's, Piper's phone had been going off all day. It seemed like everyone she had ever met was trying to contact her. There was a video circulating the internet that was making her a lowkey celebrity. In said video, she was standing on the street beside King while his car burned in the background. The caption read: *Unknown suspect tries to bomb New Orleans private investigator. Is he "hot" on the trail?*

Classmates from her university courses were leaving messages on her phone. Her professors had also left messages offering extensions on her finals. Journalists from all over town wanted to know if she had an official statement for the articles they were rushing to print.

Henry came by the office and hugged her hard enough to pop her head half off her shoulders. People from the The

Wild Cat, people from high school. Cops. The DA's office. Everyone wanted to know what she'd seen. To hear the story one more time.

She'd heard from everyone except Dani.

I guess the news hasn't made it to New York, she thought glumly.

Piper didn't recognize the number on her cell phone's screen, so she let it ring to voice mail.

The supply closet swung open and Dani marched out.

It was so unexpected that Piper had to blink several times before she could be sure she wasn't having some sort of exhaustion-induced hallucination.

"Piper Lynn!" When Dani reached her, she pulled her out of her chair and hugged her hard. "I've been trying to call you for hours but your phone's been busy."

Lou closed the supply closet door behind her.

"I had to beg Lou for a ride just to check on you. I had to see you with my own eyes."

"I am also alive," King said as he ended one call before answering another.

"I'm glad," Dani said, giving him a sheepish smile before turning back to Piper. "I was so worried. That video is horrifying. You're just standing next to a burning car. It could have exploded again, you know!"

Piper didn't know that, but she didn't care. She was just thrilled Dani had come back.

"Wait, what did you tell Izabelle when Lou showed up?"

Man, I wish I could've seen her face.

"She doesn't know I'm gone. We were at the MoMA and I told her I was going to the bathroom."

"She thinks you're at an art museum right now? You didn't even tell her you wanted to check on me?"

"What do we know about the bomber?" Dani said.

Piper pulled away from her. "I'm sorry, did you come back for me or for the story?"

Dani gave her a withering look. "You. Obviously."

"You're not really back, are you? Otherwise, why would you lie to her?"

"Why are you mad at me?"

"I'm mad that you were in New York with *her* when you should've been here with me."

"I *am* here with you. Right now. I came as soon as I could."

"I find that hard to believe. The bombing was hours ago." Piper could hear the bitchiness in her own tone.

Lou went around them and took a seat at Piper's desk.

Dani's eyes were wide with concern. "I've been trying to call you for—"

"Don't get too comfortable," Piper said to Lou. "You're taking her back."

"My feet hurt," Lou said, putting her boots on the edge of the desk.

King ended another call and stood. "You two, *out*."

He pointed at Dani and Lou.

"The feds are going to be here to interview Piper and I in about thirty seconds. Someone at the precinct called to give me the heads-up. They're walking over now."

Dani frowned at her. "I'll call you."

You'll try, Piper thought. But at least she was able to stop this thought from leaping out of her mouth.

Dani gave her a lingering look before following Lou into the supply closet and closing the door behind her.

Piper exhaled, clasping her hands behind her neck. She felt like a child.

What the hell was that? I was a second away from a full-blown tantrum.

In her heart, Piper knew that Dani wasn't really choosing

Izabelle over her, but she couldn't seem to convince her emotions of that. Something about this situation reminded her of her mom, how Piper was always put second or third to whatever drug or man her mother was feening for at any given time.

"Listen," King said. "I don't know what that was or what's going on, but I'm going to need you at your best for this interview. They're going to ask if we—"

The bell above the door rang as the two agents walked into the Crescent City Detective Agency.

Whatever warning King had wanted to give her wasn't coming.

The male agent offered a bright smile. The female agent's lips stayed pressed in a thin, unfriendly line. Her eyes slid over Piper and fixed on King.

"Are you Robert King?" she asked.

"That I am. How can I help you?" King remained standing, offering his hand across the desk.

The woman shook it without letting an ounce of pleasantness seep into her features.

We know who's gonna play bad cop, Piper thought.

"I'm Agent Smith and this is Agent Anderson. We're from the FBI."

Piper visibly relaxed her shoulders. It required a conscious effort, but she knew they'd noted her body language the second they'd seen her. King had taught her that misdirection was necessary when it wasn't possible to hide her real emotions.

They already knew she was tense. But she could change what they thought she was tense *about*.

"Oh thank *God*. If I have to talk to another journalist I'm going to *puke*," Piper said, releasing her breath in a sigh of relief. "You're gonna help us with the bomber case, right?"

"As of now you are both relieved from that case," Agent

Smith said, her eyes cold. "You are to surrender any materials you have, any evidence, and we will need to interview you both, separately, to ascertain any information you have."

"That doesn't seem fair—" Piper began.

King held up a hand. "It's their right. Bombers are considered terrorists. Now that it's confirmed there is a bomber, it will go to the federal level. Isn't that correct?"

"Correct," Agent Anderson said. Piper thought his smile looked too perfect. Either they were veneers or that guy had braces all through high school. "The police chief has already accepted our jurisdiction and we want to work quickly. I'm sure you understand the urgency. Our number-one objective is that we have no casualties."

Good cop confirmed, Piper thought, mirroring Agent Anderson's smile. *You fake ass.*

"If we can get those files first, please."

Piper didn't like the feeling of handing all her work over to someone else, knowing full and well she'd never get so much as a thank you for her time.

"All that work for nothing," Piper said glumly.

"Cheer up," King said. "Maybe they'll let you interview them."

Piper hesitated. She wasn't sure why King was forcing this angle. When she searched his face, it remained relaxed, unreadable.

Piper decided to go with it.

She lit up, affecting the perfect picture of enthusiasm. "Oh yeah! Did you know I'm thinking about applying to the FBI? I mean, you guys probably already know everything about me. You're the FBI, right? I'm finishing up my bachelor's in criminology right now. I'm even learning Spanish. Does it say I'm learning Spanish in my file?"

The good cop raised his eyebrows. "*¿Verdad? Cuánto tiempo has estado estudiando?*"

"*Un año y medio. Mi pareja es latina.*"

He clapped. "Not bad. She's pretty good, right, Smith?"

"Passable," Agent Smith said. She was flipping through the manila folder with the bomber's letters in them.

"Does it say *passable* in my file?" Piper asked.

"You don't have a file, Ms. Genereux."

Piper forced a pout while glancing at King.

She wasn't sure she'd gotten the cue right. Was she playing the bubbly enthusiast well or not? King wasn't even looking at her. His eyes were fixed on Agent Smith as she flipped through the bomber's letters thoughtfully.

"White said he already gave you those," King said.

"The first two. I see there's now more."

"But you didn't open an investigation when he came to you the first time."

She turned her cold gaze on King. "We couldn't substantiate his claims."

Good cop wrinkled his nose at Piper. "A burning car changes things."

"Does it? Are you invested in catching this guy now?" King didn't hide his skepticism.

Are we doing good cop, bad cop, too? Piper wondered. It felt like it.

Agent Smith snapped the folder shut. "You had a long and distinguished career with the DEA, Mr. King. I can respect that. I ask that you afford me the same respect and assume that not only do I intend to do my job but that I intend to do it well."

Damn.

"We trust you," Piper said. And she meant it.

Something flickered across the agent's face, but it was too quick for Piper to be sure of what she saw. Gratitude? Relief? Annoyance?

"I want to interview you first, Mr. King." She gestured at

him with the folder. "Anderson will interview your assistant at the coffee shop around the corner. Then we'll switch."

Everyone in the room knew there was no real choice. Agent Smith was running this show.

"Fine," King said, keeping his tone cool.

"Sounds good to me!" Piper decided she too would play her part and pulled open the door. "After you, Mr. Anderson."

20

King hid his relief. Though they hadn't had time to prep their story, he felt that he'd steered Piper in the right direction. If she was focused on being the eager recruit, she would drive the pace of the interview with her own questions. Hopefully that would keep her from sharing anything that might paint them in a dangerous light.

"I'll be direct with you, Mr. King," Agent Smith said, turning her blue eyes on him.

"I'd prefer that," he said, matching her icy demeanor.

"I want to know if you can be trusted to drop this case. As I understand it, Detective White has become a personal friend of yours, since you moved to the city. That's the reason he came to you for help after we declined to open a case."

"I like to think he came to me because I have a certain skillset, but yes. I suppose it helped that he trusts me."

"Are you capable of separating your feelings, and any sense of loyalty you have to Detective White, from the situation?" Another piercing blue gaze.

They had a word for stares like that. Eagle-eyed. Her unblinking gaze definitely had a raptor-like quality to it.

"If you're asking whether I will help my friend, should he come face to face with the bomber again, yes, Agent Smith. I will put my neck out for him without hesitation."

"Even if it costs you? We can revoke your license and charge you with willful interference. Bar you from ever having an agency again. You could even spend a year in prison. You won't be of much use to Detective White or anyone else in prison," she said without blinking.

King crossed his arms. "I'm not sure it's against the law to help one's friends, Agent Smith. Citizens are allowed to run into burning buildings last I checked."

"Aren't you concerned for your own safety?" she asked. "The bomber blew up *your* car. That's more aggression than he's even shown Detective White."

King couldn't argue that point. The bomber clearly wanted to warn King off. It made him more certain that he hadn't been wrong about the red Honda or about the onlooker in the red hat. But it also meant that the bomber was ready to pull the kill switch if anyone tried to get between him and White. That obsessiveness didn't bode well for White's life expectancy.

"You may think whatever you want of me, Mr. King, but it's clear that if you continue to run interference between White and the bomber, you could very well get hurt. I don't think that bomb was meant to be a warning. I think it was intended to kill you. That tells me that you've seen something."

King refrained from looking away or swallowing. Anything that might make him appear guilty.

She waved the folder again. "And I don't think it's in this folder. You saw something while tailing White and that provoked him. What was it?"

King wanted to lie. He didn't want to hand over evidence to someone who'd been so dismissive of his friend's well-being from the start, who he felt now was only interested in mopping up the glory.

Yet he knew that it wouldn't do anyone any favors—himself included—if he fought Agent Smith every step of the way.

If she already knew he'd been tailing White, someone had been talking. It was possible that it was White himself.

"I tailed White for several days," he said. "I saw a suspicious car, and I think the bomber knew I'd spotted him."

"He?" Smith pulled a pen from her pocket and began writing directly on the manila folder. "You're sure the suspect is a male?"

"Tall. Slender. Wore a red hat when I saw him on the street outside the precinct, but I couldn't get a decent look. He kept himself covered. The car was a red Honda with a ding above the headlight. Small. Could've been from a rock or hail. A baseball. It's hard to say."

"Model?"

"I don't know. Sedan. Civic or Accord if I had to guess."

"Several of the officers at the precinct said you interviewed them. Did you turn up any details there?"

King leaned back in his chair, his arms still crossed. "No. I was pursuing the possibility that it was an officer or someone who works in the building, someone who would have access to the stationery and White's desk, but no one there has a red Honda."

"How would you know that?"

Want to know what database access a little ol' private detective has access to? he thought.

"All vehicles are registered with parking. You have to have a permit," King said. "No one's registered a red Honda sedan at the precinct. No officers, no janitors. No one. I didn't find a connection, but help yourself," he said. "The issue is motive. Very few people have a reason to hurt

White. Most of his hate comes from the criminals he's convicted."

"Yes, we're checking that angle," she said.

"I'm happy to hear it." And he meant it. "Can I ask what you've found?"

"No."

"Will you keep White informed, at least? He's concerned for his family. He's got two daughters at home," King said, unable to hide his irritation.

"Then he'll have more time to spend with them. He's been asked to take a leave of absence until we solve this."

"Asked." King snorted. "That's one way to put it."

The pen froze in her hand. She turned those ice-blue eyes on King.

"If you are *such* a good friend, Mr. King, you *should* convince him to leave the city for a while. Take his daughters to the Grand Canyon or Disney World. You know better than anyone that the bomber is fixated on him and is not afraid to kill. The safest place for him is far away from here."

She leaned forward, a ghost of a smile on her lips.

"Let's be honest, Mr. King. The real appeal of this case is the media attention. You'd be the most famous detective in the city if you were the one to solve this."

King almost laughed. *So that's what you think of me.*

Her assessment told King more about the kind of men she was used to dealing with than anything. And he had no interest in changing her opinion of him. Better for her to think him an egotist than to know the truth.

About the cold cases he solved with Lou, Piper, and Dani.

About the kill lists he provided Lou for the ones that think they got away with their crimes.

About his loose connection to a certain *capo dei capi* in Florence.

"You've got me there. It would certainly improve business

with a case like that to my name," King said. "But you're right. The most important thing for me is White's safety. I'll talk to him."

"Good." She pulled out her phone and typed something. "I'm glad we understand each other."

A BLOCK AWAY, AGENT ANDERSON LOOKED UP FROM HIS cell phone, interrupting Piper's fifty-sixth question about what it was like to be an agent for the FBI.

"I'm just saying, if I have to go undercover in a foreign country, at the very least they should let me pick out the wig I want to—"

"It's my turn to ask the questions, Ms. Genereux," he said, his tone shifting from companionable to sharp. "What does your boss have to hide?"

Piper swallowed. *Shit.*

21

Lou was tired of standing. It had been the three of them together, Konstantine, Louie, and Stefano, staring at the city map for nearly an hour. Konstantine was arguing that they held the upper hand and should be forcing Modesto Detti and his men to move to the place of their choosing. Stefano, frustrated by his early efforts to catch the rival off guard, didn't want to waste time with such maneuvering. He didn't want to take a chance that Detti might slip away again.

She sat down in one of the dining room chairs, propping her feet up on the nearest seat.

They both turned to look at her.

"I'm tired of listening to you argue," she said. "Even when it's in Italian it's exhausting."

She sounded cross even to her own ears. She wondered if maybe she was overdue for a snack.

Stefano pointed at her. "She is our best asset. Use her."

"Use me," Lou said. *Anything to wrap this up.* "But buy me a pizza first. I'm hungry."

Konstantine stepped from the door, pulling out his cell

phone. When he came back, he put a bottle of limonata on the table in front of her.

"Matteo is bringing your pizza, *amore mio*. He'll be here soon."

I would be faster on my own, she thought. But that also meant getting back on her sore feet.

Instead, she poured a glass of limonata. She took a sip. This was the sweet one without alcohol.

Konstantine frowned at the city map again.

"Fine. If Lou can get as close to him as possible and drop a pin, marking his location, then we can surround the building and go in. That's what you want?"

"*Sì, sì.*" Stefano clapped loudly, once. "That's what I want."

"He can't have more than a hundred men," Konstantine said, rubbing his jaw. "Anything bigger than that and he wouldn't be able to hide as well as he does."

"We have close to ten thousand men and women in the city," Stefano said.

"I don't think we need to bring ten thousand people to this fight," Konstantine said. "Three hundred will be enough."

Lou could tell his patience was wearing thin. She sympathized with Stefano's fury. If she could have brought an army down on Angelo Martinelli, the man who pumped her father full of bullets, she would have.

"I will put the rest on reserve," Konstantine said, softening. "Once we know which building Modesto's in, we will decide how many to send. We can move hundreds easier than thousands."

"How many can you move?" Stefano was looking at her.

"Without having eaten?" she said grumpily. "Zero."

"We are not going tonight, *amore mio*."

Apparently, there were still several days left to this funeral business. That morning, family from other parts of Italy had arrived to say their goodbyes, extending the rites.

"I don't know how many," Louie said. "I've never tried to move more than a few people at a time."

"Then take me," Stefano said. "I will go with you."

"The second time, you mean," she said. "After we have his location."

Konstantine tapped the map. "Let's pretend he's in Arceti, for example. It would take us fifteen or twenty minutes to get everyone there and in the building. Assuming he is protected by his men, we would have to fight our way through to him."

"Or appear beside him, I pull the trigger"—Stefano made a gun with his first two fingers—"bang bang, and then we are gone again. Our people can mop up the rest."

They had all agreed that every single one of Modesto's followers had to be killed as well. Modesto might seem like the most ambitious, but that didn't mean there wasn't a second or third-in-command that wouldn't continue the crusade if he fell.

"Come to Florence, challenge us, and die," Stefano said, shooting his finger gun again.

The doorbell rang and Lou pointed at the door. "Pizza."

Konstantine was halfway to the stairs when Lou heard Matteo calling up to her.

"*Strega! Strega!*"

Konstantine reached for the pizza, but Matteo shot around him, bolting for Louie.

His dark little head appeared, smile bright. He ran over to her, holding the box proudly. "I have for you, *Strega*. I have for you!"

Louie took it, placing a kiss on his cheek. "*Grazie.*"

His face turned bright red. He pressed his hand to his cheek as if he could keep the kiss there forever.

Konstantine pushed some money into his hands and ushered him to the door, shushing him away in rapid Italian.

"Goodbye, *Strega!*" He waved over his shoulder.

Lou waved back, opening the pizza box on the dining room table. She took out a slice and shoved half of it into her mouth in one bite.

Stefano wrinkled his nose in disgust.

"Look away then," she said.

She'd polished off the first piece of pizza and started another by the time Konstantine had come back.

He looked at the map one more time.

"Lou will go first, mark the location, then she will come back for you and me, and we will kill Modesto on the second pass. It will be a quick in and out."

Lou had doubts that Stefano could be quick about it. She knew the temptation firsthand of wanting to exact as much pain as possible on the person who took a loved one.

Lou gave Stefano a look, her brow arched. "Are you okay with that?"

He said nothing.

"I think it would be better if instead of taking Stefano to Modesto, I brought Modesto to you," Lou said. "That way Stefano won't have to choose between risking our lives and satisfying his need to torture his sister's murderer."

"Stefano has more control than that," Konstantine said.

Lou only arched her brow higher.

Stefano said, "I agree with *La Strega*. I would like time with him."

"If that's the objective, then does dropping a pin matter?" Lou asked.

Konstantine looked to the map again. "It does if we want to wipe out his reinforcements."

"What if they're not all in one place?" Stefano looked ready to steal a slice of pizza. Lou had to refrain from growling at him. Instead, she simply pulled the box closer.

"Then we hunt them one by one. That's an easy choice," Louie said. Her compass would help her to locate the strays.

Konstantine tapped the map. "We have the warehouses across the river. You can hold him as long as you want there. No one will hear him screaming."

"*Sì, sì.* I know where they are," Stefano said. "That is good. I want to do that."

Lou wiped pizza sauce off the corner of her mouth with a thumb. "Then I'll go once, and I'll drop a pin and get a sense of what the numbers are and also how accessible he is. Because it's possible that he's keeping himself surrounded."

Each of the Martinellis had been hard to snatch too. She'd had to drive an entire car into the bay outside Baltimore just to get Angelo alone.

"Once you have the numbers, you can mobilize your people to the marked location and I'll take Modesto and drop him off to Stefano. Who I assume will already be at the warehouse with his tools."

"Then I want to be part of the party who goes to the location," Stefano said. "I want to kill his people in front of his eyes."

Lou had serious doubts that Modesto gave half a damn about his people, certainly not as much as Stefano cared for his sister, but it was pointless to say so.

"Fine. I can wait to take him until after you raid the place," she said.

"No," Konstantine said. "It's more likely she'll catch a stray bullet with more guns in the room. You take him first to the warehouse. I will be there. I will hold him until Stefano is ready."

"Alone?" she asked.

"No, with our people," he said. "No one needs to see you."

She didn't like this plan. If it was too dangerous for her, then it was too dangerous for him.

"Can't I just wear the vest?" she asked. Her anger was finally receding. The pizza was doing its work. She took another generous drink of limonite.

"A vest is not enough, *amore mio*," he said. "I would want to put you in complete body armor with plates."

"Sounds cumbersome. It'll be better if I can actually move my arms and legs."

"When?" Stefano asked. "When do we do this?"

"I will get the reinforcements ready and clear the warehouse," Konstantine said. "When will your family be returning to Bologna?"

"Saturday. Everything will be done by Sunday."

"Sunday then," Konstantine said. "*Bene?*"

The relief was visible on Stefano's face. He balled a fist and struck his palm several times. "*Sì, sì. Va bene.*"

His phone buzzed in his pocket. He pulled it out and looked at the screen before taking the call.

"*Sì, sono qui. Sì. Sì. Sto tornando ora. Dieci minuti. Okay. Le prendo io.*"

He ended the call. "I have to go. I'll be late for dinner and my grandmother needs her medicine."

Konstantine embraced him. "*Porta pazienza, fratello. Ci siamo quasi.*"

Stefano clapped him on the back. Once they drew apart, he put a cigarette between his lips but didn't light it. He wasn't allowed to smoke in the villa. Konstantine's rules.

He threw a wave to Lou. "Good night, *Strega*."

"Night," she said, leaning back in her seat.

Once he'd gone, Konstantine lifted her feet from the chair, placing them on his lap. He massaged one, then the other, pressing his thumb into the sole of her foot.

"I am worried, *amore mio*. I don't have a good feeling about it. What if something happens? What if he is ready? What if you're hurt?"

"I'm not even sure what we agreed to there. You guys argue too much."

"*Amore*—"

"If I'm fast enough to grab King before a bomb goes off, I can be fast enough to stay out of Modesto's reach," she said.

He released her feet and went down on his knees beside her chair.

"*Promettimi che sarai veloce.*"

"I promise," she said.

He kissed her hands and rested his head on her belly. Their daughter kicked him in turn.

"Finally," Lou cried. "You had that coming."

He pulled back, laughing. "*Perdonami, mia regina.*"

And I will be quick, she thought. *Because our lives depend on it.*

As much as she was enjoying the tender moment, she needed to go. She cocked her head, sensing something.

"What is it?" he asked, placing another kiss on her stomach.

"I don't know," she said. "But King needs me."

Konstantine's face pinched with concern. "Another bomb?"

"No," she said, rising from her seat. "This is something else."

22

King took his time walking back to his apartment after his interview with Agent Anderson. As he'd expected, Anderson had played the good cop. He used a lot of placating words, working hard to assure King that he *understood* what it was like to be protective of his people, his friends. He *knew* King was only doing what he thought was best. But King didn't *have* to worry. He had every reason to trust them. They were the *good* guys.

King pretended to soften to this style of questioning, offering up a little more information than what he'd given Agent Smith. It was useless shit, of course, bits from the interviews as well as what the cop had told Piper in the bar about someone checking out White's car.

It didn't matter. He didn't believe that Agent Smith bought his act. He could tell from the moment she'd sat down across from him that she was like King. She'd seen too much to believe that people would simply do the right thing. The only difference between them was Smith still invested in her career, in playing by the rules.

King was long past that point of return.

As he crossed the threshold for Fortunes and Fixes, the chandelier moaned and flickered, giving the impression that a ghost was circling overhead.

Mel looked up from the crossword puzzle she was doing behind the counter.

"How did it go?" she asked, putting her pen in the spine and closing the book.

"They want me to walk away from the case."

"Not a bad idea," Mel said. "I'm not sure it's safe for you to keep going."

"You're probably right. White might be disappointed, but it's the right thing to do." That's what King said, even as he pressed a small piece of paper into Mel's palm and gave her a look.

There was a small twitch in her brow, but otherwise, he thought she'd done a good job of hiding her reaction.

"Do you think you can check out my shower? It's dripping," King said.

Here the brow twitch was a bit more pronounced. Likely this was because King had never asked Melandra to do maintenance on his apartment in the years that he'd rented it. If there was ever a stopped sink or leak, he fixed it himself, or if he couldn't, he was still capable of making the call and getting someone over to look at it. And he paid those bills.

But he needed to give Mel a reason to come to his apartment.

"I can come look at it now," she said, her fist still tight over the note King had written before leaving the office. He'd stretched a scrap of paper over his thigh under the desk. "Just give me a minute to lock the door so no one pops in."

"Thanks."

He was already wishing for Lou as he mounted the stairs, rounded the landing and slipped his key into the lock.

He wasn't surprised when he opened his apartment door to find her already there, leaning against the doorframe, her mirrored sunglasses pushed up onto her head.

He pressed a finger to his lips to signal his desire for silence.

Lou didn't even blink. She only regarded him with impassive eyes.

He heard Mel coming before she entered the apartment behind her and closed the doors. The bangles on her wrist jingled musically as she approached.

When she looked from Lou to King, her brows only rose higher. "Tell me about this leak."

He pressed his finger to his lips before saying, "Let me show you."

This part was harder only because King's bathroom wasn't large enough for three people. It could barely accommodate him on the best of days, but still he went into it and turned on the shower, hoping the sound of running water would interfere with any listening devices that may be pointed at his apartment or the shop.

He'd known he'd be under surveillance even before he left the agency. Sure enough, he'd seen the van parked on the curb beside the convenience store, with an inconspicuous laundromat decal stuck to its side.

Once the three of them were crammed into his bathroom, King motioned for Lou to turn off the lights. She did. The drop-kicked feeling he hated so much seized his guts as he was squeezed from one point in reality to another.

When the world reformed around them, King wasn't sure where he was. An empty office building? It had an open floor plan with the makings of a cubical farm spread about. Some of the desks were still wrapped in plastic and outside the window were enormous skyscrapers bathed in moonlight. A city pulsing with lights.

"Where are we?" he asked.

"Korea," she said.

Melandra went to the big windows and looked out over the city. "This is lovely and all, but can either of you tell me what the hell is going on?"

She held up the piece of paper King had scribbled on.

"It says 'they're listening.' *Who?*" she asked. "The feds?"

"This would be easier if we had Dani and Piper here too. I'd rather only debrief everyone once."

Lou looked down and away as if listening to something. "I can get to Piper but not Dani."

"Fine. We'll have to catch her up when she gets home."

Lou left without another word.

"Are you okay?" Mel asked. Her eyes looked wet with the city lights sparkling in them. King resisted the urge to reach up and move a strand of hair out of her face.

"We just need to be careful," he said. "Or I'll be the second man you visit in prison."

She clucked her tongue. "Don't say that! Don't you dare."

Piper was still screaming when she appeared in the office space, making them both jump. In one hand she was holding a bag of tortilla chips. Then she saw them standing together and groaned.

"Gee-*zus*. Lou! I thought I was being snatched by the bomber. Don't sneak up on a woman when she's snacking, man." She shook the crumpled bag at her. "Not cool!"

Lou only stuck her hand down into the bag and grabbed a handful of chips.

"Whoa, where are we?"

"Korea," Lou said around a mouthful of chips.

"And *why* are we in Korea?" Piper looked from Lou to King and Mel.

"The FBI is going to be tracking us for the foreseeable

future. You need to assume all conversations from here on out are being recorded. All your searches public."

"Public," Piper scoffed. "That's not fair. I—I mean I have interests."

When they only looked at her, her face began to turn red.

"Look, it's just some fanfiction, okay. Some very specific, very *niche* fanfiction. But no one needs to know about it."

"It doesn't matter. They'll be tracking your searches nonetheless. And while they can collect audio from the street, it's also possible they may snag some video as well. Lou, you need to be careful with how you come and go."

"I'll let Konstantine know," she said.

King sucked his teeth. "Tell him to use a light touch if he doctors something. Agent Smith is the type to dig. If you suddenly start disappearing from footage or it gets corrupted every time you show up, she's going to start asking questions."

"There's a solution for that too," Lou said around another mouthful of chips.

Piper tried to take the bag back and Lou held it out of reach.

"Fine. Feed the baby, I guess."

"We need to be careful," King said. "I believe her when she says she'll prosecute if she thinks we're interfering. I don't have any interest in going to prison."

"I wouldn't let anyone stay in prison," Lou said.

"Thank you, but I'm also not interested in living the rest of my life as a fugitive," he said.

"What are we going to do?" Piper asked.

"I want to get us some burner phones. Anything to do with the bomber case—" He looked to Lou. "Or any of our other cases that we don't want them to know about, we use the burners."

"They'll notice if you stop talking on your phones alto-gether," Mel said, adjusting the bangles on her wrist.

"Yes, we'll have to keep talking about the normal stuff. Meals. Cases that will hold no interest for them. But nothing that we don't want the FBI to know. Nothing about the bomber. Nothing about serial killers. Nothing about the mafia. Nothing about Lou at all."

"Can they track burner calls?"

"They could create a zone if they had the phone the call went to," King said. "But if we keep the burners out of their hands, we should be fine. But it would be best if we text because there's still the possibility that they're using parabolic mics. If you've got to make a call, try to run interference. A loud radio, a running shower. Something."

"Your shower is still running," Lou said.

"Small price to pay."

"Them thinking the two of us are showering together?" Mel asked, lips pursed. She motioned for the chips and Lou handed them over.

Piper opened her mouth in protest but no sound came out. She simply stood there opening and closing her mouth like a fish out of water.

King felt the heat rise in his face at the thought of show-ering with Mel, their slick bodies brushing against each other.

"They won't think that," he said. He turned to Lou. "If I give you some cash, can you get us the burners?"

"Don't need the cash," she said, finally giving Piper back the bag. "How many do you want?"

Piper looked into her nearly emptied bag with a pout. "Now it's just the broken ones on the bottom."

"Six. One for each of us, including Konstantine. If he needs one."

"He doesn't," Lou said. "I'm not sure I do either."

"What about White?" Piper asked.

King hated to admit that he didn't want to give White a burner. Given the emotional state he'd been in the last few times King had seen him, it didn't feel like a great idea. It was more likely to feed his paranoia rather than ease his mind.

"No, just us," he said. "In case we lose one or have to ditch it. I'll have to ask you to keep an ear out for White, Lou. If you think the bomber's planning something—"

Piper pointed at the belly. "You can't expect that of her."

"I don't *expect* it," he said. "But if you can help without getting hurt. Please step in."

"I'll keep an ear out." She slid her glasses down over her eyes.

"That's what you said last time," Piper said, frowning into her chip bag again. "Then that killer got you. *Worst* day ever."

"Get the burners. Take one to Dani and let her know what's happening," King said. "The rest of you, please be careful. The bomber is still pissed off at me. I think he's smart enough to keep his distance now that the feds are all over this, but it's possible he'll plant another bomb. Because we're always in the same spaces, I need you guys to *stay alert*."

"Roger that, boss," Piper said.

Melandra didn't say anything, but she didn't have to. It was enough to see the concern in her eyes. And looking at her there with the city lights shining on her hair, King realized why he could never leave New Orleans.

He could admit to himself that when he retired and left St. Louis, he'd had only one intention. To escape his depression and loneliness by drinking himself to death.

Then he'd met Mel. She'd offered him not only a place to live but friendship. The first real friendship he'd had in decades. That feeling had only grown as Lou, Piper, Dani, and White entered his life. But it was Mel more than anything else that made New Orleans feel like home. She was part of the magic of the place.

Mel took his hand and squeezed.

"Don't worry, Mr. King," she said. "Everything is going to be all right."

He really hoped she was right.

23

Piper looked at Mel and King holding hands and thought, *This is a disaster.*

It took everything she had not to yell *no* into their faces. Instead she gave Lou's arm a tug and whispered, "Leave me at King's. I gotta say something."

Piper wasn't even sure she'd heard her until she found the three of them back in King's bedroom, the shower running in the adjacent bathroom.

Lou had already left.

Lady was still barking across the hall.

"I'd better go check on her," Mel said. She glanced at her watch. "And if I open the shop back up now, I can get another two or three hours of the evening rush in. I'd love to move these fifty Mother Mary candles I've got."

King didn't hide his disappointment. "I'll come down in a few and—"

"Your shower is running," Piper said dryly. In her mind she was rapidly forming the argument she wanted to make. "You better turn it off."

King pressed his finger to his lips.

Right. The feds. Piper had already forgotten in the face of the horror she was watching unfold before her eyes in real time.

The longing in King's eyes as he watched Mel walk from the apartment—*watched* her—it was too much.

Piper pushed him into the bathroom with a furious wave of her hand.

Once the door was closed, she stopped him from turning off the water. "Man, come on!"

King's brow scrunched. "What? What's wrong?"

"You don't think I can see that?" Piper fought to keep her voice low. She knew this pounding water throwing icy mist into the air around them could only be doing so much for her.

"*That!*" She jabbed her thumb over her shoulder toward Mel's apartment. "Are you *kidding* me?"

King's face darkened. "If you've something to say, Genereux, just say it."

Piper rubbed her forehead, trying to abate the headache forming there. "Look. As someone who has slept with many of her friends"—*Almost all of them*—"it's not worth it, man," she said. "It's going to ruin your friendship."

"Melandra and I are mature enough."

"No," Piper hissed. "*No.* No one is mature enough once the feelings start flying, and then what's going to happen to us?"

Confusion seeped into his features.

"What's going to happen to *us*?" She made a circle with her hand. "We have a good thing. All of us. We're an amazing team. You can't be messing that up with those puppy dog eyes."

"I do not have puppy dog eyes." King swatted away the shower curtain trying to cling to him.

"You do," Piper insisted. "And it would be a Christmas miracle if Mel hasn't noticed yet."

King's face brightened at this prospect. It was then that Piper knew she was in trouble.

Man, he's too far gone.

"Look. If she hasn't given you any reciprocal signs, please just drop it. *Please?*" Piper put her palms together. "I will get on my knees and beg you if I have to."

He seemed to pull himself together then. He straightened, running a hand down the front of his shirt. "I never said I like her like that."

"We are too far into this conversation for you to pull that card now," Piper said flatly. "You like her. I know you like her. It's very possible that Mel also knows, and if she does and hasn't said anything, what do you think that means, Romeo?"

"You and Dani work fine together."

"Because we like each other. It goes *both* ways. And trust me, I put up a fight at first. There was plenty of resistance. Are you even *trying* to resist?"

"Of course I'm resisting," he said defensively. He flinched. "You don't think she likes me back?"

Shit.

Piper puffed out her cheeks and held her breath for a count of five.

"Listen. You're a lovable guy. I didn't mean to imply otherwise. I'm sure that you know from Beth that you've got charm."

At least his face softened a bit at that.

"But Mel had a horrible marriage for, like, her *whole* life. She ain't ready, man. She's free for the first time in forever. If you go and try to ruin your friendship by telling her how you feel, she's gonna feel like she lost a friend, or worse, she's gonna feel like she's gotta hop into a relationship with you just to keep you. But she's *not* ready for that. She's not, and you're going to make it weird."

"I'm not going to make it *weird*," he said. "I wasn't planning on putting her on the spot or anything."

"But you do have feelings for her. You're admitting it *right now*."

King ran a hand through his hair. "It is something that may have very recently come to my attention, yes."

Piper pulled at her face before looking up at the sky. "Why? I beg you why? How could you let this happen?"

"She's smart, she's brave, and beautiful, and—"

King's phone began ringing. He pulled it from his pocket and frowned at the number.

"I'm just saying, please let her take the lead on this and—"

"Hello?" King said, taking the call.

Piper was about to say more, but he covered her mouth with a fierce look of concentration on his face. Then he was furiously turning off the shower.

"Hello?"

They stood in silence, with only the sounds of the stray droplets hitting the bottom of the tub.

"Is that you?" King whispered. "I can hear you breathing."

Oh shit.

"Where are you?" King looked up, his gaze distant.

He made a motion with his hands, but he didn't need to explain. Piper saw the danger as soon as he did. She rushed from his apartment, out into the hall, and down the stairs just as the door to Melandra's Fortune and Fixes was flung open and Agents Smith and Anderson marched in. No one was playing good cop anymore.

The agents started at seeing her.

"What are you doing here?" Agent Smith asked.

"I asked her to run the register while I started dinner in my apartment," Melandra said.

Melandra stood at the top of the stairs with Lady at her

side. The lithe Belgian Malinois went down the stairs, eyeing the agents suspiciously.

Then she put her body between Piper and the agents.

Good girl, Piper thought, giving her erect ears a scratch.

Piper turned to the agents to see if they'd bought the story. Even if they hadn't, it didn't matter.

"We've got a surplus of Mother Mary candles if you wanna buy some," she said.

They were pushing up the stairs to King's apartment.

They reached the landing the same time King opened the door.

"We heard the call," Agent Smith said instead of greeting him.

"Come in," he told her. "I'll tell you what he said."

24

"Take this too." Konstantine went to the safe in the living room and unlocked it by pressing the passcode into the keypad embedded in its formidable steel face.

Inside there were four laptops that he kept ready for moments like this. All were wiped clean of traceable and identifying information. "He can do his work on this. If they take it, tell me. I have a remote detonator."

Lou slipped the burner phones he'd already handed her into the pockets of her leather jacket as she crossed to him.

She reached for the laptop and he moved, holding it out of reach.

It was such a boyish move, but he was delighted that she indulged him.

She leaned her body into his at an angle so the stomach wouldn't push them apart, and pulled him into a kiss. She took her time, exploring his mouth with her tongue before taking his bottom lip between her teeth.

"Payment enough?" she asked, smiling.

"No, but you can settle the account later."

"So generous," she said, and took the laptop from him.

Then she crossed to the empty closet and closed the door behind her.

He knew she was gone by the pop in his ears, a slight shift in pressure.

Konstantine stood where he was, alone in the living room, for several minutes after she left. He slowed his breath. He let the weight of his legs settle, feeling the carpet sink beneath his socks.

He grappled with the fear choking him. Never in his life had he known such uncertainty, such helplessness. He trusted Lou. He really did. He believed in her strength, her instincts, and her will to survive. But the baby was an unknown.

Children were unpredictable.

He loved her already, without question, but he did not know her the way he knew her mother. And when he thought of how small she was, how fragile, a mixture of terror and defensiveness overtook him that he couldn't even begin to articulate to Lou.

It was possible, and *dio piacendo*, that one day she would be as indestructible as her mother. But that day might not come for a long time. He wanted to safeguard, above all, her childhood.

She would be loved. He felt confident of that. But would she be safe?

Could they make her strong without subjecting her to the horrors that had made her parents strong?

Questions like these circled his mind day and night, causing him deep unease.

He thought he had done a good job of hiding the war raging within him from both Stefano and Louie. He was sure that she'd seen his concern, and his insecurities about their safety. But he had hoped that she had not seen the depth of the conflict.

Did Lou know what it was like to both long for their daughter's birth and be terrified of it? To hope that she had her mother's gifts so that she could use them to protect herself, and also worry how she might use such power?

He knew Lou thought he was worried about the pregnancy. Perhaps even about the precarious nature of birth, though even in that regard he knew Lou was better equipped than most. She was young and healthy—which said nothing of the healing abilities La Loon had given her.

But did she also know that he was more afraid of the ever after?

He didn't know how he would feel when he held that tiny body in his hands. If joy or terror would overtake him.

He had worked—in every possible way—to be a better man than his father had been, than even Padre Leo had been. But would it be enough to make him a *good* father?

He didn't know.

His phone rang.

He ran a hand down his face and removed his cell from his pocket. "Pronto."

He listened with disinterest as one of his suppliers described a delay in Cape Town. There were three freighters rotting in the port with almost fifteen thousand kilograms of cocaine sitting in holding.

Konstantine assured him he would handle it and ended the call.

And what if she judges us?

Konstantine had asked Louie this late one night. They'd finished their lovemaking and lay sweating and entwined in the afterglow of it. He hadn't been guarding himself or he would have never said his thoughts aloud.

What if she doesn't like that her father sells drugs?

Lou had shrugged him off. *What if she doesn't like that I'm a murderer? What will she do? Try to stop me?*

It was true that he saw *that* confrontation as more problematic than his own. In truth, if his daughter looked him in the eyes and asked him to walk away from this life, Konstantine would do it. He would make sure a successor was in place, and that his commitments were honored.

But he would do it. Happily.

He could only hope that he would never have to referee between Lou and their daughter. That was a game he was not equipped to play.

His phone rang again.

"Come to the church," Stefano said.

"Why?" Konstantine asked. He didn't like his tone. Stefano was somber by nature, but rarely did it hold such coldness. "What's happened?"

"*Vieni, vieni. Ma sii preparato,*" he said.

Konstantine decided to take the Maserati rather than walk. It would be faster. He backed it out of the garage onto the narrow street running parallel to the Arno River, before speeding north.

As he navigated around pedestrians and mopeds, the church came into view, and he parked behind a stone wall, keeping the car out of sight.

When he entered the church, he was struck by how cold it was despite the heat of the day.

These idle thoughts evaporated the moment he spotted the corpse sprawled on the stone floor. It was at the base of the altar as if it were an offering to the Virgin. On the first pew sat Stefano, pressing a cold rag to Nario's face.

The boy had a split lip and a swelling eye. Konstantine was certain it would be black by tomorrow.

"What happened?" Konstantine asked. To the boy, "Are you all right?"

Nario gave a stiff nod but hissed.

Konstantine walked around the corpse, searching its face,

or what was left of it. Half of its skull was gone, clearly blown off.

"Did you do this?" he asked. Nario had always been a fighter, but he didn't think the boy had killed anyone before. He wasn't even sure he'd shot anyone before. He was only sixteen, the oldest of the children in his care.

"She did," Stefano answered, nodding in the direction of the Virgin.

For a moment Konstantine thought it was a joke.

"She'll be right back," Stefano said.

Then a shadow separated from the pillar beside the altar.

Lou.

"I couldn't grab another," she said. "I barely got this one."

She pointed at the dead man on the floor. She looked displeased with her kill.

"What happened?" Konstantine was still struggling to understand what was going on.

"One of Modesto's men got ahold of Nario. I think they wanted a hostage."

"How many were there?"

She shrugged. "Six or seven."

"*Hanno detto che mi avrebbero tagliato il cazzo e te l'avrebbero spedito*," Nario said, wincing again.

It was a sight, Stefano babying the boy. He was not nurturing by nature.

"I think the arm is broken," he explained, pulling the ice back from his face.

"Did they see you?" Konstantine asked her.

"They saw me, but after I blew out his brains they ran like rats."

Nario snorted. "*È stato meraviglioso. Penso che uno si sia incazzato.*"

The stiffness of his torso gave Konstantine the impression

that maybe the arm wasn't broken. Maybe it was a dislocated shoulder. In either case, he was bearing the pain admirably.

"I thought you were with the detective."

"The feds have him," she said. "I had to leave everything in Mel's apartment."

"And you knew Nario was in danger?"

He looked at the corpse again. She really had made a mess of him. No wonder the others had run. Seeing the top of his head come clean off must have been very motivating.

"I knew," she said.

"*Lei lo sa sempre. Così dice Matteo. Immagino abbia ragione.*"

I do not have to be afraid, he thought. *Her power will hold. If she can hear the cries of children across the world, she will always know if our daughter is in danger.*

A knot in his chest loosened, but his unease didn't leave him completely.

25

Dani loved New York. She loved the food. She loved the people. She loved the art and conversation. She *should* be having an amazing time, except that nothing could get Piper out of her mind. It didn't matter if she was eating the most delicious meal she'd had in weeks or was looking at a sculpture so gorgeous that she could have wept. Her mind kept circling back to Piper and the hurt look on her face when she'd asked, *Did you come back for me or for the story?*

The meetings had all gone well, and yet—

Me or the story.

The editor-in-chief and team in Izabelle's department had all been kind and accommodating. They were generous with their praise, even if she did still sense a coldness beneath their smiles. And yet—

Me or the story.

As she walked the streets, she could easily see what her life would be like here. Exhausting but exhilarating. The only problem was that she couldn't picture Piper here. She couldn't imagine how she would have time to continue her work with King and Lou.

If she was in New York, chasing a Pulitzer, she definitely wouldn't have time to be digging for corpses in a snowy forest at night. In a city this large, the work would be double if not triple her current load.

Where did that leave her?

Me or the story.

The accusation took her back to when she'd met Piper. When she'd been tasked by her boss to find out more about Louie. Dani had been willing to cozy up to the cute shop girl in hopes of getting the story that would promote her from assistant to editor.

But it had been Lou's bullet through his head that had opened the door for *that* promotion.

And because of Dani's deception, she and Piper had started dating on shaky ground, and only after Dani had managed to convince her that her interest was genuine, that Dani hadn't, in fact, only been using her to get ahead.

Now it felt like they were circling back to the start.

Me or the—

"*Hello?*" Izabelle waved a hand in front of her face. "Earth to Daniella. Come in, Daniella. Are you there?"

Dani blinked, the world coming into focus around her. Izzy stood beside her on Eighth Avenue. There was a cinema to their right, closed this early in the day, and a jazz club across the street, with five lanes of traffic rushing between them.

Izabelle shrugged one shoulder, her clutch slapping her hip. "Did you even hear me?"

"Sorry. I think I'm a little tired," she said. This was a lie, but believable. They'd been walking most of the day.

Izabelle frowned and pointed up the street with her clutch. "Let's get a coffee. There's a good place up ahead."

Izabelle held the door open for her, and Dani thanked her while crossing the threshold. The frosty air conditioning struck her, immediately cooling the sweat on the back of her neck.

"Iced caramel macchiato?" Izzy asked.

"I'll get it," Dani said.

Izzy waved her away. "It's fine. Grab us that table by the window."

There was only one open table in the whole place, so it was easy to spot. She watched Izzy get in line behind the others before turning to the window. People rushed past, everyone's steps strident and hurried.

It was very different from New Orleans. In the Big Easy, no one was in a hurry. Sometimes they would get a tourist who might have forgotten they were on vacation taking the streets by storm, but most people found the pace of the city relaxing. Even King, who had been the fastest walker she'd known, rarely accelerated above a stroll these days.

Would she become like them if she moved here? Always focused on the next place she had to be. The next thing she had to do. Rushing through her life?

Dani looked at her phone for the dozenth time that day and saw her message to Piper was read.

But no reply.

She'd become lost in thought when Izabelle put the coffee down on the table in front of her. "One caramel macchiato."

"Thanks," she said. "I'll treat you to the next one."

"I like treating you," Izzy said, her smile bright. It made Dani think of all the years in high school she'd had braces. She supposed it had paid off well. "If you lived here, I could take good care of you all the time."

Dani ignored this comment. She had adamantly denied Piper's assertion that Izabelle was still into her, but it had become harder to ignore since coming to New York.

The flirtatious comments were nearly constant.

"You could be happy here," Izabelle said over the rim of her own coffee. "You'd be appreciated."

"I'm appreciated in New Orleans," she said. And she was. Not just at *The Herald* but in her work with Lou and the team.

Izabelle arched her brows. "At that tiny wreck of a paper? You're wasted there."

"I'm not wasted anywhere," Dani said firmly. "I'm there because I want to be."

"It's not—Christ." Izabelle jumped.

Dani turned, following Izabelle's gaze to find Lou on the other side of the large window. She was standing in the middle of the sidewalk, looking at them. The flow of foot traffic gave her a wide berth, as if she were a rock parting the river.

A man with a cell phone pressed to his ear said something and Lou turned, looking at him.

He moved several feet away before hurrying past her.

Lou nodded at the entrance.

"I'll be right back," Dani said.

"What? Why—"

Dani exited the coffee shop and met Lou on the sidewalk in the sunlight.

"Hey," she said, stopping short of her. "Is everything okay?"

"I'm supposed to give you this." Lou pushed a phone into her hand.

"Why? What's happening?"

"The feds are watching King and Piper. If you need to talk to them about anything related to me or our cases, use the burner."

Dani frowned at the phone in her hand. But also a spark of hope ignited within her. Maybe Piper was just avoiding using her phone because of the feds, worried Dani might say something.

"Nothing about our work on the main channels. Got it."

Lou dipped her head. "Is that the ex?"

Izabelle scowled at them through the window.

"Yeah," Dani said, suddenly embarrassed.

"She looks like she wants to fight. Should I offer?" Lou asked with a bright smile.

"No, please." Dani choked on a laugh. "You're as bad as Piper."

"If you change your mind, let me know." Lou turned to go. Dani knew she was looking for some patch of darkness thick enough in these sunny streets.

"Wait," Dani called after her. "How is she?"

"Are you asking if she's still mad at you?" Lou slipped her hands into the pockets of her leather jacket. Her sunglasses hid her dark eyes. "You should ask her. Our numbers are in the phone."

Dani didn't stop her for a second time. It wasn't that Lou was above running interference—she'd done it before—but it was clear that she thought they would best be served talking it out.

The very idea made Dani's stomach turn.

It was still twisting when she retook her seat across from Izabelle.

"Who the hell was that?" Izzy failed to keep the emotion out of her voice.

Dani made up the first lie she could think of. "An informant on a case I'm working."

"How the hell did she know where you were?"

"I told her the area I'd be in. She said she'd find me."

Izabelle pushed her coffee away. "I don't like it. She looked like bad news. Do you really run with people like that?"

Yes.

"What story is it?"

"I can't tell you," Dani said.

Izabelle pressed her fingers into her forehead. "Does this have to do with your hospitalizations?"

Dani felt as if someone had kicked her in the guts. "Excuse me?"

"Your mom told me about the hospitalization. Something happened and you got hurt. Then you checked yourself into a psych ward—why? Was it trauma? Or to hide from someone? That woman"—she pointed to where Lou had stood minutes before—"she looked like *mafia*, Dani."

Dani snorted. "Why do you say that?"

"That was a Ferragamo jacket and Armani boots. She looked like she'd crawled out of a trash can but she was wearing at least five thousand dollars."

Of course you'd know the brands, you snob.

"And her jacket was bulging. Was she carrying a *gun*?"

Izabelle hadn't mentioned the belly. Lou was hiding it well, but Dani should have known that Izabelle would notice the guns. Her family were big into the Second Amendment. Izabelle had at least three handguns in her own apartment. And those were only the ones that Dani knew about.

"Your mother was worried about rape, but I did my home-work. You weren't raped. But you were beat to shit and you lost a finger. You know who removes fingers? The fucking mafia. How deep are you in this?"

Dani hadn't thought of Dmitri Petrov in a long time. She hadn't even had a panic attack in a long time, and she wanted to keep it that way. She opened her mouth to tell Izabelle so, but her mind snagged on a detail.

Dani circled back. "When did you talk to my mother?"

"A few weeks ago."

Weeks ago. Before the awards ceremony then. Maybe

even before Izabelle's editor had emailed Dani the informal offer.

Dani held up a hand. "Why the hell would she talk to *you* about that? And what makes you think you can go digging through my medical records?"

Dani knew she could do it. Like her parents, Izabelle wasn't above throwing money at a problem. Everyone could be bought for the right amount.

Izabelle held up her hand. "Don't get mad. We were just worried about you. I told your mom that I would find out what happened. I didn't tell her about the finger."

Dani's shoulders relaxed.

"I won't lie, D. I have to agree with her. If Piper's got you running with the mafia—"

Dani couldn't contain her laugh then. "Piper doesn't have me *running* with anyone."

"Your mom said that the minute she came into your life, you changed. You—"

Dani's mind started putting the pieces together.

Izabelle talking to her mother. The job offer that came out of nowhere. Not just from anyone but from Izabelle's very own department. The encouragement to move to New York.

Dani's heart kicked in her chest. "It was you? All of this was *you*?"

Izabelle's lips pressed shut. "I care about you. If your mother calls me and tells me that you're going to get yourself killed, what did you expect me to do? Hang up on her? I *love* you, Daniella. If you're in trouble, I'll help you. I'll keep you safe. You can start over, have a better life here. And if your own mother thinks you need to get out of New Orleans, of course I'm going to—"

"Oh my *god*, it *was* you."

Curious baristas snuck looks in their direction. The patrons closest to them were also watching, their ears perked.

"Lower your voice," Izabelle said.

"You went to your boss and told him to make me an offer. It was all orchestrated to give me a reason to move to New York."

"I might have suggested—"

"*Ugh.*" Dani pushed back her chair. It scraped angrily across the floor.

"Dani!"

Dani didn't look back. She marched out of the coffee shop, away from Izzy and her coffee abandoned on the table.

She could barely think around her fury.

She threw her head back and yelled at the sky, "Louie!"

Izabelle called after her, "Please, let's talk about this."

"No. I'm leaving."

"Where will you go? Back to New Orleans? She doesn't deserve you, Dani. You're better than that."

"How *dare* you." Dani clenched her fists until her joints ached. She was so close to throwing a punch, she could see red. There was no need to ask who *she* was. Izabelle could only mean Piper.

"She's a million times the person you'll ever be," Dani said.

Izabelle flinched as if slapped. But her hurt and disappointment were short-lived, folding into anger as a dark form slid into Dani's periphery.

She turned to find Lou standing here. "You okay?"

"Get me out of here." Dani's face was hot with her anger. "Before I do something I regret."

"Dani, wait. You can't just—"

But Lou was already guiding her into the dark alley.

"Anywhere but home," Dani said. "I can't see Piper. I need to think and—"

"Dani!" Izabelle was following them, but it didn't matter.

"Just go, please!" Dani begged her.

Then they were gone.

LOU PULLED DANI FROM THE NEW YORK ALLEYWAY, WITH its stench of piss and hot garbage, to her lake. The air was much cooler here, the sunlight diffused beneath an abundance of cloud cover, giving everything a gray overcast.

Lou decided not to tell Dani they stood a few feet from the place where she'd blown her ex-boss's brains out after learning he was Petrov's lapdog.

It didn't seem like the time for that show and tell.

Dani fisted her hair, her face pinched. At first glance Lou thought she was pissed—and maybe she was. But it was quickly folding into heartbreak, tears forming in the corners of her eyes.

"I'm so *stupid*," she said, her lower lip quivering.

"We both know you're not," Lou said plainly. "But if someone told you that you were, I'll take care of it."

Lou could use a nice warm-up to the main event with Modesto.

"I should've seen it. It had my mother all over it, how could I be so *blind?*"

Lou's back was starting to ache again. It was annoying how quickly the pain came on these days. It was tolerable—Lou had endured worse—but she didn't understand why carrying a child had to be so backbreaking. Did all women feel this way? Or was her child heavier than most?

"I wasn't offered that job because of *me*. It wasn't because I'm an amazing journalist or—"

"You are an amazing journalist," Lou interjected.

"Or because I deserve to be recognized—"

"You do deserve recognition." Though Lou had no idea

why anyone would want such a thing. It brought too much attention.

"It was because my mother wanted to get me out of New Orleans. She didn't care about making me happy. She just wanted to get me away from Piper and—"

The tears spilled over her cheeks then.

Dani wiped at them with her sleeves.

Lou pulled her into a hug, as close as she could despite the belly pushing them apart. She held Dani while she cried.

"I *really* thought it was because of *me*. Because I'd earned it."

Lou could do nothing else except hold her while she cried. She suspected killing Dani's mother or even the woman that Piper had called her *rival* was too strong of a response to this situation. Besides, they hardly felt like sport. More like shooting chickens in a pen.

"You have guts and you work hard," Lou said as Dani pulled away. "Even if the world never sees it."

Dani opened her mouth to refute the compliments, but Lou pressed on.

"It's because of you that we've put people like Gein away. Killers. Pedophiles. You've done more in the last couple of years than most journalists accomplish in their whole lives."

Lou knew the words weren't sinking in. It was too soon. Dani's disappointment and the sense of betrayal from her mother too fresh.

She gave Dani her space, standing silent beside her as they watched the placid lake. A fish leapt up and ate a fly before disappearing beneath the surface again, leaving ripples in its wake.

"All my life I've been trying to prove that I deserve things because of who *I* am, not because of who my parents are or what *they've* done. I know that sounds like such a pathetic rich-girl thing to say—"

"No," Lou interjected.

"I just feel stupid. *Ugh*, and I'm going to have to tell her she was right." Dani covered her face with her hands. "Piper knew Izabelle wanted to get back together. *Ugh*. Izzy even said 'I love you.' She doesn't even say that to her own parents. How could I miss it?"

Lou couldn't pass judgment. She'd ignored Konstantine's longing stares for a while before she'd caved to his affection.

"Piper won't care about being right," Lou said. "She'll just be glad you're home."

"Are you sure? She was pretty mad."

"Because she thinks Izabelle is right. They have that in common."

Dani frowned at her, swatting a mosquito away. "What do you mean?"

"They both believe she's not good enough for you." Lou had recognized this insecurity in Piper long before she'd confessed to it over drinks in a dark New Orleans bar.

The worst part is I agree with her mom. I'm not good enough for her. But I want her anyway. Is that selfish?

Lou had told her no.

"I decide what's good enough," Dani said flatly. "No one but me."

"Tell her that," Lou said. "She might need to hear it again."

And every day for the rest of her life until she believes it.

"You don't think she'll be mad if I come back now?" Dani asked, hopeful.

Lou snorted. "I think she'll take one look at your pitiful tear-stained cheeks and give you whatever you want."

She watched as Dani warred between the idea of being seen as pitiful and the desire to win Piper over.

Lou turned her compass in Piper's direction. She listened, her ears straining to get a sense of the place. She thought she caught a hint of Henry's voice, the scrape of wooden chairs across a floor.

"I think she's at The Wild Cat," Lou said. "It'll be better to drop you off there than at the apartment. The feds will be less likely to question where you came from."

"My stuff is still at Izabelle's."

"I'll get it," Lou said.

Dani hesitated. "Can you do it without her seeing you?"

Lou rolled her shoulders, trying to ease the tension in her back. "I *can*. It won't be as fun, but I can."

26

Piper arranged the chairs around the table. Overnight they were stored upside down, the seats resting on the tabletops. Before opening, each had to be pulled down and turned right side up.

It wasn't the most exciting way to spend her evening, but she'd promised Henry that she'd help him set up for his show tonight, and after they'd gotten his set design into place, the bartender had asked if they'd help with the chairs, given they were shorthanded.

Even though Piper was exhausted, she would rather be in the bar than alone at the apartment, confronted by Dani's absence, wondering what she was doing with Izabelle. Whether or not she was slowly being charmed by the interloper's moves. Whether or not New York was looking more and more like home and—

I mean, if she loved Izabelle once, she could fall in love with her again. And maybe that's the kind of life she—

Someone threw their arms around Piper's neck and squeezed.

Piper looked up, startled. But she recognized Dani's scent

and the long dark hair. Then she saw Lou slinking toward them, her eyes hidden behind her mirrored shades.

"Dani?" She pulled back, trying to get a good look at her assailant. "God, are you okay? What happened?"

It was clear that she'd been crying. Her beautiful eyes were puffy and red, her cheeks wet.

"What *happened*?" Piper demanded.

Of course she was assuming the worst. Izabelle put the moves on her. Or maybe they even had sex. Piper could imagine it all. The drinks. The city lights. Falling into Izabelle's bed without a single thought for Piper.

"I'll tell you at home," Dani said. "Can you please take me home?"

Home. Something in Piper unclenched when she heard that. It was the way Dani had said it. If she was really about to confess to cheating, she wouldn't have said the word with so much warmth or longing, would she?

"Yeah, okay." She waved to the bartender. "Sorry, but I could only do half. I have to go."

He took one look at Dani and Lou and waved them on. "No problem. Thanks for the help."

Only Lou didn't follow them out of the bar. When they were on the street and Piper looked back, she saw they were alone. Maybe she had somewhere else to be. Or maybe she didn't want the feds to get a good look at her.

Either way, when they got back to the apartment, it was just the two of them.

As soon as Piper closed the apartment door behind them, Dani launched into a nearly incomprehensible story. It was hard to follow her not only because of the speed in which she talked but also because the longer she spoke, the more emotional she got.

Yet Piper was able to piece together the gist of it. New York had been a ruse. Her mother and Izabelle had conspired to sway Dani away from her dangerous life in New Orleans. The job was only a pretense to get her away from here.

From *her*.

Piper was hurt, but not surprised. Dani's mother hadn't liked Piper from the start. Somehow she'd conflated two events in her mind—Piper and Dani meeting with Dani's brush with death.

It didn't matter that Piper had nothing to do with that. It had been Dani's ex-boss that had put her on Petrov's path.

"You were right," Dani said, wiping her nose on her sleeve. "I bet you want to say 'I told you so.'"

It was tempting. Piper did feel slightly vindicated knowing that she hadn't been crazy.

But she couldn't relish the win when Dani's face was steeped in pain.

Instead she went and got her a box of tissues, handing them over. "I'm sorry they lied to you. That sucks."

And it did. Piper didn't like being lied to either.

Dani rubbed her nose until it was red. "You're not mad at me?"

"No," Piper said. "But they're right. You deserve the success you're dreaming about, and it will be harder to come by here. You know that. And I'll be honest. I don't think I'll ever leave New Orleans."

That fact was becoming more and more clear now that Piper was face to face with the feds. She'd always wondered if an agency path was really the right job for her. It was cool as hell, the prospect of becoming a profiler. Hunting killers, looking at crime scenes. But the ideas in her head weren't matching up with the reality she wanted for herself.

She didn't want to be told where she was going to live.

She didn't want to jump through hoops and red tape or play by someone else's rules. She supposed in that way Lou and King were ruining her. She liked doing things their way.

Even profiling itself seemed less cool when she considered the fact that her best friend could just *take* her to the killer if she asked. No need for all that conjecture and speculation. No need to put more lives at risk while she raced against a clock.

But maybe Lou wouldn't always be here.

Was that "maybe" enough to build a life around?

"Not without you," Dani said.

"What?" Piper surfaced from her thoughts.

Dani grabbed her face. "It's not success if it's a life without you. If I have to choose between you and a Pulitzer, it's an easy choice."

"Shut up," Piper said, even though her insides were rapidly becoming jelly. "All you ever talk about is your Pulitzer. 'When I get my Pulitzer. When they give me my Pulitzer. When—'"

"I don't care about that."

A blatant lie, but Piper supposed it would ruin the romance if she called Dani out on it.

"You mean more to me than a Pulitzer, Piper."

It was clear that Dani believed that. Her eyes were too round, too earnest.

"Even if I can't live in New York with you? Even if I don't become an agent, or a lawyer? If I'm forever this poor, unedu-cated, backwoods—"

"You're not listening to me," Dani said, cupping her cheeks again. "I don't give a *shit* about any of that. Be a PI forever if you want. Work cases with King. I just want to be with you."

Piper could see it. Working with King until he died—because let's be honest, that man wasn't going to give up the ghost unless he was a ghost himself. Piper was already making connections with law enforcement around the city. It would be easy for her to show proof of having worked as a PI for at least three years—the minimum for Louisiana. There was also a forty-hour training course she could take and pass, but that was it. Her criminology degree, her experience, her connections, the course—that would be enough to keep doing what she loved.

"I'd have to at least finish law school if I want your mother to accept me," Piper said.

"Fuck her."

Piper held up her hands. "I'd rather not if it's all the same to you."

"I'm so mad that she went behind my back and called Izabelle. *Izabelle.* Do you know that when we were dating all my mother did was call our relationship a *phase*. Now she's calling her up like—" Dani's words devolved into a growl.

"Forget about them. What they did was dumb. They don't know anything." Piper pulled her closer until Dani's head rested on her shoulder. "You've stood up to mob bosses and psychopaths. You're amazing."

This earned her a weak smile.

"I still feel stupid," Dani admitted. "I can't believe I didn't see through them sooner. The job offer came out of nowhere. I really should have been suspicious. If something seems too good to be true, it usually is. I should've known it wasn't because I'd earned it."

"Hey." Piper went over to the bookcase and pulled Dani's award off the shelf. She put it directly into her hands. "Your mom didn't have anything to do with this, did she?"

"Not that I know of," Dani said.

"See? That was all you."

Dani's smile was wider now.

"And there will be more," Piper said. "You're not even thirty. By the time we're King's age, we're gonna need a whole room in our house just for your awards."

"You think so?"

The hope in that voice made Piper's heart ache.

"I *know* so. We might even need a second house."

Dani laughed even though the tears were still in the corners of her eyes.

She came up onto her toes and pressed her lips to Piper's. Piper could taste the salt from those tears.

"Thank you," Dani said. "Thank you for loving me."

"It's easy," Piper said. And that was the truth.

27

King was getting tired of repeating himself. He didn't like having the agents in his apartment. Part of it was the weed that he kept in an old Sam Cooke album. They had no reason—or right—to sort through the vinyl stacked beneath the record player, but King knew if they got close enough to the record player, they might smell it.

He'd managed to keep them in the kitchen at the little table for the length of the interview, but Agent Anderson's eyes kept roving. Every time they did, King's mind made a compulsive list of the things he had in the apartment that he shouldn't.

Burner phones.

An unregistered weapon and ammo.

The eighth of weed.

Nothing that could get him into big trouble, but enough for them to make his life harder than it needed to be.

Enough that his desire for them to leave was like a fingernail scratching at the back of his neck, dividing his focus.

But he couldn't force them out now. That would look suspicious.

"I've told you everything," he said. "I'm not sure what else you want to know."

"Just take me through it one more time," Agent Smith said. Her blue eyes were red at the edges. King knew that look well. He'd worn it himself during his years at the DEA. She was burning the candle at both ends. She was going to hit a wall soon if she wasn't careful.

Maybe they're taking this more seriously than I thought.

"I just want to make sure I'm not missing anything, Mr. King," the agent said.

"Okay," he said, feeling a wave of sympathy for her despite the fact that this was still the woman who'd threatened him with prison just a few hours before. "I asked my landlady to come up and look at my shower. It's got a drip."

"We should question her next," Agent Anderson said, leaning back in his seat.

A swell of defensiveness rose in King. He wanted to tell them to leave Mel alone. But that was just another thing they would look at more closely. Instead he mimicked Anderson's body language, leaning back in his chair as well, affecting an air of casualness.

"By all means," King said. "Whatever ends this interview."

Mel can hold her own. I don't have to worry about her.

"You were looking at the shower when the call came in?"

"No, we'd finished and were just talking."

Because that was when they were in Korea. Of course, King couldn't say that.

She met his eyes. "About?"

"A whole lot of nothing," he said. "We're friends. We often share highlights from our day when we see each other. She wanted to know if I was coming over to watch *Drag Race* later."

Smith arched a brow. "*RuPaul's Drag Race?*"

"But you're straight," Agent Anderson interjected.

Taking an interest in my sexuality, are you? King wondered if they'd explored the possibility that King was so motivated to protect White because they were in a clandestine affair.

King laughed at the idea. They both looked at him.

"I didn't realize you had to be gay to watch the show," he said.

"Your landlady, Ms. Durand, left and the call came in."

"Yes, she was already gone when I got the call," King said.

"Then?"

Then as if you haven't made me say this ten times already.

"At first he didn't say anything. He was just breathing. White said he liked to do that."

No point in hiding that detail. He knew White had already told them so.

"But he spoke to you," Smith said. "He hasn't spoken to White."

That was true.

"He said, 'I want to know why.'"

I want to know why.

Why what? King had asked.

Why would you help him? Why would you help someone like that? You're a good man.

How do you know I'm a good person? King had asked.

I read about you. I know you helped that girl who wanted to kill herself. You stopped her.

He'd been talking about Zoey Peterson. But that had been Mel's win, not his.

White was there that night. He helped too, King had said instead. *He's a good man too.*

That had earned him several beats of silence.

Then the bomber had said, *You're wrong about that.*

There was one thing about the voice that King hadn't

shared, and maybe Smith knew it. Maybe that's why she kept insisting he tell her the story over and over again.

The voice had been young.

Not a child, but young. Late teens, maybe. It aligned with what the cop had told Piper in the bar. But if the bomber was a kid, that was enough to give King hesitation. What the hell had White done to a kid?

Again his mind turned toward Melandra's cards, old and worn as they were. They'd seen war. They'd seen slavery and liberation. They'd been passed hand to hand for generations. He was starting—despite his best efforts—to believe that they might know a thing or two about the world.

The insult isn't in the bomber's head.

It was just enough to make King worry he might be working the wrong side of the case. He cared about White, and he sure as hell didn't want a bomber on the street—in any case, he had to be stopped before someone got hurt—but maybe there was more to the story than King knew.

"Were you able to trace the call?" King asked. "Was he on long enough for you to trace it?"

Agent Anderson sucked his teeth. "No, we weren't even able to hear him that well. We believe it's because you were in the back of the apartment and—"

"Thank you, Agent Anderson," Smith said, her blue eyes cold. She was clearly pissed at her partner for oversharing.

Who was King to get involved in a couple's dispute?

She turned those eyes on King again. "He didn't say anything else? Didn't give you instructions or express an interest to meet?"

"No, no, and no."

She snapped her notebook shut. "If that changes, will you let us know?"

There was something to her tone. Almost a desperation. She was hoping for an ally, but King wasn't what she was looking for. His allegiances were elsewhere, and they both knew it.

"Of course," he said. "But we both know *you'll* know if he does reach out."

Disappointment flashed through her eyes. "It's imperative you remain cooperative, Mr. King."

He couldn't suppress a laugh. "I'm not sure how much more cooperative I can be, Agent Smith."

They rose from the table and relief washed over him. He wanted them gone. He wanted to be alone with his thoughts. With what Piper had said. And with the memory of Mel running a thumb across his knuckles as they'd held hands in the half-assembled office building, the moonlit skyline at their backs.

He opened the door for the agents.

"We'll be in touch," Agent Smith said.

"I'm sure," King replied.

His breath hitched. Melandra was behind the counter. Piper was nowhere to be seen. Maybe she had somewhere to be or maybe Mel had sent her away.

Either way, Agent Smith stopped at the register and King could only watch, battling with another wave of protectiveness.

But they didn't interrogate her. They only handed her copies of their business cards before leaving the shop, the moaning chandelier signaling their departure.

King closed the door and rushed through his apartment to the balcony. He slid the door open as quietly as he could and stepped out, keeping to the shadows.

There they were.

Agents Smith and Anderson cut a path up Saint Peter, weaving through the crowds forming now that the heat of the day was dissipating.

He followed them, keeping to the shadows. He hoped

that the ferns lining his balcony would make it hard for anyone to see him.

They were half a block up when they stopped beside a large van advertising a laundromat. They didn't open the sliding door on the van's side.

Agent Smith climbed behind the wheel and Agent Anderson took shotgun.

King was sure that if he went and threw open that sliding door, he'd find other agents and tech equipment galore, with mics pointed in his direction. He wasn't sure they could pick up Piper's apartment from this distance, even though she was just around the corner, above the agency.

That meant they might have two vehicles tailing them. Hell, maybe more.

He filed this information away and crept back inside, trying to keep his profile as slim as possible.

He locked the balcony door behind him. Then he went to each of his windows—one in the bedroom and one in the bathroom—and locked them too. If they did decide to climb the fire escape and scale the balcony, King didn't want to make it easy for them to sneak into his apartment.

The temptation would be high.

Once he felt certain he'd done what he could to prevent a break-in, he used his burner to page Lou.

She stepped out of his bedroom a moment later, pushing her mirrored glasses up on her head.

He motioned for her to come forward, and she did, pulling him through the shadows without having to be asked.

God, he hated that feeling. The drop-kicked launch of his soul as it was sucked through the void. It was unnatural.

He swore as his feet found steady ground again. They were in the middle of nowhere, beneath the shade of an enormous tree. Some kind of evergreen.

He'd reached out to steady himself by grabbing the tree trunk. His palm came away sticky and smelling of sap.

"My dumping ground," she said simply, as if sensing his confusion. "I miss coming here. I brought Dani here earlier too."

He wasn't sure what to say. *Sorry you haven't been able to murder anyone lately.*

"Two things," he said. "First I need to give you some things to get out of my apartment. Maybe Mel does too."

He suddenly remembered the gun she had, the one she'd shot Lou with, in fact, but couldn't remember if it was registered or not.

"I can't guarantee the agents won't come back with a warrant, and there's some things I'd rather they not find."

He could keep his registered gun for protection. No need to give that up. But some of his fake documents, the weed, the extra burners—one wasn't enough to pin a whole case on, especially not when he could ask Lou to switch it out for him even if they tried to excavate the call log—but most importantly, the two unregistered weapons.

"And the second thing?"

He hesitated. If Piper knew what he was thinking, she'd be furious with him.

Lou seemed to already know. She grinned. "Is it dangerous?"

"Yeah," he said. "I was wondering if we could go to the bomber's place."

"You didn't ask before because...?"

"Piper told me not to put you in danger. You and the baby."

Lou acknowledged this with a nod. "Konstantine and I have recently reached a new agreement."

"About danger?"

"Our original agreement may have been...unrealistic. Given the lives we lead."

"Is there a way we can do this but with you being extra careful?" Because it wasn't that King wanted her to get hurt either. He'd promised Lucy, the love of his life, that he would always look out for her niece. He wasn't about to shit on that by getting Lou killed.

"I can try to listen," she said. "It's not a guarantee."

"Then what happened with Gein?" King asked. Because if she could listen ahead, how had that psychopath been able to entrap her?

"My compass still worked then. I was looking for a kid and I found him," Lou said. "I just hadn't expected the kid to be waiting to stab me with a syringe full of sedatives."

King looked out over the placid lake. Something in the distance crossed from one patch of trees to another. He couldn't tell if it was a bird or something that could leap.

That would be a big squirrel, he thought. And suddenly wanted to leave this patch of wilderness sooner rather than later.

"I only want to go to his place if he's not there," he said. "If he's there, let's not chance it."

Lou's eyes slid down and away. Her head cocked slightly, as if she were listening to something.

"I hear a ticking clock," she said. "No movement, no voices. No breathing."

"Can you tell if he's in the same location?" Because King would rather that they not risk running into the guy.

"No, when I focus on the bomber, my attention is drawn somewhere else. But it's hard to say how much distance is between the two places."

Then he could be heading home for all King knew.

"You still got that pin thingy on your watch?"

"Yes."

"Then let's pop up, drop a pin, and get out of there."

She reached out and grabbed his arm. Before he could prepare himself, he felt that horrible drop again before he was squeezed through the darkness back onto solid ground.

He shuddered.

The room was markedly cold and dark.

Thick blankets had been pulled over the windows. Only a thin line of light from around the edge fell across a rumpled bed.

The AC unit duct-taped into the window hummed, drowning out the sound except for the ticking. Lou had been right about that.

He found the clock affixed above the closed bedroom door.

Lou's face lit green as she began tapping on the face of her watch. Its scant light gave King an odd sense of the room.

Small. Only enough space for the twin bed, a dresser, the cluttered desk. There wasn't even a closet. The carpet was a thick brown shag.

On the desk were a couple of framed photos, but it was too dark to see the subjects clearly and King didn't want to touch anything.

There was also the smell. Body odor. King wondered when the guy had last washed his sheets.

Lou pulled a phone out of her pocket and began snapping photos. King lifted his hand to stop her but changed his mind. Lou seemed to already know what he was thinking.

"They're not tracing my phone," she said. "I can document what I want."

"Just don't send them to us," he said. "And don't touch anything."

If the feds did find this place, it wouldn't look great if their prints were collected along with the evidence.

"Are we *telling* Piper that we came?" Lou asked.

"As long as we come back safe, it won't matter. She can berate us after the fact."

Lou reached out and grabbed his arm suddenly, pulling him off balance. Just before he fell back into the dark, he saw the bedroom door opening.

But they were gone before he could get a look at the person's face.

When the world reformed, they were on a street between two buildings.

"Was it him?" King asked, breathless.

"Yes," she said. "But I didn't know that by the footsteps. I checked the compass the second I heard someone coming."

Heard someone coming.

King hadn't heard anything over the hum of the air-conditioning unit and the ticking clock.

The joys of getting older, he thought.

When he was twenty years younger, he would've noticed the faintest creak of a settling house. Of course, firing guns and a love for blasting The Rolling Stones had also been unkind to his hearing over the years.

He peeked out at the street, trying to look for any sign of where they might be.

He still didn't recognize it. There was a pharmacy, a shoe store, a grocery store. A block up there was a four-way stop. They could've been in any mid-sized city. The signs were written in English. That was his only clue.

"I've got his address," Lou said. She was scrolling through her phone. "But only a couple of these pictures came out. I'm not sure they'll be of any use to you."

"It's okay," he said. "I'll work with what I've got."

She slipped the phone into his pocket. That's when he realized she still wore her mirrored shades. How in the hell had she seen in that room with her shades on? He'd barely been able to make out anything but the vague shapes of the furniture.

"We should move your things sooner rather than later. I'm busy tonight."

It took him a minute to realize she was talking about his weed and unregistered guns.

"Sure. Let's do that next. Could you also drop me off somewhere? Europe should be far enough away. Amsterdam, maybe?" He wanted to find a café with good Wi-Fi, out of the FBI's jurisdiction. Then he could use the address and photos they just took to figure out the identity of the bomber without the feds breathing down his neck.

He told Lou his plan.

She frowned. "How will you pay for the coffee? You can't use your credit card."

"Cash?"

She opened her wallet and pulled out two fifty-euro bills. She pushed it into his hand.

"You don't have to—"

She cut him off.

"You can pay me back," she said. And before he could protest, she pulled them through the dark.

28

Piper didn't *have* to be at the agency. She told herself this for the third time as she looked out the window wistfully at a group of girls stumbling past. King had told her—via Lou—that she could work from anywhere today if she wanted to. She was even invited to hang out with him in Amsterdam.

But the truth was that she was worried about Dani. She didn't want to go too far away in case she needed her. At this very moment she was meeting with her mother for lunch, two blocks up at the high-end Creole restaurant where everyone wore tuxedos and drank Bloody Marys at all times of the day.

Piper knew she should feel triumphant. Izabelle's efforts to convince Dani to abscond to New York had failed. But instead, there was a bitter taste in her mouth. It hurt, more than she cared to admit, to know that Dani's mother had been behind the ruse. Yes, Izabelle had been a willing participant, but her mother—Piper had hoped she was growing on the woman.

That maybe with time she would even come to acquire the woman's respect, if not affection.

It made her stomach twist, knowing that despite her best efforts, her girlfriend's mother still had such a low opinion of her.

The bell above the door rang and Piper looked up, half expecting to see Dani with news about how the lunch had gone.

But it wasn't Dani. It was Agent Smith. And given the pinched look of her face, she was *pissed.*

"Where the hell is he?" she said.

Smith could only mean King.

"I don't know."

"You're lying."

Technically, she was right. Fine, Piper would play the half-truths game if she had to.

"He said he was going to do some work in a café. He didn't tell me which one. I don't know the name, so I can't tell you."

This was the truth. The agent didn't call her a liar for a second time, but it was clear she didn't love this answer either.

"We searched his apartment—"

Of course you did.

"—and his cell phone is there but we can't find him anywhere in the city."

"He doesn't have a car. Most people can't leave a city without a car. I don't have one to loan him and you don't have a record of him renting one, do you?" Piper said.

Now that she knew the agent could read her like a book, all Piper could do was to keep stating the obvious.

Smith glared at her. "All of his known contacts are presently accounted for."

Meaning no one could have given him a ride. Except for the contact the FBI didn't know about. Louie Thorne.

"He didn't drive away," Piper said. "And you would know it if he'd gotten on a plane. So relax. He'll be back soon."

"Call him," she said.

Piper frowned at her. "You know I can't. His cell phone is at his apartment."

"Call his other number."

"Agent Smith, if you can't find him, you're just going to have to wait for him to come back."

The agent gave her a long hard look. "Give me a list of places that he likes to go."

Piper groaned. "Ma'am, with all due respect, I'm trying to get some work done here. Some of this is time sensitive."

"Aren't you worried about his safety?"

"No," Piper said. "He said he was working and that he'd be back. He's only been gone for like an hour. That's not enough time to get into trouble. I'm sure he's fine."

"If he's working on this case, I—"

The door to the agency swung inward with such force that the bell hit the top of the door, cutting its ring short. Agent Smith turned, her hand going to her gun.

But it wasn't an attacker.

It was Dani, swearing in Spanish.

Her mother was on her heels.

"Please don't shoot my girlfriend, Agent Smith," Piper said, equal parts grateful for the interruption and worried that this was about to get ugly. Well, *uglier*. "Her mother, though—"

Agent Smith released her gun. "Are you Daniella—"

She was looking at Dani, clearly about to ask her a question, but Dani's mother held up a hand in the agent's face.

"Excuse me," she said, her face fierce. "*I* am talking to my daughter. Thank you."

Agent Smith's eyebrows rose.

Piper was frozen in her seat. She wasn't sure what the proper reaction to such a situation would be.

Agent Smith looked equally pinned. She stood on the other side of the arguing couple, her gaze sliding from the mother to Dani, back to Piper.

Piper pressed her lips in a thin line and shrugged.

The heated exchange between Dani and her mother raged on. The Spanish was so fast that Piper couldn't follow it.

But she did catch bits of the conversation.

Future.

Happiness.

Secure.

Izabelle.

Class.

Piper couldn't be sure if Dani's mother said Piper had no class or if she was saying that journalism as an occupation had no class. Maybe both?

Her mother threw up her hands for the hundredth time. "If you insist on being a *journalist*, at least choose someone—"

In English, Dani screamed, "I'm going to *marry* her, Mother. It's happening! *Está hecho y me importa una mierda lo que pienses!* You hear me? *Y viviremos aquí en este apartamento hasta que muramos.*"

For a moment her mother only stood there, stunned. One of her hands cupped her cheek as if Dani had slapped her.

Dani's chest was heaving, her face red.

Piper felt equally stunned.

Marry me?

"*Dios ayúdame,*" her mother said.

"Excuse me," Agent Smith said, trying to interject again. It was only then that Piper remembered the agent could speak Spanish. Shit. She'd probably understood more of that conversation than Piper had.

Dani's mother whirled on her. "Who are you? What do you want?"

"I'm Agent Smith with the FBI. And—"

"No. *No más.*" Mrs. Allendale threw her hands up over her head and marched out of the agency.

That only left Dani.

Agent Smith turned to her. "Do you know where King is?"

"No," Dani said. "Excuse me."

Piper could tell that Dani was on the verge of tears. And not the sad kind. The furious kind.

It was the same kind of tears she'd cried for hours the night before while Piper held her and she ranted about how betrayed she felt that her mother had gone behind her back. To *Izabelle* of all people. How tired she was of fighting her mother for what she wanted. How impossible it felt to convince the woman that she deserved to chase her own dreams without her interference.

"Babe—" Piper half rose out of her seat.

"I can't." She held up a hand and Piper stopped where she was. She'd wanted to come around the desk and hold her, but it was clear that Dani didn't want to be touched.

Piper could respect that.

"I need a nap," Dani said, crossing to the edge of the room and pulling open the door to the apartment above. "We'll talk later."

The door shut behind her, leaving Piper and Agent Smith alone in the agency.

The silence hung in the air, buzzing between them.

"I didn't realize there was an apartment up there," Agent Smith said. "It's not on the schematics."

"One bedroom, one bath," Piper said. "About eight hundred square feet."

"Are you hiding King up there?"

Piper had expected this. "No. I wasn't lying when I said he's not here."

"I can get a warrant."

Of course you can.

"There's no need for that. If you've really got to, just go up and look." Piper rubbed her forehead. A headache was forming behind her eyes again. She felt like that was happening a lot these days. "Just don't bother Dani, okay? She's probably crying and the last thing she needs is someone invading her space right now."

Agent Smith gave her yet another long hard look. Piper had the distinct feeling that she was used to people spilling their guts under a stare like that.

Piper said nothing.

"I don't think he's up there," she said finally. "But if I find out you helped him interfere with the case, you'll go to prison with him. You realize that, right?"

You can try, Piper thought.

Because she knew Louie would never leave her in a place like that. Of course, escaping prison probably meant spending the rest of her life exiled in Italy, going off radar with the help of the Italian stallion.

Fuck it. Piper could live with that.

"He's not trying to mess up your case, Agent Smith. Are all agents this paranoid?"

"Only the ones who stay alive."

Piper snorted.

The agent was still watching her. Piper didn't care. Her attention was on the closed apartment door. She wanted to comfort Dani. It stung that she couldn't. When Dani was pissed, she wanted to be alone. Piper had learned this about her since they started living together.

Of course, that didn't make it easier.

Smith's expression turned icy. "You understand that he's in

trouble, right? That bomb was made by an amateur, but in a lot of ways amateurs are more dangerous. They're reckless. Unpredictable. And King *is* his target. He only threatened White, but with King there was an actual bomb. You see the difference?"

Piper's heart kicked. This little speech would have scared her if she didn't know that King was safe in Amsterdam.

Hell, it's scaring me anyway.

Agent Smith knew it. She nodded, as if satisfied. "When you see him, tell him to call me. It's urgent."

"Will do," Piper said.

Smith pulled open the door. But she didn't leave. She turned back to Piper, her face blank and tone even. "I don't think you have what it takes to be an agent."

Piper's throat tightened. "That's your professional opinion?"

"If you were a federal agent, you'd be expected to put the case above your partner. Whether that be your professional partner or your life partner. Obstructing justice in order to protect the people you care about would only get you fired, arrested, or killed."

The door swung shut behind her.

Piper couldn't be sure if she'd just been complimented or insulted.

She fell back against the chair, the remainder of her focus leaving her as a sweeping exhaustion overtook her.

With the agent gone, Piper had only her thoughts to contend with.

I'm going to marry her, Mother.

Had Dani meant that? No. Surely she'd just been speaking out of anger.

Maybe she just wanted to piss her mother off.

Yeah, that was it. Piper rubbed her eyes.

"Time for a break." She grabbed her keys, phones, and

wallet off the desktop. She decided that she needed a coffee. Yes, she could make it herself using the coffee station against the wall, but she also needed a walk to clear her head.

And this office was still buzzing with the emotional charge of all that yelling. Hopefully it would be gone by the time Piper got back.

She locked her laptop in the desk for safety and checked her pockets again, making sure she had everything she needed.

Her eyes fell on the closed apartment door.

Then she stepped out of the office into the darkening streets and locked it up tight behind her.

29

K ing was starting to feel the jitters from the coffee even though he'd only had two cups. He wondered how much stronger the coffee was here, and was glad that he'd passed on the space cake that the barista had offered him. It had been tempting purely for the sake of the novelty. He'd never had weed in Amsterdam before. But no. He needed his wits about him as he continued his investigation into the bomber's identity.

Now that he had an address, it was easy to ascertain the names of its inhabitants. Jonathan and Sylvia Harman had bought the house in the nineties and lived there with two sons, Sawyer and Clyde. Old-fashioned names. The red Honda was registered to the woman, Sylvia. But King was sure he'd seen a man behind the wheel. And Jonathan was almost fifty, much older than the person King had seen and talked to. That left the sons.

The oldest was nineteen and the youngest was thirteen.

The thirteen-year-old couldn't drive a car, let alone make a bomb. That left Sawyer as his prime suspect.

King did another search, seeing what he could turn up on him.

Then, on a whim, he did a search for Sawyer Harman and Richard White.

An article popped up.

There was White, shaking hands with a tall lanky kid with a bright smile. Below, the caption read: *Fresh crop of NOCHS students join the PeeWee Patrol. The summer program teaches local students from low-income areas the importance of law enforcement roles within the city.*

It's part internship, part mentorship, Detective Richard White told Channel 3 News. *I love doing it. We get a great group of kids every year. And it's tied to a scholarship program at the University of New Orleans, which we're very proud of.*

The article was from three years ago.

King found it hard to believe that White had done something so terrible as to turn a sixteen-year-old kid into the bomber.

What the hell happened?

But the address matched the pin Lou had dropped. And here was a clear connection with a resident at that address.

He searched, trying to find more to the story.

But there was nothing.

Both parents were alive. The little brother was on the President's List at his middle school. There weren't many public records of Sawyer.

He'd graduated with a low GPA just last spring, a year late. He worked as a night janitor in the precinct, which would have given him access to White's office. He had no criminal background. From no charges to a bomber felt like a leap, especially at such a young age. There was mention of him in a short obituary for Rhett Harman, his grandfather. Sawyer and his family were listed as the surviving relatives. The grandfather had died at seventy-five, but there was no mention of how he passed. King assumed at that age it was probably natural causes.

And that was it.

That's all he could find.

The insult isn't made up.

Mel's words came back to him. King looked between the two photos of his suspect. The first when he was sixteen, eyes bright, smile big, as he shook Detective White's hand and grinned at the camera.

The second was a driver's license photo taken last year. So much had changed, but most noticeably, the light had gone out of his eyes. His face had been round, almost boyish in the first photo but had grown gaunt and haunted in the second. It was hard to believe that only a couple of years separated those two shots.

Hell, it was hard to believe that it was the same kid.

White. What the hell did you do?

King took his burner phone off the table and shot Lou a text.

She appeared at his table two minutes later, her mirrored sunglasses hiding her eyes.

"Did you get your guy?" she asked.

"Yeah, but I don't like it. He has means, but I don't know the motive. I need to talk to White."

"Let's go now."

King hesitated. He didn't want to take Lou to the conversation. In fact, he didn't want to bring anyone to this conversation. The questions he would have to ask White were going to be hard enough. Bringing an audience might just feel like an attack.

"Actually, can I just leave the laptop with you and go alone? If you can drop me off that would be great. Uh, but not *in* the house."

King didn't want to try to explain to White how he had

just magically appeared in his house. The alternative was to let him think he'd snuck in, which might breach White's trust.

"Just try to get me as close to his house as possible," King said. "I'd prefer to walk up and knock on the door like a normal person."

"Sure." Lou took the laptop and nodded in the direction of the bathrooms behind her.

King rose and followed her to the back of the shop. They stepped into the bathroom together and Lou shut the door without turning on the light.

King had expected a warning, but what he got was the sudden, drop-kicked feeling of falling through a crack in the world only to find himself squeezed out the other side.

King opened his eyes, trying to get a sense of where they were, realizing that he was lying on his back in the dirt.

He lifted his head, looked at his feet. "Are we under the porch?"

"This is as close as I could get you and keep you out of sight," she said, releasing him.

"Thanks," he said. But silently, he'd made a note to be more specific next time.

As close as you can get me where I'm still vertical.

"I have to go. They're waiting for me," she said. "You can make your own way home, right?"

"Yeah. Who—" He'd wanted to ask who was waiting for her. But when he turned back, she was gone. He spoke only to the darkness. "Don't worry about me."

He had no choice but to army-crawl out from under the porch with little to no dignity.

He was too old for this and he knew it. His back ached by the time he pulled himself to standing—oh so slowly—and brushed the dirt off his pants.

He looked around the quiet street, at the cars parked in a line on the curb.

He spotted the FBI immediately.

Lucky for him, the guy behind the wheel had fallen asleep. His head was lying against the headrest.

King thought about going over there and tapping on the window, but that seemed cruel. He'd been on many a long stakeout himself. And he had fallen asleep too. Getting two hours of sleep spread out over two days wasn't for everyone.

King let the agent sleep and walked up to the front door.

He rapped on the door, then rang the doorbell. He couldn't remember if White had fixed the bell or not. He knocked again.

"White, it's me," he called. "It's King."

Just in case he was under the impression that King might be a solicitor, or a politician.

But he knew White was there. He'd seen the SUV in the driveway.

He knocked again. This time King heard the footsteps before the door opened.

It was White, peeking through a slim crack. "What?"

Well, this is a less than friendly welcome.

"I came by to give you some information," he said. "About your bomber."

"You can call me," White said, and tried to close the door.

King stopped it with a hand.

"No, I can't. The feds are watching you and tapping our phones." King pointed at the agent asleep behind the wheel. "I was worried I wouldn't be able to tell you anything in case they're recording the house, but there's no one else. I don't know how much time we have so—"

"Let him in," a voice said.

The hair rose on the back of King's neck. "Who's that?"

White didn't answer. But his eyes were wide with fear. He mouthed, "*Go.*"

"Detective White," the voice said, a low warning. "Let him in or you know what'll happen."

King could've run.

His gut told him to. But there was fear in White's eyes as he stepped back, moving so that King could enter the house.

"I'm sorry," White said.

King didn't know why until he was in the foyer, with the door closing behind him.

There was the kid at the end of the hallway, where it opened on the living room.

It was Sawyer.

He was wearing his red cap, making the shadows under his eyes more pronounced. He had a gun pressed to Ayisha's head, White's oldest daughter.

She was crying, her eyes pinched closed.

"You really are a good cop. Mr. King. A better cop than this joke," Sawyer said. "You found me before the FBI did."

"What are you doing?" King stood where he was, trying to take in the scene. "I thought you were mad at White."

"I am," Sawyer said with a bitter laugh. "It's pretty obvious that I'm fuckin' mad, ain't it?"

"Then why are you pointing a gun at Ayisha?" he asked, doing his best to keep his tone gentle and even despite his pounding heart.

"Lock the door, Detective White."

White reluctantly turned back and twisted the lock. The deadbolt clanged into place.

King tried again. "If you're angry at White, then why are you pointing a gun at her?"

Sawyer released the girl and turned the gun on King instead. "Better?"

30

Konstantine was on his knees before the Virgin Mary. It had been a while since he'd prostrated before her like this, praying with all of his soul.

Please watch over her and our child. If a life must be taken, let it be mine.

Please.

Please.

Konstantine repeated the prayer over and over in his mind until his knees began to ache from being pressed so long into the stone floor. He didn't care. He didn't have much time to make his wishes known. Stefano was readying the men. Lou said she needed a few moments more to help King.

They would both be back soon, and the night would begin.

Benedetta madre. I will give anything. My life. But please keep them safe and—

He became aware of a shadow in the corner of his eye.

He turned, expecting to see Lou. But it wasn't. It was Matteo.

He waved the boy forward. "*Dovresti essere a letto.*"

"I heard you come into our room," he said.

"I'm sorry if I woke you." Konstantine had only wanted to check on the children once more before he went out to confront Modesto. It eased his mind to know they were safe.

Matteo was getting taller. Konstantine thought he'd shot up almost a foot in the last few months. He still had his soft round face, but he was beginning to look less like a child. This realization caused a small pang of sadness to rise up unexpectedly.

Matteo searched his eyes questioningly. "*Che c'è?*"

"You're getting tall," he said. He placed an affectionate hand on the boy's head before giving his shoulder a squeeze. "I was wondering if you would get taller than me."

"*Lo spero.*" Matteo stood up straighter, his smile wide.

Konstantine chuckled. "*Vai, vai. Torna a dormire.*"

He saw Lou in the corner of his eyes even before Matteo, now in a good mood, turned away from him, taking off in the direction of the dormitory.

Once he was out of sight, she stepped forward.

She smiled down at him. She glanced at the Virgin Mary then back at him. "I thought I was the only woman you got on your knees for."

He accepted her hand, allowing her to pull him to standing.

"What did you pray for?" she asked.

"The baby. *Sempre.*"

She seemed to accept this. He knew Lou did not believe in the things he did. She'd once told him of the ghosts she'd seen. But she spoke of the dead as if they were only a possibility. Ghosts that may or may not be the result of her imagination. She did not have his faith.

The phone in his pocket buzzed. It was a text from Stefano.

Siamo pronti.

To Lou he said, "They're ready."

"Should I go now then?" She turned as if she would step right into the patch of darkness pooling just out of Mother Mary's glow.

"Wait." He grabbed her wrist. "Wait a minute."

She came closer, willingly stepping into his arms.

"I remember the drill," she said. "I pop in. I drop a pin. I come back to you and give you the address. Then I take you to Stefano and the others. I stay close so that I make sure Detti doesn't get away. And to save your ass if this goes sideways."

"If it isn't safe to help me—"

"That's exactly when I will be helping you," she said coldly. "Save your breath."

"You must be careful, *amore mio*."

"*You* must be careful. If you don't want me stepping in, then don't give me a reason to." She held his gaze in challenge.

He knew there was no point in arguing with her. That was why he'd prayed to the Virgin. Konstantine thought his luck would prove better with her.

She must have seen the worry on his face, because she wrapped her arms around him, squeezing him.

"We will keep each other safe," she said.

He softened against her, burying his face in the nape of her neck. He loved the smell of her. The steadiness. A soft kick struck his stomach and he laughed into the crook of her shoulder.

"At least it's not my kidneys," Lou said. He heard the smile in her voice.

Konstantine's phone buzzed again. He sensed Stefano's agitation even before answering.

"It's time," Lou said.

"*Sì.*" He placed his hand on her stretched belly one more

time. "*Vai.*"

She stepped away from him and was gone.

Konstantine looked away from the darkness where she'd disappeared and turned to the Virgin Mary again, her hands stretched out in offering.

Please watch over her and our child. If a life must be taken, let it be mine.

Please.

Please.

Let it be mine.

LOU STEPPED THROUGH THE DARK OF THE CHURCH, committing Konstantine's face to memory. She was getting used to that particular expression. It was the way someone looked when they didn't want to let something go but they had to.

She found it amusing.

Perhaps because she was not as worried about her own safety, or the safety of her daughter, as he was. She had every intention of being quick. She'd decided that very afternoon, before she'd gotten the pull from King, before they'd finalized the last details of their campaign against Detti, she knew what her strength would be tonight.

Speed. She would simply be too fast for him.

She would spend no more than a second in each patch of darkness. Watching, taking measure of her prey. She'd used such tactics before with great success. Yes, it was quite different than lying in wait for a target so that she could snatch them when they came within range, much like a spider.

No, she wouldn't be able to snatch Detti tonight. He was promised to another, and she would stick to the plan. Unless—

There was only one reason why she'd break her promise and put a bullet in Detti herself. And that was if he threatened Konstantine.

If he got a chance and took it, well, then all bets were off.

Stefano would just have to forgive her. Or not.

Speed.

She relaxed into the darkness, trusting her compass to guide her to Modesto, no matter where he hid in the city.

And just like that, the world softened around her, and she slipped through it. The sight of the church and the Blessed Virgin disappeared, and in its place, large swaths of plastic formed.

There was a face beneath it.

This struck her. For a moment she thought she was looking at a dead body, perhaps suffocated.

But it wasn't a body. It was a sculpture. The face beneath it bloodless, colorless.

A wind ruffled the plastic and Lou realized by the echoing quality to the sound that she was in a dim gallery. The night spilled through the high windows above, throwing gray shadows across the floor. Small lamps had been lit and clustered near the center of the chamber.

She spotted Detti immediately, his face illuminated by the nearest lamp. He was sitting at the foot of a statue, leaning forward, one hand braced on his knee. He was speaking to someone over the phone, his eyes pointed down and away from her.

From where she stood, she recognized only the words for *left* and *right*.

Sinistra.

Destra.

Perhaps he was giving someone directions.

Konstantine had only wanted her to pop in and out, but Lou planned to do better than that. She wanted them to be well prepared. If she could help it, they would lose no one tonight.

She moved from shadow to shadow, counting the men as she went. More than a few wore guns in holsters, resting against their ribs. Still more had them tucked into the waistbands of their pants.

She counted forty men in all, with almost a hundred guns between them. A skeleton crew. Surely Modesto didn't plan to wrest Florence from Konstantine's control with *forty* men.

She retraced her steps, but her count was the same.

This will be easy, she thought, relief washing through her. *They'll be crushed.*

Modesto ended his call and reached for the bottle of wine at his feet. As he did, he looked up suddenly, meeting Louie's eyes.

She slipped. The gallery was gone and in its place was Konstantine's office. He was also speaking into his phone, and it gave Lou a strange sense of time warping around her.

"Did you get my pin drop?" she asked.

"Yes, he's in Pitti Palace."

Lou frowned. "That's a major tourist attraction."

"Not the West Wing, at least not now. It's closed for renovations."

That explained the plastic draping she'd seen over the sculptures.

"The Pitti Palace isn't far away," Louie said. Something about this fact unsettled her. She'd hoped that she was going to find Modesto on the other side of Florence, or perhaps even in its suburbs, not at their back door.

"It doesn't matter. He doesn't know where we are."

Are you sure about that?

"Is Stefano and everyone ready?" she asked. "We need to get moving. I think he saw me. That might make him run."

"They already left. As soon as I got your pin, I sent them

on." He checked his watch. "They might be there by now."

He pulled a key from a drawer in his desk and went to the large wardrobe in the corner. Lou watched as he opened it, pulling the doors wide.

Of course it was full of guns.

"Why have you never showed me this toy box before?" she asked, sliding up beside him.

He smiled. "Pick what you want."

She had her Berettas already in the shoulder holsters at her sides. And while it was useless to put anything below her waist, slow as she would be to pull it with her belly in the way, she chose a shiny pair of Benellis before filling her pockets with ammo. She checked whether each gun was loaded and found they were.

"What?" Konstantine asked. "Why are you smiling like that?"

"It feels good," she said. He probably thought she meant holding the Benellis, but no. Lou was talking about the sheer volume of weapons on her body. It had been a while since she'd had an excuse to carry more than a pistol or two. And while she wasn't wearing her full arsenal—a shame—even just the extra pair of guns was comforting.

She took a moment to relish the feeling, the promise of battle.

When she opened her eyes again, Konstantine was wearing a Kevlar vest, a gun at each hip and pistols in his hands.

"Are you ready?" she asked him.

"*Sì*." He offered her the vest.

She took it. "Wrap your arms around me."

He did, his neck aligning with her lips. She pressed a kiss there.

"For luck," she whispered, and pulled them through the dark.

31

King sat on the loveseat, opposite White's wife and girls. Ayisha was released and rushed back to her mother's side.

"Are you hurt?" King asked them.

White's wife, Dana, shook her head. There was fury in those eyes, and her jaw worked as she cradled her crying girls.

"Physically, *no*," the bomber said. "Not yet anyway."

"I thought it was White you were angry at," King said. He couldn't look at the girls. Seeing them cowering at their mother's side made his chest ache unbearably. The acid rose up his throat. He swallowed but it didn't really help. "I thought he was your target."

"He is. All of this is *his* fault," the bomber said. He pointed the gun at White, using the barrel to motion toward the chair. "Sit down. I don't like you *lurking* in my periphery like that."

White obeyed, walking between his family and King, taking a seat in the adjacent chair. And there they were, all together, each forming the side of a square—the bomber, King, White, and the girls.

"Why don't you let them go," King said. "The girls don't need to be here."

"I suppose you'd be the one to walk them out, valiant as you are?" The bomber sneered. "Ever helpful. So *loyal*."

King heard the derision but couldn't understand the source of it.

"Are you mad at me too?" he asked.

The bomber's jaw began working. Not a good sign. He pointed the gun at King. "Yes. You could say that."

"Can I ask why?"

"Because you made everything *bad*. It wasn't supposed to be like this."

King waited, hoping for an explanation.

"I was having *fun*," the bomber said. "We were enjoying ourselves."

He motioned to White with the gun as if he expected the detective to agree.

"Then you had to go and get involved."

"I asked for his help. That was on me," White said. "I took your threats seriously, Sawyer."

"As you should," the boy hissed. "But for a minute there it was almost like——it was like it should be."

King was sensing a subtext here but was struggling to put the pieces together.

"I'm sorry if I offended you, Sawyer," he said. He did his best to keep his tone even. "I was just trying to help a friend."

"How can you be friends with someone like that? *How?*" The bomber's face pinched. The whirlwind of emotions playing across his face made King's stomach knot. He didn't want someone emotional pointing a gun.

"What did he do?" King asked. "What did White do to you?"

"Why don't you tell them?" the bomber said. "Tell them what you did."

"Sawyer, I've done everything you said. Please just let my wife and kids—"

"No!" The bomber pivoted the gun from White to the girls. "They stay. I want them to know what a shitty human you are. They should know what you did."

"I want to know what he did," King said. This was true, but what he was really hoping was that the bomber would turn the gun on him instead.

Please don't let him shoot the girls, King thought. He couldn't watch two little girls be murdered in front of his eyes tonight.

Louie, where are you?

He was wishing with his whole heart that Lou would show up. If she could just appear behind the bomber, serve as enough of a distraction for King or White to rush him and get the gun, that would be enough.

But no matter how hard he wished it, she didn't come.

Where are you?

That filled him with a terrible thought. Maybe Lou had heard him. Maybe she had sent that compass of hers ahead and had found the situation too dangerous to come into.

That didn't bode well for them.

"Cops are supposed to be honorable men," Sawyer said. "You were *supposed* to be an honorable man."

"Sawyer, I—"

"Shut up! Shut up!" He pointed the gun at White. "I'm tired of your lies. All you ever told me was lies."

"I never lied to you. I—"

The gun went off.

32

Lou felt the column form at her back for only a moment before she heard the gunfire. Konstantine pulled away from her even before her boots fully settled on solid ground. She released him, turning her attention instead to the dark hallway around them.

A man appeared around the corner. He reached for his gun and Lou shot him before he even pulled it free of its holster.

"The look on your face, *amore mio*," Konstantine whispered. "Wear that one in bed for me next time."

She chuckled. "You'll have to earn it."

"I will. *Prometto.*"

She couldn't deny that it felt good. She hadn't taken a life in months. She hadn't even worn this much firepower pressed against the curve of her waist in ages. With the gun warming in her hand, she was beginning to feel like herself again.

Lou spotted Stefano in the gallery below. That's when she realized they were actually up on the balcony. The man she'd shot must have been hoping to take the high ground and attack Stefano and the others from above.

"I'll stay here and guard the high ground," she said. "You go cover Stefano."

"*Bene.*" Konstantine brushed a kiss across her lips, then touched her stomach as if for luck.

Lou stayed where she was, her attention splitting between the shootout below and the stairs leading to the balcony.

She spotted Modesto behind a carved Venus. He was well guarded, a solid wall at his back and no angles with which he could be surrounded. His closest men—seven or eight—had taken the sculptures in the rows ahead. This line was doing a good job of keeping Stefano and the others at bay.

Lou raised the pistol and shot the one closest to her.

The top of his skull popped off, splattering brains across the plastic protecting the statue at his back.

She was able to take a second and third man easily enough, clearly the first line.

Stefano's men advanced.

Still the angles were not in their favor. The statues were good at absorbing bullets, each hit spraying chunks of stone across the gallery floor.

Lou didn't mind.

She emptied one Benelli, taking out three more of Modesto's men as she did. A bullet grazed her shoulder and bit into a column beside her as she pulled the second Benelli, raining stone onto the floor below.

Four men rushed forward from the landing above the stairs, probably hoping to take Lou at a charge.

She emptied the second Benelli. Three chest shots. Two headshots. She didn't *have* to empty the gun, she knew. But it had felt good to do it. To hear that satisfying *click click*.

Rather than reload, she threw the empty Benellis away and drew her prized Berettas.

She searched the gallery below, finding Konstantine immediately among the fray. He had blood trailing down his right arm, but even from here Lou could see it was a flesh wound, the rivulet of blood hardly something to write home about.

Still, the sight of it angered her.

She took out five more of Modesto's men from above, spilling brains across column after column.

She spotted Modesto nearing the back.

But there's nothing back there.

No exit. And his men were dwindling.

Lou's compass began to spin and pull. She registered King's concern at a distance, but she pushed it away, trying to focus her attention here and now.

Something was wrong.

Why was Modesto backing himself into a corner?

Why did he have so few men defending him? And the dwindling numbers weren't replacing themselves.

That couldn't be right.

Where was everyone else? Surely Detti couldn't be so stupid as to believe he would overtake Konstantine's men with so few people.

Another man came up the stairs. Lou shot him with barely a glance.

No one followed him.

They're only sending enough people to keep us busy.

Lou stepped through the dark, abandoning the balcony for Konstantine. She appeared beside him in the gallery below. She pulled him through the dark before he could fire his shot. When the world reformed around him, the bullet sailed into the dark, targetless.

"We have a problem."

He lowered the gun. "What is it?"

"This is all wrong. Look." She gestured at the gallery below. At her view of Modesto in his stronghold at the back of the church, Stefano and his charge carving a slow path forward. Now there were no more than two or three rows of statues between them. Soon they would all be against the far wall.

"Yes, he is cornered," Konstantine said. "Good."

"No. They're just buying time." Lou was sure of it. She hadn't forgotten the way he'd executed Stefano's sister and her children. That was cold, exacting, and precise. That Modesto wouldn't back himself into a corner or waste bullets. And he sure as hell wouldn't provoke a group as large as the Ravengers only to come to the fight under-prepared.

"You said he was part of the Naples family."

"The Celesti."

"Then he knows this game. He's been mafia all his life. He wouldn't do something this stupid."

She saw Konstantine weighing her words in his mind. He rubbed his jaw, biting his lower lip.

"This is a distraction," she said.

"From what?"

"I don't—" Alarm cut her words short. It felt like a hook was jerked through her navel. She'd registered King's fear first, but it was quickly swallowed by the fear of the children.

The children.

Before she even stretched her compass out into the dark, searching, she could hear their screaming in her ears.

"The church," Louie said. "They're attacking the church."

"Go." He pushed her gently. "*Go.*"

"This is a trap. Get Stefano out of here," she said. Then she was gone.

THE BULLET BLEW A HOLE THROUGH THE ARMREST OF White's chair, scattering stuffing into the air. King drew back reflexively, even though the armrest was a good two feet away.

"Tell another lie, Detective White, and the next bullet is going through your chest. Then they can watch you die."

"Sawyer," King said calmly, his hands held up in front of him as if he were trying to soothe a raging animal. "Why don't you just tell us the story? I don't know it. Dana doesn't know it. Why don't you just tell us?"

Because what they needed most right now was time.

Lou wasn't coming, that was clear, and King tried to remain calm about that. It was possible she was held up with something equally important, though at the moment he struggled to imagine something more pressing than the situation he'd found himself in.

That left the FBI. And the fact they hadn't charged in yet was entirely his fault. He was the one who'd given them the slip by going to Amsterdam. And he was the one who hadn't bothered to wake up the agent sleeping outside.

If he died here and now, he had no one to blame but himself.

The cell phone in his pocket began to buzz.

He reached for it and Sawyer turned the gun on him. "*Don't.*"

"You know the FBI has been following me," King said. "If I don't tell whoever is calling I'm all right, it'll be suspicious."

Sawyer sucked his teeth. "If you say anything stupid, you're *dead*."

King quickly pressed accept before it could go to voice mail.

Sawyer jabbed the air with his finger while mouthing the word *speakerphone*.

King obliged. This wasn't his burner. That meant that Piper was already going to watch what she was saying.

"Piper?"

"Hey, man, where the hell are you? Agent Smith is breathing down my neck."

"I'm hanging with Johnny and White down at the watering hole."

Piper paused. "How many drinks in are you?"

"Just one. But there's a few of us chillin' here. So we might be tied up a while."

"Okay. Roger that. I'll tell her so she gets off my back."

"Thanks, Genereux."

Another long pause. "Be careful out there, boss."

"You too," he said, doing his best to keep the emotion out of his voice. "I'll see you soon."

Sawyer snatched the phone away, ended the call, and tossed it across the room.

"No more fucking calls," he said, retraining the gun on King.

That was fine. King preferred that he be the target. It was easier to imagine his own death than be forced to watch someone else die in front of him.

Besides, he'd done what he could. He'd tried to alert Piper and the FBI to his whereabouts. That was the best he could do.

"I'm still waiting for that story," King said when Sawyer's attention started sliding toward the girls again.

"You know, in a way it's funny," Sawyer said, though there wasn't an ounce of humor in his voice. "I only applied for the PeeWee Patrol because of my granddad. He was the one who loved all that crime stuff. When I was a little kid, we used to watch *all* the crime shows together. All the movies. He was a religious man, but he loved to write mysteries on his typewriter. He'd spend the afternoons typing while I read on the floor of his office. When he was done, he'd read the chapter from that day. He had a pretty good story about a monk who went around solving crimes. Too bad nobody published it."

"Movies?" White looked unwell. There was sweat standing out on his forehead and he looked ready to throw up.

"Yeah, movies. *Speed* was my favorite. That bomb on the bus scene was *sick*."

Sick like you, King thought, but said nothing.

"The old movies were the best. My grandad loved *Se7en*, with Morgan Freeman. It was pretty good, but *Speed* is still my favorite. Keanu is a legend."

King understood now why Sawyer's letters had been old school. Magazine cutouts and letters. That *was* the stuff of crime shows, things he hadn't seen in decades.

"My grandad used to tell me that becoming a cop was my ticket out of here. That if I became a detective like those guys in the movies, I had a chance at a real future. And I wanted to make my granddad proud. He was the only one who ever cared about me. My parents don't give two shits about me. They look at me and they see a fuckup. But my grandad, he loved me. He believed in me. At least he did until you went and fucked everything up."

Sawyer pointed the gun at White.

"When I told him that I'd been accepted to the PeeWee Patrol, he was over the moon. He was so proud of me."

Sawyer's eyes filled with tears.

"He was so happy. For *me*."

"Sawyer, I—" White began.

"Shut up!" Sawyer shook the gun at him. "Shut up or I swear to God, I'm going to shoot you in the fucking face!"

White didn't say anything more.

"I *idolized* you. You promised me the scholarship. *You* said, 'Don't worry, Sawyer. I'm going to do everything I can to get you that place at UNO.' Only you didn't, did you? You gave your letter of recommendation to Maggie Brooks. And you looked so smug on the stage at the ceremony when you handed her the little *certificate* and the little *award*. And you know where I was?"

"Sawyer—"

"I was in the fucking audience with my grandad, watching you give away what you promised to me. I'd told *my* grandad I was getting that award, and then you went and made a liar out of me. A liar to the only person who mattered."

"Sawyer—"

The boy crossed the room and struck White across the cheek with the gun. Again and again. And again.

"I did everything you asked of me! I jumped through every hoop and did every stupid little—"

King leapt up from the couch and grabbed Sawyer.

"Go!" He shouted at the girls. "Go! Go! *Go!*"

Dana grabbed her girls and bolted for the front door.

King wrestled the young man to the ground, and White, with his bleeding and swollen face, held his legs.

King expected Sawyer to fight back, throw a few punches.

But instead he went limp beneath King.

And he was smiling.

"I wouldn't be too rough with me, Mr. King," he said.

King sat up, moving back. He wasn't afraid of being shot —he'd thrown the gun across the room.

Now he was afraid of something else. Very afraid.

Sawyer pulled open his shirt, popping several buttons to reveal the bomb strapped to his chest.

"I'd be really careful if I were you."

33

Louie stepped from the darkness into a world of flames. Bodies littered the ground. Faces she recognized. Konstantine's people. Everyone had been slaughtered where they'd stood.

The children.

Her compass pulled her toward the Blessed Virgin. Arms stretched forward, she shone bright like a beacon of hope even while the pews, floors, and rafters burned. The whole place smelled of smoke. She heard a tremendous crack and stepped aside in time to miss a chunk of wood tumbling from the ceiling to the floor at her feet.

Ash flew into the air, causing her to turn her face away.

And the heat on her skin was too much—she couldn't stay.

The children.

A man cut the corner leading to the kitchen and Lou snatched him by the back of his neck. Without thinking she twisted hard, feeling his vertebrae crack in her grip.

A semi-automatic submachine gun clattered to the stone floor. She slowly bent and picked it up just as a wave of men spilled through the adjacent hallways, blocking her path to the Virgin statue.

She knew the children were hiding there. Of course they were.

How many times had Lou caught the children beneath her, sharing their stories at the end of the day? Countless.

I'm coming, she thought. *Hold on. I'm coming.*

She opened fire. Bullets sprayed the room in a sweeping arc from left to right. She aimed a little higher than she needed. It made her targets smaller, but with this much ammo it hardly mattered. It mattered only that a stray bullet didn't strike low, potentially hitting a child.

"*La Strega!*" someone screamed. Lou didn't know where the voice had come from.

When they opened return fire, she was gone.

It was easy to move in this place. The flames, though plentiful, were not strong enough to overtake the darkness.

She found solid ground again at their back, cutting a line of gunfire across their spines. Their bodies arched, bucking forward.

She caught sight of Matteo, sticking his head out.

"Stay down!" she screamed.

He disappeared beneath the Virgin again.

But not before the men on the other side of the nave caught sight of him.

Lou bled through the dark again, striking one on the back of the head with the gun.

A few feet away a man trained his pistol on her.

Lou had a momentary flash of fear. A knowing that *that* bullet was going to strike true.

Right in the gut.

Then something happened.

The light of the fire suddenly burned brighter in front of her. For an instant it was too bright to see anything.

Lou took a step back and found that darkness eluded her. She was pinned in place.

The man's aim faltered. His finger squeezed the trigger, but the bullet went wide, striking the stone wall over her shoulder.

What the hell was that?

She placed a hand on her stomach, trying to quell the strange fluttering there.

It didn't matter. There was no more time.

Men were spilling in from all directions. There were too many. This was the real siege.

With the strange light gone, Lou stepped into the darkness, finding the world again behind the Blessed Virgin.

She bent down, lifting the fabric. She said a silent prayer of thanks that this piece of cloth had not caught fire, driving the children out into the gunfire.

She was met with a dozen fearful faces.

"Come on," she said, waving them into her arms. "We can't stay here."

The fire was getting too close, the smoke too thick.

Little arms wrapped around her, clutching her.

"Hold tight."

She pulled them through the dark with her. It didn't matter that her arms were not big enough to hold them all. They clung to her and to each other.

That was enough to move them from the burning church to the villa miles away.

They stood in the living room, quiet.

Lou listened, her muscles skittish. If the Celesti family had really been watching them this whole time, it was possible they knew where they lived. That the villa wasn't safe.

But there were no footsteps.

Lou didn't sense any danger here.

Still she held up a hand, signaling that the children should wait where they were.

Quickly she moved through each room. She checked each crevice and closet. But there was no one. The security system remained on with no notifications. No one had moved in this house for hours. They couldn't be lying in wait.

She loosed a breath and went back to the children.

They weren't there.

"Matteo?"

A little head popped up from behind the loveseat. Several more mimicked him. It gave Lou the impression of meerkats or prairie dogs.

"Is everyone here?" she asked, doing a headcount. They were missing two.

"Gabriella." Matteo made a motion with his hands. First together, then apart. "Separate," he said.

"You got separated." Lou was already casting her compass out, searching for the girl. To her relief, she felt her alive, if afraid. "Anyone else?"

"Nario," he said, his lips pressing into a thin line. "He fight. He fight. We run."

But reaching out for Nario returned nothing but the cold whisper of death.

He hadn't survived.

Lou could see the scene clearly in her mind's eye. Nario, who slept closest to the door of the dormitory. The oldest boy in the bunch. He had done what he could to buy the children time to escape when the gunfire started.

Lou placed a gentle hand on Matteo's head.

"I have to go," she said. Then, seeing the doubt in his eyes, she tried to use her shaky Italian. "*Vado per Gabriella. Vado per Konstantine.*"

"*Sì, sì.*"

"*Rimani qui.*" She looked to all the children. "*Rimani qui.*"

"Okay," Matteo said. "Yes."

She disappeared where she stood, the living room still dark. She hoped that the villa remained safe until she could come back for them.

Gabriella, she told the darkness.

And the world opened up once more.

She was in Konstantine's office. There was his desk. Two men were tearing it apart, looking for something.

Lou shot them both in the head and turned to find Gabriella in the grip of a man who had his gun pressed to her temple.

"Don't," the man said in English. "Don't—"

Gabriella bit his hand and threw an elbow into his gut. It bought the moment Lou needed to blow his brains across the wall, his head knocking back as if punched.

Gabriella ran into her arms.

Lou pulled her through the dark without stopping.

"Gabriella, Gabriella!" The children surrounded her. But Lou couldn't stay for the happy reunion—she needed to be with Konstantine.

Now that she'd seen the church, she understood just what the Celesti were capable of.

Hold on.

Hold on, I'm coming.

34

Stefano couldn't hear him. Konstantine yelled his name again, but he didn't stop. He didn't turn. He kept leading the charge, taking their men deeper into the gallery, toward the back wall, the corner Lou had warned him of.

"Stefano! *Aspetta!*"

A spray of bullets forced him to duck behind a statue. He watched it absorb the attack, the marble cracking and splintering before his eyes, dust rising into the air.

Konstantine knew he had to get Stefano out of here.

The danger was clear now.

The more Konstantine thought about it, the more he realized that it was very possible—in fact, *probable*—that Ettore had lied about Modesto's exile. That the brother didn't come here looking for a new city where he could stake his claim. But rather, that he was doing reconnaissance for the Celesti.

Konstantine could see the shape of it now. How smart it was to send Modesto ahead. Not only to get a sense of

Konstantine's power in the city, the size of his army, the numbers, but to identify and track who was closest to him.

They must have been watching long enough, if they'd managed to find Stefano's sister.

Even that kill would have been strategic. Provoking Konstantine's second would test their bond, prove whether or not Stefano was truly loyal to him. Would he obey Konstantine's orders even when the hit was so close to home?

But Konstantine didn't believe that Stefano was the only one being tested. What had Vittoria said?

Detti is boasting that if he kills La Strega, *he will be the new Master of Florence.*

But was it really Detti who had those ambitions? Or was he simply executing the ambitions of his brother-in-law?

If the Neapolitan crime family wanted to grow, to absorb Florence and Konstantine's empire, maybe Detti simply thought he might be rewarded for playing his part. That he would be the one to reign from Florence as an extension of the Celesti stronghold.

All of it seemed plausible. Worse, he wondered if Vittoria was trying to warn him of the real threat and he'd simply missed it.

He wants to know if she is really immortal, fratello. *Why would he ask such a thing?*

And why wouldn't she warn him? The only thing standing between her throne and Ettore Celesti's ambitions was Florence. And she did not have his numbers. If the Celesti took Florence, it would be in her best interests to surrender out of hand or be massacred.

Then there was the matter of Nario. It occurred to Konstantine now that they hadn't intended to take the boy for a mere ransom. They'd intended to torture him for information.

If Ettore was willing to do that, to torture a sixteen-year-old kid, then he was willing to go to war.

I should've seen it.

I should've known and killed Modesto right away. My caution will cost us.

It was impossible to know how much Modesto had already told Ettore before killing Stefano's sister. It was possible they'd been watching Konstantine for a long time.

It was *more* than possible that war was coming no matter what he did.

If Florence and the Ravenger empire was what Ettore Celesti wanted, there would be little Konstantine could do to deter him.

Konstantine heard Stefano swear and stole a glance around the pillar. He was bleeding from his shoulder. Konstantine couldn't tell from this distance if he'd been shot somewhere vital. The room was too dark, and even Stefano's clothes, black as they were, gave him no clue to how much blood had been lost.

I have to get him out of here.

It had to be.

Otherwise, why this gallery?

Why a *renovated* gallery?

Because if it comes down, no one will be surprised. The people will say only, meno male *it was closed.*

Konstantine made a run for it. He drew gunfire but no bullet struck him. He made it to Stefano, colliding with him, knocking him back against the statue's base.

Stefano cursed.

"We have to go," Konstantine said.

Stefano pulled away from him. "No. The bastard is right there. Load my gun."

Konstantine didn't. He gave him one of his own instead.

"It's a—"

Movement in the corner of his eye made him turn. For a moment he only saw the pistol, level with his eyes. Then the gun disappeared, a boot striking the gunman hard in the ribs. He flew sideways, striking the statue. His head made a sickening crack when it connected with stone.

Before she turned back, Konstantine felt the gun pressed into the side of his head, firm against his temple.

"Easy, *Strega*." Modesto's voice was low, very close to his ear. "I wouldn't make a sudden move if I were you."

35

King stared down at the bomb strapped to the boy's chest. His mind blanked, dilating to take in the scene and yet comprehending nothing. He was frozen. His eyes traced the wires emerging from the silver box. The explosives looked like clear cylinders filled with something. Accelerant? He had no bomb training so he wasn't even sure what he was looking at.

But it certainly *looked* like a bomb.

What had Mel said?

You're going to come up against your worst fear.

And here it was.

"I'd be careful," Sawyer said, his grin bright. There was a mania in those eyes that would have scared King if the bomb itself hadn't emptied his mind, leaving only the consuming fear.

He thought, *I've come full circle.*

I was supposed to die in that first bombing with everyone else.

Death won't miss a second time.

"Take a step back," Sawyer said. He brought his hand up

and showed the detonator held in place only by his thumb. "Step back or I end it for all of us now."

Slowly, King moved away from the boy.

"You too, Detective White."

White did as he was told. He settled back into the armchair while King took his place on the loveseat.

Mel had said something else. Something to remember when this moment came.

But it wasn't surfacing. He truly felt as if his skull had been scraped clean.

Come on, he thought. *Come on, think.*

"Let's take it down a notch," White said. He was using his *easy there* voice. The one that all cops had when trying to talk someone down from a ledge.

"You took everything from me and now there's nothing," Sawyer said.

"That's not true," White countered. "You're young. You have your whole life ahead of you."

The boy sneered. "There's no coming back from this."

"That's not true," King said, finding his voice at last.

"Shut up. You don't know anything."

"No one's died," White said. "I haven't been hurt. My wife and kids aren't hurt. You let them go. We'll tell everyone you let them go."

The boy pointed at King as if expecting him to agree. "I already set off the bomb. I blew up his car."

"But I wasn't hurt," King said. "No one got hurt."

White held his hands up in front of him, palms out. In something akin to a *stop* or perhaps *wait* gesture. "We can come back from this, Sawyer. We *can*."

"No!" the bomber shouted. "You're not going to take this from me too."

"We're not—"

"Shut up!" He shook the hand holding the detonator and the breath left King.

He felt hot all over. He was certain with every cell in his body that he was about to die.

"He was the only one who cared about me," the boy said again. "He was the only one and he died thinking I'd *failed*. Because of *you*. We're going to fix that."

"Sawyer—"

"All I've got left is a story. A good story. A story my grandfather would've liked. A story about—"

"Sawyer, *please*," White begged.

"—about justice. About a bad cop who got what he deserved. He'll be proud of me for that."

"I'm not a bad cop," White said. "I didn't—"

"I did everything you wanted! I worked so hard and did everything you asked, and you lied to me. You promised me a future then you took it away. *You* did that!"

"I'm sorry," White said. He rose from his place on the sofa and started toward the boy. "I'm sorry, Sawyer, I really am."

He approached slowly, watched as Sawyer's lip quivered, his face breaking open with his heartbreak.

Then King saw how it was all about to go horribly wrong.

White was about to betray him again. The kid thought he was getting a real apology, a confession, but King knew better.

"White," King said. "Wait."

But White didn't turn around. He kept his eyes trained on the boy. The worst part was King saw him weaken, saw the boy's desire to be forgiven by his hero.

"I wanted him to be proud of me," the boy said. "I wanted you to be—"

White lunged for the detonator with one hand, collapsing on top of the kid.

"No!" King screamed. But it didn't matter. The explosion launched both White and the kid skyward. They hit the ceiling above and the house rumbled and shuddered.

King had only a moment to look up before the world came down on top of him.

36

Lou's focus wavered. It was under attack by King's terror vibrating through her mind. She couldn't go to him. She remained where she stood, all of her attention on the gun pressed to the side of Konstantine's head.

Then King's terror cut off abruptly.

I'm sorry, she thought. *I'm sorry.*

"What's the plan?" Lou asked. "You kill Konstantine and become king of Florence?"

"He will make me king, yes." Modesto spoke in heavily accented Italian, but the English was good enough.

"He won't," she said. "Because you're dead. Pull that trigger and you're dead."

"Pull it, don't pull it. I am dead either way, no?"

"You're smarter than you look," Lou said.

Detti snorted. "You will not beat him."

"Of course I will," she said. "I'll be killing him right after I kill you. Then I'll kill his wife. Your sister."

Lou watched the fear and doubt pass through Detti's eyes.

"You made sure of that the moment you attacked the

church. The children." She took off her shades so he could see her eyes. "It doesn't matter if you pull that trigger or not, I'm going to *gut* him. Right after I kill you."

Modesto licked his lips. "If I kill him, you will die. You are tied."

She smiled as if he'd made a joke. "Is *that* what you believe?"

More superstition.

Lou had heard this story before, from little Matteo's lips. That Lou was a witch, a demon tied to Konstantine. That he'd sold his soul in exchange for her power.

"You thought if you killed Konstantine, *I* was going to die? Because we are in some sort of pact?" she asked. "You think I'm a *demon?*"

"*Sì,*" he said. "You are."

"No," she said. And smiled, intentionally showing a lot of teeth. "I can do things to you a demon never could."

There. She saw the fear she wanted.

A fear that rapidly multiplied, his eyes darting back and forth, searching her face. The gun in his hand began to shake.

"But you care for him. He is the father of your child."

Lou tilted her head. "Is he?"

She took a step toward him and Detti stepped back, pulling Konstantine with him as if now he sought to use him as a shield.

He really believed it, she realized. *He actually thought that if he could kill Konstantine I would just disappear. What a bunch of horseshit.*

She wondered who'd told him something so stupid.

Then again, maybe that was really how it looked to the people who didn't know her. That she was more ghost than human.

Or, Lou thought, it was more likely that Celesti fed him this lie, knowing it would get Detti to sacrifice himself the way Celesti needed. Because anyone who came to Florence would likely not come out alive. Who would agree to such a mission? Unless, of course, he thought that he might win.

"Ettore lied to you," Lou said. "He was the one who told you that you only needed to kill Konstantine, didn't he?"

Modesto's eyes were wide with fear. "*Sì.*"

"He told *you* that if you could just get your hands on the man, just one man, then the demon would be powerless."

"*Sì, sì.*"

Lou tsked. "You know what *I* think? I think your brother-in-law wants us to kill you."

"Ettore said he would consider it a courtesy," Konstantine said.

Lou shrugged, as if to say, *See?* "Were you really on such bad terms?"

Modesto's eyes widened, the realization of his situation washing over him.

"You won't die," he said. "If I shoot him?"

"No," she said. "I probably won't even die if you shoot *me*."

His aim faltered. Konstantine seized the moment, throwing up an elbow, hoping to knock the gun away.

It went off, the shot echoing through the gallery.

Lou grabbed Detti by the throat. She pulled, yanking him to his knees and pressing one of her Berettas to the side of his head.

"And why would a demon kill you with a gun?" she said. "Why not my hands? My teeth? My *claws*?"

She stopped short of calling him a gullible idiot.

"I don't know! I don't know!" Modesto screamed.

Lou fought against the urge to pull the trigger. Oh, she wanted to. Her skin itched to do it. And if he had pulled the trigger on Konstantine, then Stefano be damned. Lou would've torn Modesto apart.

With the last of her self-control she said, "Stefano."

"I'm here, *Strega*."

He was at her arm, raising his pistol.

"You better hurry up before I forget my promise." Lou released Modesto, knocking him back to give Stefano a clear shot.

Modesto turned his wide, fearful eyes on Stefano. He brought his hands together in front of him as if in prayer. "*Per fa—*"

The gun went off.

Modesto's brains were blown out the back of his head, across the plastic protecting the nearest statue.

Lou watched the tension in Stefano's body leave him. He crossed himself.

"*Per Ilaria. Riposa in pace, sorella.*"

Stefano kicked Modesto's corpse and spit on it, hurling Italian curses at it.

Konstantine squeezed his shoulder. As he turned his head, Lou saw the blood coming out of his left ear.

"I think you ruptured your eardrum," she said. But she couldn't hide her relief. "Better deaf than dead."

"It is ringing, yes." Konstantine touched his bloody ear and hissed. "What about the children?"

Lou hesitated. "Almost all of them are safe."

Konstantine must have seen something cross her face. "Who?"

"Nario," she said. "Matteo said he sacrificed himself so they could run."

Konstantine's face pinched. Slowly, he nodded. "Good boy. He was a good boy."

"The others are in the villa."

Konstantine was nodding, but he turned away. Lou knew it hurt him to lose Nario. He'd been so close to reaching adulthood. To getting out of this world and starting a life of his own. More than once, Lou had heard him ask the boy about professions and schools, insisting that he pick a dream and follow it even though all Nario wanted to do was stay with the Ravengers.

"What are all those sirens?" Stefano asked.

Now that they weren't shooting their guns, it was impossible to miss them.

"Probably for the church," she said. "They tried to burn it down. I didn't get everyone. I killed a lot of them, but not everyone. The children were my priority."

"Could it have spread?" Konstantine asked.

"The fire? Probably. It was pretty bad. Though the stones weren't really burning yet. It was mostly just the wood."

Konstantine typed a message in his phone. "Take me there, I want to see."

"What about this?" Stefano pointed at the mess they'd left in the gallery.

Konstantine waved the phone at him. "I just called Guido and his team. They're on their way. *Amore mio*, please take us to the church."

Lou reached out and gently clasped their arms.

What greeted them was a funeral pyre. She released them as they stepped forward from the dark street toward the blazing cathedral.

Stefano pulled a cigarette from his pocket and lit it. "The fucking bastard."

Konstantine stared at the flames, a quiet fury playing across his face. He said nothing.

He didn't need to.

Lou knew what this was.

It was an invitation to war.

37

K ing felt like he was being crushed. When he licked his lips, he found a gritty film coated them. It tasted salty. He needed to cough, but that need struggled against the base of his throat.

His chest wouldn't rise. Something was pushing hard against it, keeping him flat on his back. He tried to move, but nothing happened. His arms didn't budge. And he hurt. Everywhere he hurt.

Hold on.

Please hold on.

There was movement. Air. Flashing lights and voices. All of it brief before a consuming darkness overtook him.

Don't give up on me.

Please don't give up.

Who was speaking?

It felt like he was the only one left in the world—a world of crushing darkness and pain.

He couldn't even remember where he was. What had he been doing?

Hold on.

Mr. King.

Robert, please.

Robert.

He felt a cool hand on his, and with this touch all the pain evaporated. He opened his eyes.

"Lucy."

She smiled, bright in the sunlight. "Hi, handsome. Fancy meeting you here."

He grabbed hold of her, never wanting to let go. "God, I missed you."

She pulled back, tilting her head coquettishly. "You always did know how to make a girl feel special."

She felt so real. The warmth, her smell.

"You still love me after all this time?" she asked.

"Of course I do," he said. "I never stopped."

"Then I'm sorry to be the one to tell you, but you can't stay."

"I don't want to go," he said. He didn't care if he sounded like a petulant child. It was the truth. "This is better. Let me stay."

Because now that he was beside her, he could finally admit to himself just how hard it had been to live without her.

"I don't make the rules," she said, and pushed her fingers through his hair. "You'll have to wait a bit longer."

"No." His voice cracked, dry. This was no dream voice. No conversation in his head. "No, wait, Lu—"

"No what?" someone asked. "What's he saying?"

King turned toward that voice and found three faces.

He blinked several times until his vision focused.

It was Melandra, Piper, and Lou who stood over him. And he knew that smell. It was burned into his memory after all the time he'd spent with Lucy during the last months of her illness.

Antiseptic.

He could have told them where he was even before he looked down and saw his feet covered by the hospital blankets. The rails of a hospital bed surrounded him.

His eyes fixed on Lou. "You."

"Why does that sound like an accusation?" Piper asked. "*We* didn't know you were going to get bombed."

"Where were you?" he asked her.

"Saving Konstantine's life," Lou said. There was no apology in that voice.

That was fine. King didn't need one. He'd been more afraid that she was hurt and that was what had kept her from saving the day. Besides, she'd already saved his life once this week. He couldn't ask too much of her.

And if she had stopped the bomber, he would've never had the chance to have that precious moment with Lucy, even if it was a dream.

Lucy.

"I'm glad you're okay," King said.

"I'm glad *you're* okay," Lou countered.

"*Yeah*, I'm going to need *all* of you to stop dancing with death," Piper said. "We're about to have a baby on the premises."

"Konstantine has declared war on the Neapolitan crime family. The Celesti."

"Wow, okay. Not the direction I was hoping for. Are you *trying* to make me raise this baby on my own?"

A hand squeezed his. It was Mel, running a dark thumb over his knuckles.

"How do you feel?" she asked.

"It hurts," he said. And that was the truth.

Mel lifted the button for the morphine drip and gave it a couple of pumps. "Hopefully this will help."

"Thank you." King's body felt warm all over. He turned his hand so their palms touched. "How do you feel?"

"We watched them carry you out of the house on a stretcher, man," Piper said. "It was terrifying. We thought you were dead."

"I told you he wasn't," Lou said. "They would've covered him with a sheet if he were dead."

"Yeah, but he *looked* dead. It was terrifying," Piper said. "Dani was here earlier but left to get us lunch. What happened in there?"

What happened?

King searched his memories.

Slowly they surfaced. Fragments, out of order. The girls crying. Ayisha with a gun to her head. Sawyer. The bomb strapped to his chest. White leaping forward and yanking the wires out—

"White," he said. "Is he dead?"

"He's in a coma," Mel said. "His hand was pretty mangled. It'll probably never work again, but they managed to keep his heart beating despite the shock. Thanks to his wife. She ran back into the house after the bomb went off."

"She was crazy brave," Piper said.

"How is he alive?" he wondered. "The wires."

"Agent Smith said it was another shitty bomb. Whatever the kid learned off the internet, he didn't make it very well," Piper said. "But White's gonna have a lot of burns. There was some kind of acid in the bomb that gave it the explosive quality. God, what did she call it? Some kind of acid that starts with a 'P.' *Ugh*, I can't remember."

"I'm sure his wife will just be happy that he's alive," Mel said.

"Do they think he'll wake up from the coma?" King asked.

"They don't know yet."

"And the kid? Sawyer?"

"Dead."

King was sorry to hear that. Even though it was clear he needed help, that more than a few wires might have been crossed in his head, King wouldn't wish an ending like that on anyone. And he'd been so young.

Mel squeezed his hand and King looked at her.

"You scared me, Mr. King," she said. Tears stood in the corners of her eyes.

"I'm sorry," he said. And he meant it. "But you were right. You were right about everything."

Piper leaned forward, inserting herself in the conversation. "What are we talking about here?"

"I read the cards." Mel gave her a brief recap of what the cards had told them about the case. Then she turned to King. "What did White do? What was the betrayal?"

He told them.

Piper frowned. "Wait. White got blown up over a scholarship? That seems extreme."

"I don't think it was really about the scholarship," King said. "It was about White humiliating him in front of the most important person in his life. People who experience severe forms of public humiliation will often feel helpless. I think *that* more than anything pushed the kid in the wrong direction."

King was still certain they were going to learn of some mental illness as well. PTSD at the very least. Now that his identity was uncovered, it would only be a matter of time before the story was all over the news.

Piper gave him a strong hug. "I'm just glad you're okay, man. Using the code was not fun. Not at all."

The code. That was right. He'd warned Piper about the bomb when she'd called.

"As soon as I realized what was going on, I reached out to Agent Smith and asked if she knew where White was. She said they'd last clocked him at home and I was like, are you *sure*, and of course, that pissed her off. But then I was like, if he's really at home then you'd better get someone over there because King says he's with White and the bomber's got them hostage."

"How did you get to the house?"

"Dani drove us. Me and Mel. Lou came later. She was there by the time they'd dug you out. We all got to see you hanging on to life by a *thread*. So thanks for that collective trauma."

"I'm sorry," King said again.

He took Mel's hand and brought it up to his lips. He kissed it.

And she looked as surprised as he was.

Maybe the morphine was hitting. Or maybe he'd been too close to death not to take a few chances.

A knock on the door stole his attention.

They all turned.

It was Beth. She had a bouquet of flowers nestled in the crook of her arm.

She looked from King to Mel to their clasped hands.

Then she said, "Am I interrupting?"

38

Konstantine stood outside the ruined church. He thanked the contractors who'd come to assess the damage and given him an estimate for its repair. Then he was alone with Stefano.

"This is goodbye," he said.

"Don't be dramatic," Stefano said. "The new church is more beautiful."

That was true. Konstantine had chosen this place because it was subtle, hard to notice in an older part of the city often overlooked by passersby.

The church they were moving to was closer to the city center and safer. It was more beautiful but also easier to protect.

It also wasn't as hard to let go of this place as it had been to let go of Padre Leo's church when Nico had burned it down, doing all that he could to destroy his father's legacy.

But still, it was bittersweet. There were things that could not be replaced. His people. The ones who the Celesti killed.

Sweet and stubborn Nario, who would never be older than sixteen.

Fortunately, the statue of the Blessed Virgin was not lost. She'd survived two church burnings now, and that solidified, in Konstantine's mind anyway, that she was a good-luck charm.

She would be the first thing he would install in their new homebase. That was one virtue about the city of Florence. There were more than seventy churches around the city. It was nothing for him to purchase another and begin again.

Still, he kissed the back of his fingers and touched his heart before turning away from the charred remains.

Stefano stood at his back, smoking a cigarette and blowing the smoke up to the sky.

"The bastard will get what he deserves," Stefano said. "Don't worry about that."

"I'm not," Konstantine said. And he wasn't. With Lou at his side, he knew they would destroy the Celesti family. He only hoped that the cost to do so wouldn't be too great.

That was why he'd insisted on sending the children away. Lou had been resistant to the idea, which had surprised him. He took it as proof of her maternal instinct that her initial desire was to keep the children close.

But Konstantine knew the boarding school well. Matteo and the others would be very safe there. It was remote and difficult to reach.

The Celesti will never find them. And war is no place for children.

With a war on his doorstep now, the children would be far safer at the school than running the streets of Florence. At least until this was over.

And if you don't survive it?

He'd asked himself this question many times in the last few days. He always arrived at the same answer.

I have to.

For our daughter.

For our future.

But still doubt nagged at his mind. He believed with all his heart that Lou would survive. That was her nature. He knew now that his initial fears about her safety during her pregnancy had been foolish. She'd gone into the church, rescued the children, and shot down the Celesti men as if they were rats. Then she was back in time to save him from Modesto's gun.

She was incredible.

He was less confident in his ability to survive.

Men like him died all the time. Capi did not have long lifespans.

His father. His brothers, none of whom had made it to forty.

And why should he get more time when children like Nario were buried every day?

His heart clenched.

"*Che c'è?*" Stefano asked. "Why do you have that face?"

"Nario," he said.

"That wasn't your fault," Stefano said.

"He was mine," he said. "My responsibility."

Stefano flicked his ash on the street. "*Non hai iniziato tu questa guerra.* Don't blame yourself."

It was hard not to whenever he closed his eyes and saw the boy's shy smile.

"The Celesti will pay," Stefano said. "We will kill every last one of them."

"Not the children," Lou said.

Konstantine turned and found her at his elbow. He hadn't heard her approach, and there was too much light in the street for her to simply appear.

"We'll have to displace them."

Stefano snorted. "Rehome them? Like puppies? *La Strega* has a heart."

She said nothing.

"What did you learn?" Konstantine asked. Because Lou had already started her hunt. Konstantine had told her they could wait, gather their forces, and most importantly, bury their dead.

Lou didn't care.

She wanted to hunt the Celesti now.

"You're right," she said. "He's well guarded. He won't be easy to get to."

Konstantine had expected as much. Ettore Celesti was like his father. Old-school capo. His entourage would be hundreds deep. More than that, he would have a strong hierarchy in place. It wouldn't be enough to kill Ettore. They really would have to wipe all of his generals and the Celesti heirs off the map as well.

"He didn't even fuck without an audience," Lou said. "I did take two of his entourage though. I grabbed them on my way out."

"Couldn't resist?" Stefano chided. "Now he'll know you were watching."

Lou pointed at her stomach. "I'm not getting any smaller. It would be easier to take him now than later. Can you see me grabbing him at nine months pregnant?"

Konstantine wasn't sure they would make much progress against the Celesti in just two months. There wasn't much time before their daughter would be born. And once she was here, then what? Lou would likely need time to heal from childbirth. She might heal faster than most women, but she *would* need to heal.

They had to stay ahead of the Celesti for at least the next few months, for the window when Lou and the baby would be the most vulnerable.

"It may take time to draw him out into the open, *amore*

mio," Konstantine said, watching the movers put the last of the boxes on the truck.

"You're telling me I'm going to have to satisfy myself with low-hanging fruit until we can get Ettore?"

"Low-hanging fruit?" Stefano repeated.

"*Quelli che può raggiungere facilmente*," Konstantine said.

Stefano snorted. "Americans and their idioms."

"Where are they now?" Konstantine asked. "The fruit."

"Their bodies are at the lake. I wanted to check on you before I crossed."

That was her way of saying she'd sensed his concern. He supposed he would have to get used to that. If he was being honest, he liked it, knowing that Louie always had one ear tuned in his direction. It was probably the closest to an *I love you* he was ever going to get.

"I am okay, *amore mio*," he said. He took hold of her and buried his face in her neck. "I will see you when you get home."

She returned his embrace before throwing a wave at Stefano.

He returned it. "*Strega.*"

Once she was gone, Konstantine turned to Stefano. "Do you want to get dinner?"

"No. *Voglio scopare*," he said. He nodded east, in the direction of his favorite casa chiusa. "I'll see you later."

They hugged, clapping each other on the back.

"*Ciao, ciao.*"

Konstantine stood there until Stefano turned a corner out of his sight. Only then did he start walking toward the Palazzo Vecchio, alone.

39

L ou stood on the Alaskan shore, two bodies at her feet. She felt happy, light. She couldn't remember the last time her mood had been this high. The deep satisfaction that had been eluding her for months had returned.

She'd known for a while that she needed to kill, had gone back and forth in her mind about the implications of this need and being a mother.

But now, after recommitting to the task, seeing how her mood was instantly improved, she could see clearly how deeply entwined her need was to her peace of mind.

At least there were plenty of kills on the horizon.

She knew Konstantine worried about the war. The costs would likely be high.

But Lou couldn't lie—least of all to herself. The promise of a fight excited her.

It even made her a little nostalgic for the old days, when she'd hunted every member of the Martinelli clan to the ends of the earth. For years.

She would do it again if that's what it took.

Maybe I'll finally get to use the flamethrower.

She grabbed a stiff leg with each hand and dragged the corpses into the lake. She waded out into the silvery water until it was chest high. Then she dove. It was cool on her face. Refreshing.

She relished it until the water began to warm and darken, the gray hues morphing to blood red. Lou kicked for the surface and found La Loon waiting for her.

The white mountains sat in the distance beneath its hazy yellow sky. The twin moons glowed like radiant eyes, ever watchful. The patina of Blood Lake was calm except for the waves she cut as she made her way to shore.

She dropped one corpse while still in the water, so that it would be easier to swim. As soon as she dropped the other one on shore, she heard the screeching. The death knell of Jabbers greeting her.

Only it wasn't one screech.

A second joined. And a third.

Her panic spiked and she only had time to pull a gun and take one step toward the lake before the ink-black foliage broke open and there they were.

The offspring. Three of them.

They surrounded her. Their screeching strident, almost fervid. Lou stood perfectly still, her hand on her stomach. She had a gun, but what good was that going to do her when they moved like liquid smoke, faster than any creature in her world.

This is how we die, she thought.

Torn apart by Jabbers's offspring.

But they didn't tear her apart. They whistled and clicked and sniffed. But there were no snapping jaws, no claws.

All of their attention shifted to the corpse on the embankment.

Jabbers pressed her head into Lou's shoulder by way of greeting.

With relief, Lou placed a hand to that large head, holding tight to the beast while her children tore the body apart.

"I hope you plan to tell them that they should only eat *dead* human," Lou said, her fear dissipating.

Jabbers's nostrils flared before she dragged a tongue over Lou's arm.

Two of the offspring threw their heads back as if sniffing the sky. Then they dove into the lake, only to surface with the second body between them. A fight ensued.

Their sense of smell must be incredible, she thought. How else had they known there was a body in the water?

"I'm glad you like it," she told the offspring, still leaning her weight into Jabbers's strong shoulder. "Because there's about to be *a lot* more where that came from."

40

Piper wiped her hands on her black slacks for the third time.

"Stop that," Dani said. She pulled her toward the restaurant. "You have no reason to be nervous."

"What are you talking about? *Of course* I have every reason to be nervous."

They were meeting Dani's father for lunch. He'd been the one to issue the polite invitation, but that hadn't made Piper feel any more settled about the whole thing.

Surely this was about the feud between Dani and her mother. Piper could only imagine—and *boy* did she imagine—all the things her father might have to say on the subject. Perhaps he was here to persuade Dani to come to her senses and leave the white-trash would-be detective for the more sophisticated life they'd fought so hard to build for her.

At least the restaurant wasn't as pretentious as the one Izabelle had brought them to. It was a simple Caribbean place that Piper had visited more than a few times. The decor was colorful and the music had a very island feel, with upbeat tunes sung in Spanish.

Alberto Allendale was already at a table in view of the door when they arrived. He waved them forward. Dani dismissed the hostess with a few kind words.

This is it, Piper thought as she stood at the edge of the booth. *We had a nice run.*

He stood up as Dani and Piper slid onto the bench opposite. Piper had let Dani slide in first, more out of her desire to be closest to the door in the event she needed to escape, and less out of any sense of chivalry.

He gestured at the basket in front of him. "I ordered Yaniqueques. They're delicious. Try it, try it."

Piper took one dutifully even though her stomach was too sour to eat.

Dani, however, was not amused. "If you've come to tell me—"

"No, no." Her father shook his head. "I haven't come to tell you anything."

Dani hesitated. "Did she send you?"

Her father laughed. "She doesn't know I am here. I came because I wanted to come."

His English was very good though the accent was there.

He reached for their hands. He took Dani's easily. Piper had to fight the urge to pull away, half believing it was a trick.

He gave them both a squeeze.

"You do not need it, and you did not ask for it, but I wanted to give my blessing."

Piper choked. "Excuse me."

"Your mother says you want to marry. Good, good. Be happy."

He patted their hands and released them.

Piper sat stunned. She hadn't recovered from her shock when he asked, "When do you want to do it? I am busy in September and October, but I will cancel any appointment if—"

"Papa, we're not getting married *now*."

He frowned. And the disappointment on his face was so honest that it touched Piper's heart.

"Because of Mama?"

"No," Dani said. "I mean, the time is bad. We'll do it in the future. We'll do it later."

He looked to Piper, clearly expecting her to say something. But Piper didn't know what to say. She hadn't been aware that Dani had even considered marriage before she'd yelled at her mother about it. Even then she'd thought it was just something Dani said to piss her mother off—not something she was serious about.

"When do you want to do it?" he asked her.

Piper looked at Dani, a silent cry for rescue.

Dani fell into a slew of Spanish so quickly that Piper couldn't keep up, and she got the distinct impression that was on purpose. The only part she'd caught was "*no he propuesto porque—*"

I haven't proposed because—

But whatever reason Dani had given was lost on her.

Piper's face felt like it was on fire.

The waitress came.

"Can you order for me?" Piper's throat was tight. "I don't know what's good here."

"Do you eat meat?" her father asked.

"I do."

"Good, good."

Dani and Mr. Allendale ordered while Piper sank into the pit of her thoughts.

I haven't proposed because—

I haven't proposed because—

Piper was sure the *because* must have been followed by some reservation on Dani's part. Was it Piper's lack of financial prospects? Was it the shady ex that had put her off? Or maybe Dani just didn't feel like their futures were compatible.

That maybe she really *had* only brought up marriage to piss her mom off. And now she needed to tell her father the truth so that he didn't take this any farther.

Was that why he looked relieved?

The waitress left.

"I need to use the bathroom," Dani said. "Baby, can you let me out?"

"Yeah, okay."

Piper stood up, moving out of the way.

Then it was just the two of them in the booth.

"Piper, do you know why our last name is Allendale?" he asked, tearing a Yaniqueque in half and dipping it in some kind of sauce. "Why not Hernández, López, or Martínez? I always thought I looked like a Cruz. It sounds cool, right? *Alberto Cruz.*"

He smiled, doing his best to draw Piper out of her thoughts.

"No, I don't know."

"It's because my great-great-grandmother, Amaya, fell in love with a Scottish emissary, Angus Allendale. Their love was *forbidden*," he said passionately. "Because he was not of her tribe, he was an outsider, and for him because he was a man of God. *But* they married anyway. Their forbidden love is the reason I am here today. And the reason Daniella is here. You see?"

The knot in Piper's chest loosened.

"Forget about what my wife said," he said. "*I* know that sometimes good things—*very* good things—come from the love that was not supposed to be."

He reached across the table and patted her hand.

"Now eat." He pushed the basket of Yaniqueques toward her. "You're looking too thin."

When Dani came back, Piper had half a Yaniqueque in her mouth. A moment later, the food was on the table, lightning quick.

Dani unrolled her silverware.

"Don't worry about money," her father said.

"I wasn't worried," Dani said defiantly. "I have no intention of taking another cent from her. And as soon as I find another car, I'll be parking the SUV in the driveway."

"Keep the car. And you don't need her money. You have my money. My money is your money," he said.

Piper continued shoving black beans and plantains into her mouth, and some kind of shredded spicy meat that she was fairly certain was pork but she couldn't be entirely sure. She was only happy to eat whatever Dani forked onto her plate.

Mr. Allendale nodded approvingly.

"Oh, that reminds me!" He put down his fork. "Did you bring it?"

Dani reached into her bag and pulled out her award. Her father accepted it over the table, pulling it up close to his face to look at it. He had to lift his glasses to read the smaller print.

"Journalist of the Year." He pursed his lips. "Very nice. I am sorry I was not there for the ceremony. I am so proud."

"It's okay, Papa," Dani said. "We weren't there for very long either."

An hour later the three of them were standing on the street outside the restaurant. Mr. Allendale gave them both warm hugs and patted them on the back.

"I am here if you need me, just a call away," he whispered into Piper's ear, and then he started up the street, walking in the direction of the black sedan parked on the curb.

The driver opened the door for him, and Mr. Allendale threw them one last wave before disappearing inside.

"Well that was a nice surprise," Piper admitted.

"Now you know why he's my favorite," Dani said.

Dani hooked her arm in hers and they started up the street in the direction of her SUV, parked in the garage a block away.

"I didn't catch all of the conversation you guys had though," Piper said.

"He was making excuses for her," she said. "Which I get, fine. But I'm not going to stop living my life just because Charles died."

That part of the conversation Piper had actually understood.

Dani's uncle had been a doctor in Doctors Without Borders. And he died in an air raid with thirteen children. Mr. Allendale had made the argument that her mother was only against her desire to be a journalist because she thought it was too dangerous.

"But I'm not *in* the Middle East, am I?" Dani fumed.

"I meant the other part," Piper said, feeling the heat rise in her cheeks. "I didn't catch what you said after '*no he prop-uesto porque...*'"

Dani turned and looked at her. "Your Spanish is getting better."

"Come on, tell me." Piper wasn't sure she really wanted to know why she wasn't marriage material, but if she didn't ask, she was going to make herself crazy wondering. "Is it because I don't want to leave New Orleans? Or because of Scarlett? Or because I'm never going to make a ton of money or—"

Dani kissed her. "Don't start with all that again."

"Then what is it? What did you say?"

Dani looked up at her through long lashes. "You really want to know?"

"Yes, and both things. I think you gave two reasons."

Piper wasn't one hundred percent sure on that, but she thought she'd heard an *and* in there somewhere.

"I told him I haven't proposed because you're too beautiful and I'm worried the competition is too steep—"

"No, be serious." Piper grabbed her.

"I am!"

"Are you kidding, *you're* the gorgeous one. Have you already forgotten about the interloper who tried to get you to abandon me for New York?"

Dani snorted. "Interloper."

"I've been calling her that in my head pretty much since the moment I saw her."

Dani rolled her eyes. "God, don't bring her up. I'm still pissed at her. You know she told my mom that I'm involved with the *mob* now?"

Piper hissed. "Well, I mean, we are mob *adjacent*. But hey, Agent Smith and the feds aren't pressing any charges, so at least we aren't *actual* criminals. Wait. Don't distract me. What was the other reason?"

Dani's smile returned. "I said you were very picky about jewelry and I haven't found the right ring, but that as soon as I did, I would propose properly."

Piper's face flushed with heat. "Have you really been looking at rings?"

"Yes." Dani pulled her close. "But you're so hard to shop for."

"You really were planning to propose to *me?*"

"Yes."

"*Me?*" Piper scoffed.

"Stop it. Of course you. There's no one but you. But I can't propose now because my mother ruined everything. I want it to be a surprise. And I also know you're not ready to be married right now anyway. But in a year? Three years? It doesn't matter. It's going to happen."

Piper hugged her, burying her face in Dani's hair.

"I hear no objections," Dani said, holding her.

"No objections," Piper said. "But you're right. Not yet."

Dani pulled her toward the SUV. "So get ready. Start preparing that little head of yours now. Because it's going to be *so* romantic. I'm going to find the perfect ring, and the perfect moment, and I'll spring it on you. I'm going to pull out all the stops and your mind will be *blown*."

She made a little explosion with her expanding hands.

"*Poof.*"

Piper laughed despite herself.

"I can't wait to see your moves."

"You will be *impressed*. I promise," Dani said, pulling the keys to the SUV from her pocket. She tossed them to Piper so she could drive.

Piper caught them and thought, *Unless I propose first.*

41

Soft afternoon light spilled through Beth's window. The living room was only boxes now, apart from the items still left on the mantel. A couple of scented candles. Cute little figurines, African dancers in motion. A clock.

King took each one down, wrapped them in newspaper. He paused, noticing that these were outdated copies of *The Herald*.

He made a note not to tell Dani about it.

"Stop that." Beth had come into the room and spotted him putting the wrapped candles into the open cardboard box. "You're beat up. You're supposed to be resting."

"I want to help," he said. "It's why I came over."

They only had a few days left together. And while sex was off the table—King's back was too bruised and sore for that—it didn't mean he wanted to pass up the chance for a proper goodbye.

Beth frowned at him. "Robert. If you don't put those Bath & Body candles down, I'm going to put you down, sir. Sit in that chair, right now."

He chuckled, relinquishing the candle. "Yes, ma'am."

She put it in the box herself while King took a seat. Slowly, he put one leg, then the other, on the ottoman, relief washing over his tired frame.

He was beat up, yes. She wasn't wrong about that. He was bruised nearly from head to toe. But he'd gotten lucky. No internal bleeding. And the acid from the bomb had mostly hit his boots, which, when returned to him, had been eaten through. The part that had reached his skin had left his feet only mildly irritated. They were raw, but he didn't think they'd scar.

"Can I at least treat you to dinner?" he said. "Whatever you want. We are celebrating the imminent arrival of your grandbaby."

Her expression changed. She was looking into the half-packed box, but King had enough experience with women to know that the conversation was about to take a sharp turn.

"Whatever I want," she said.

"Whatever you want," he said cautiously.

She came to the chair and sat down on the ottoman, throwing one arm over his legs.

"I want you to move to Orlando with me," she said solemnly. "I want you to be safe."

"Oh, I was thinking Mexican," King said.

She tilted her head. "Robert. I'm serious. You could've died."

"I'm aware," he said. The only blessing from the experience was that he'd blacked out right after the bomb went off. It wasn't like before, when he'd been awake and pinned beneath the debris for days. With nothing but his fear and panic to keep him company in the darkness.

"I guess you are," she said, her disappointment clear. "How is he?"

She could only mean White.

"The same."

King had gone to the hospital every day since his release. He mostly brought good coffee, which wasn't a staple on the hospital rounds, but he also brought some of Mel's old crossword books and games that he could play with his girls, anything to keep him entertained.

His wife had forgiven him the moment he woke from the coma. But King didn't think White had forgiven himself.

He was worried that his friend never would. That every day, for the rest of White's life, every time he looked into the mirror and saw his burn scars, every time he tried to use his hand and found it wasn't what it was before—he worried White would blame himself.

He was on leave now, surrounded by his family. But it was unclear if he was going to go back to the force. Unless he learned how to shoot with his left hand, he'd never be able to use a gun again.

"I worry about you," Beth said, placing a gentle hand on his thigh. "I wish you'd reconsider."

He wouldn't. And they both knew it.

She nodded as if he'd spoken. "Something else must be keeping you here."

Mel's face flashed in his mind. He wondered if that was who Beth was thinking of too.

He'd seen the hurt in her eyes when she'd caught him holding Mel's hand in the hospital. She'd never mentioned it since, but Beth was an insightful woman. King was starting to wonder if she suspected that he had feelings for someone else.

"It must be," King said, and gave her hand a squeeze.

With a sigh she stood, slowly, her knees popping. "I'm good with Mexican. But let's make it Los Amigos. They have the best chips."

He pulled out his phone and searched for the number. "Coming right up."

TWO DAYS LATER, AFTER KISSING BETH GOODBYE FOR THE last time, King decided to walk back to the Quarter. It was an ambitious objective considering that the pain was never far from his mind. But his back and legs did feel better when he moved. When he sat for too long, he'd become so stiff that he felt more like a corpse than a living, breathing man.

He made it half a mile before caving and hopping onto the streetcar. He rode it to the edge of the Quarter, getting off at Canal and managing the rest of the way home.

When he got to the shop, he placed his hand on the horsehead post and checked his feet, then he entered Melandra's Fortunes and Fixes.

The girl behind the counter smiled. "Hi, Mr. King. You're quite the celebrity these days. I read all about you in the paper this morning."

I read about what you did for that girl who wanted to kill herself.

King's heart clenched.

"Don't believe everything you read," he said. Then he pointed up the stairs. "She home?"

"Yes, sir. She said she wanted to start dinner."

King thanked her and made his way slowly up the stairs.

"Do you need help?" she called after him.

King pushed aside the flash of humiliation washing over him and said simply, "No, thank you."

Mel opened the door on the second knock. "Yeah, honey. Is there a prob—Oh. It's you."

He smiled. "I'm not 'honey?'"

She rolled her eyes at him. "Get in here. I've got to watch my stove."

"What are you making?"

"Red beans and rice with sausage. I've got enough for two if you're hungry."

While she cooked, he told her about Beth's send-off and updated her on White's condition, expressing his fear that he might never recover emotionally.

"I don't know, Mr. King. You were quite the mess when you arrived at my door, looking like a half-drowned puppy. You turned out all right."

He leaned against her counter. "You think so?"

She stirred the rice, knocking the spoon against the pot to clear it.

"So you moving to Florida on me?" she asked. "Is this you telling me that I need to find a new tenant?"

"Would you be sad if I left?" he asked.

"Would I be—of course! Listen to you. This man."

King offered her the hand towel when she gestured for it.

"I want you to read my cards again," he said.

She arched a brow, moving the rice off the burner. "Are you a believer now?"

"It helped with the bomber case," he said. "You never know. Maybe it can help with my love life too."

"A *love* reading." Melandra laughed. "It's always about love, money, or health. I swear, every human is the same. Here I thought you'd be the exception, by solving crimes."

"Sorry to disappoint," he said, moving aside as she pulled her card deck from her pocket. He hadn't been surprised. Of course she kept them close. Closer still after her ex-husband, Terry, stole them from her.

He gestured at the stove. "What about dinner?"

"Rice is done, but the sausage needs more time. Let's sit at the table."

King joined her, pulling out the chair opposite hers.

"Did you have a specific question about your love life?" she asked, her dark eyes searching his.

He wasn't so brazen to ask, *Do you like me back? Is there something for us in the future?*

Instead, he said, "How's it look for me? Now and in the future."

She began shuffling the cards. Her eyes were closed tight as she mumbled something under her breath. He only caught the words *we ask for guidance*.

Though who she was asking, King could only guess. Her ancestors, maybe? Since it was their deck. He'd ask her some other time, when her face wasn't fixed with concentration as it was.

She laid out the cards and was quiet for a long time.

The longer the silence stretched on, the more pinched her face became, and the more King worried that maybe this was a mistake.

He thought he was being smooth, confessing his feelings in this indirect way, hoping maybe that she might see something for them in the future. But if that was the case, why did she look so concerned.

"That bad, huh?" he asked.

"I didn't realize you were married before. *Before* Lucy."

King hadn't expected his first wife to show up in the cards. That marriage had felt like a lifetime ago. Something that had happened to someone else.

"Fiona," he said. "But that was ages ago."

"Yes, I can see that. What the cards are talking about is the condition of your heart."

The condition.

"Because I'm old?" he asked with a laugh.

"Your metaphoric heart," she said. "Fiona hurt you. And you closed your heart. Lucy was the one who opened it. Then she died and you closed it again. You started dating Beth, but your heart was closed. Though hers is open. It shows others too, I'm guessing flings or brief relationships you've had over the years. It shows me a pattern of you keeping your heart closed even though people are opening theirs to you."

King couldn't deny the accusation—for that brief moment he'd seen Lucy again, he'd felt like his emotions were going everywhere at once. If that was an open heart, he definitely didn't have that now.

It was also true that he'd dated plenty of women after his marriage fell apart. And even though Lucy had chosen to walk away from him to raise Louie after her brother died, he hadn't been bitter about that. In fact, on nearly every level he'd felt he deserved it.

It was his fault that Jack had died. His fault for not protecting his protégé better. And Lucy was the one who'd had to give up her life and freedom to clean up his mess. How could he blame her?

So yes. There was openness. And love, free flowing.

"I wouldn't say my heart is closed," he said.

"Can you say that you have felt for anyone else what you felt for Lucy?" Mel asked.

"No," he said. That was true. There was something for Mel, some kindling. But King couldn't look her in the eye and say it was the same.

"This isn't a judgment," she said, searching his face. "Take me, for example."

With pleasure.

"My whole life was living in Terrence's shadow. I loved that man even after all the horrible things he did to me, how he treated me. Lied to me, manipulated me. Took my money. *Beat* me. Even after he went to prison, I couldn't bring myself to divorce him for years because of the hold he had over me. It wasn't until he was dead that I felt truly free for the first time in my life. Because of that my heart is closed too. This is

the first time in my life that I'm finally figuring out who I am
—*me*. Without no man in the picture."

King had a feeling they weren't talking about him
anymore.

He tapped the card closest to him. It was a man holding a
heart out toward the viewer. It looked very much like King
himself offering Melandra the heart she was calling *closed*.

"The Knight of Cups," she said, a slight blush rising to her
cheeks.

"What does it mean?"

After a pause, she said, "In this case, unrequited love."

"If my heart is closed for now," he said, willing to play
along with what obviously felt like an outright *rejection*, "does
it say it always will be?"

She gathered up the cards. "Only time will tell. But my
advice is to look after your own heart first. It needs some
healing. No one wants a heart that belongs to someone else.
Even if the woman is dead."

King had his answer then.

He didn't like it. But he had it.

And though that particular door was closed—for now—
there was no reason why he couldn't keep on loving Mel, just
as she was. They were best friends, after all. Nothing had
happened—nothing ever *would* happen—to change that.

42

Konstantine sat at his outdoor table, watching the foot traffic move through the piazza. He should have been cheered by the sight of happy people enjoying the comfortable evening, particularly the three children chasing a dog.

But he hated dining alone. It did not matter how delicious the red wine was or how perfect the food. He had left the church late, having lost track of the hours while completing the many pressing tasks that required his attention.

Lou was still hunting. When she'd told him her plan, he'd been pleased.

However, he was less pleased *now*, given how it kept depriving him of a dinner partner.

She was using her gifts, her compass, to hunt down any remaining Celesti in Florence, whoever might still be left behind, tracking their movements and reporting back to their master.

She had killed nearly twenty so far. A small number, given the size of Florence. There were more than three hundred

and eighty thousand people in the city. But still enough infil-
tration to annoy him.

I've gotten too comfortable here, he thought. *I've been careless.*

Strategically, Florence didn't offer much advantage, land-
locked as it was. Everything that was manufactured in the
area had to be driven ninety-five kilometers west to Livorno.
Given the Celesti's access to better ports, there wasn't much
the city itself could offer a man like that. Only the warehouses and local businesses that catered mostly to tourists.
But he wouldn't be so bold as to target the tourists. It would
draw unwanted attention.

So no, it wasn't Florence that the Celesti wanted.

It was *La Strega*. And Konstantine. Likely Stefano too,
given that the only way to acquire the Ravengers' assets
would be to kill his second as well.

That begged the question if they should remain in
Florence at all. Perhaps it would be safer to move around,
present a more difficult target.

The children.

They'd been heartbroken when he'd told them they were
being sent away to school. He'd tried to drum up their excitement, telling them stories about the time he'd spent there,
the things he'd seen and done on the island.

It had not convinced them.

They had not agreed until it was Lou who told them they
must go. That it wasn't safe for them here. For whatever
reason, they'd taken her assessment of the situation more
seriously, especially Matteo. Perhaps it was simply that
Konstantine had been lenient with them over the years, and
they believed him to be persuadable. They'd never so much as
conceived the idea of questioning *La Strega*.

It hadn't only been the church that the Celesti had
attacked.

They'd also burned down two of the warehouses in the

west. That was costly, but not catastrophic. Konstantine was glad that he'd taken the pains to diversify his investments. Unless the Celesti planned to launch a coordinated global attack, he'd never touch the majority of his holdings. Even before Padre Leo's death, Konstantine had worked to hide most of their wealth in shell companies, masks behind masks behind masks, that were nearly untraceable back to Konstantine.

He had more economic power than the Celesti, and that's where he planned to start, adding pressure where he could. And they had more mobility, given Lou's talent.

That left only two vulnerabilities that needed to be managed, apart from the children—Lou's pregnancy and his alliances.

Konstantine wasn't sure who he could trust.

Vittoria might aid him—not out of any sort of sibling fidelity but simply because it would be in her best interests to do so.

Konstantine had to assume that Rome was at best indifferent, since they'd run no interference. And the Ravengers had burned their bridges with many of the other crime families long ago—the Yakuza, the Russians. He could count on the Riccis and the other families in New York.

But their other ties were unclear.

Too many had lost numbers to *La Strega*.

He would need to take stock of where loyalties lay. Because while it would be useful to squeeze the Celesti economically, the pain would be more complete if they could also destroy their support.

Konstantine would need help to do that.

Despite what she might think, Louie Thorne *did* have her limitations.

And their daughter would soon be born.

Who knew how long the war might last?

Konstantine poured himself another glass of wine from the bottle on the table. Then his phone began to ring.

He saw the number, paused, then answered it.

"Ettore," he said. "You'll be happy to know that your troublesome brother-in-law is dead."

Nothing.

"Isn't that what you wanted, Celesti?"

"*Sì*," the other man said finally.

Konstantine wondered if Celesti intended to play along, to act as if the losses that Konstantine had suffered were from Modesto's ambitions alone.

"I hear that congratulations are in order," Ettore said, his voice dark and melodic. "She is quite far along, *La Strega*. I assume you are the father. *Felicitazioni.*"

Konstantine's blood iced. He had hoped that no one would know of a child. That no one who'd seen her would live to speak of it. But obviously, someone had.

Then it will not do to play games, he thought.

"*La Strega* believes that you are the real enemy," Konstantine began, turning the wine glass in the light. "She says Modesto was simply your pawn. You promised him things he could never have, hoping that he would come to the city and make trouble with me."

"And you believe her?" Ettore asked.

"I will never doubt her," he said. "My only question is why you would bother starting a war with me. We aren't friends, but I didn't think we were enemies either."

"Perhaps we are tired of your reign of terror, Konstantine. Always wondering when you will send your bitch to kill us."

"No one *sends La Strega*. Surely you know that."

"And yet she comes for us," he said, his voice tight.

Clarity dawned in Konstantine's mind. So it was economic. It was true that Lou's hunting focused primarily on the factions that profited from human trafficking. Drugs, like what Konstantine sold, and guns, which he also profited from, though less than cocaine, did not bother her the same way that enslavement did. Many of the gangs had seemed to notice and had pivoted accordingly.

But from what Konstantine could tell from his preliminary investigations into Celesti's business, it remained largely dependent on human trafficking. Were fewer and fewer gangs willing to do business with the Celesti for fear of rousing *La Strega*? Was he *already* suffering economic loss? Had that provoked him into challenging Konstantine?

He could only ask.

"How is business?"

The silence that followed was so long, Konstantine thought the man had hung up, which would have been an answer of its own.

"My men say—the ones who survived—that she really does look like the devil." There was a strange, metallic clicking behind his words. Some movement in the background. "I wish I could have seen her standing there, in your burning church. A gun in her hands. Is she really that beautiful, your fallen angel of death?"

Konstantine said nothing.

"And when you fuck her, does she feel like a woman, or a serpent twined around you?"

A gun went off, the loud report garbling the line. In the background someone began to cry. A woman.

Konstantine's stomach knotted. "Perhaps we should speak another time. You're working."

"No, no trouble. *You* are my work now." The gun went off again. "You won't tell me, will you? That's okay. Perhaps I will find out for myself. Soon enough."

Konstantine waved the approaching waiter away. He took a breath, trying to still his anger.

When he was ready, Konstantine said, "Ettore, I will tell

you what I told Nico Agostino and Dmitri Petrov and Riku Yamamoto. They all said the same things to me that you're saying now. They thought somehow they could beat her."

Konstantine knew these names would get Celesti's attention. Ettore had never dared to challenge them when they'd been alive. It was good to remind him that Lou had destroyed each one in turn.

Let him remember who he is threatening.

Konstantine took a sip of his wine and said, "If you go against her, you *will* die. She will kill you and your entire family the way she did my father and brothers. She will take your children and place them with families, and one day they won't even remember your name. It will rain blood. That I promise you."

Celesti was quiet for a long time.

Konstantine looked at the phone again, making sure the call was still connected.

At last, Ettore said, "We will see, *amico mio*. We will see. But maybe I will take you with me. Maybe that is enough for me."

The phone clicked, the call ending.

From his little bistro table at the edge of the piazza, Konstantine could see no way around it.

It is war then.

So be it.

He would fight harder than he ever had before. He could see the same prize that Celesti wanted, after all. Supremacy. Ettore wanted to be the one who said he'd killed *La Strega*. That he'd defeated the Ravengers and now owned the world.

But if Celesti brought war and was destroyed, maybe this would finally be over. Maybe no one would be so foolish as to go against Konstantine or the Ravengers again.

Maybe, just maybe, he could broker the peace he longed for. For his daughter's sake.

A peace purchased with the blood of the Celesti.

He paid his bill and rose, beginning the walk home.

There was nothing else to be done for now.

Night was approaching.

LOU WAS WET, HER BACK ACHING, WHEN SHE STEPPED FROM the closet into their bedroom. In the living room, she heard Konstantine singing in a low voice, but Lou couldn't go to him. Her hair itched and there was blood on her face.

She'd just taken three more of Celesti's men.

What she needed more than anything was a shower.

He was still in the living room after she'd washed her hair and changed into soft, clean clothes.

She found him on the floor. The coffee table had been pushed away. In its place was what seemed like a hundred pieces of something in process. Nuts, bolts, legs. Lou couldn't tell by looking at the mess what it was he was assembling.

Konstantine looked up.

"*Buonasera, amore mio.*"

"*Buonasera,*" she said, and sank onto the sofa. Her back thanked her for the relief, which she increased by positioning the pillows around her just so. "What are you making?"

"*La culla,*" he said.

Lou placed a hand on her belly as her daughter stretched.

"And what is *la culla*? Pray tell."

"A crib," he said. "Or maybe a bassinet. I am not sure how they are different."

He looked up, still holding one of the legs. "How was the hunt?"

"I think I got the last of them," she said. "Florence is clean and clear."

Lou had hunted every day since the night they killed

Modesto. She asked her compass again and again, *Who is spying on us?*

Her compass had her all over the city. Sometimes her targets were in apartments near the Palazzo Vecchio—too close to their villa for her comfort. Sometimes they were farther away, nearer the warehouses. She'd taken as many as ten men in a single night and as few as two.

After tonight's last kill, there had been only silence.

It wasn't that they were no longer in danger, she knew that. It was only that there were no foxes left in the hen house, as her father would have said.

She had also kept checking for her opening with Ettore Celesti. She didn't tell Konstantine, of course. He would worry. But if Ettore made a mistake, if he so much as stepped out of his car to take a piss on the side of the road, Lou wanted to be there with a Beretta in hand.

Her daughter's future depended on it.

"Good," Konstantine said. "I don't like looking over my shoulder in my own city."

"I would keep doing it if I were you," Lou said. She might have cleared out the spies, but that didn't mean that the Celesti wouldn't send more goons to bother them. Or hell, maybe a trained assassin. Someone to rival Lou's skill.

"I do worry about you, *amore mio*. You don't want to strain yourself. What if you go into labor prematurely? Or what if they are waiting for you?"

"They're always waiting for me," she said. That was true. And it was why Lou was careful to tell her compass to hide her well. No appearing in broad view of anyone. She could travel through thinner shadows on her best days, but not now. Now she needed the darkness more than ever.

Konstantine held up the basket, looking into it. "*Così piccola. Sarà così piccola.*"

Yes, she will be small, but Lou didn't think she'd be completely helpless.

Many times over the last few weeks, Lou's mind had turned back to that strange moment in the church. She kept trying to make sense of it. To rationalize it. Was it simply the fire flaring for some explainable reason? She didn't think so. There had been an unnatural way to how the light had brightened and bent around her. And the strange fluttering in her stomach as it had happened.

She kept looking for excuses, but each attempt only drew Lou closer to the conclusion that it had been her daughter.

She'd done something to the fire to protect them. Or maybe it wasn't the fire. The air? The light?

Not that Lou believed for a moment that she could rely on such a thing.

Lou's own gift had taken time to learn, to hone. She'd been terrified of it until Lucy came along. It had been Lucy's kindness and patience which had opened up the world for her, teaching her that the darkness and the water weren't to be feared.

These things took time, she knew.

And it would be Lou's responsibility—no one else's—to safeguard her child until she came into her own power. *Lou's* responsibility to nurture her daughter's gifts even if they were different, the way that Lou's gifts had varied from Lucy's.

I will love her no matter what she can or can't do.

Konstantine stood the bassinet upright, rolling it along on its large wheels.

He turned toward her, his smile bright. "What do you think?"

Lou slid off the sofa and came to join him on the floor. She took the bassinet in her hand and moved it back and forth, the other hand still on her stomach. She imagined the nights and days ahead. Imagined her hand moving the cradle, trying to soothe the infant within. A natural hesitation rose up in her. Motherhood, she realized, scared her far more than war.

I can do this, she thought. Women became mothers every day. They even became mothers during times of war.

"So this is for Elena?" Lou asked. She watched his face closely as she said the name. She wanted to try it out on her tongue, but also she wanted to see his reaction.

In her heart she knew they'd end up with a Cia or a Rina. Maybe even a Jack—but he needed something bright and beautiful to look forward to. Especially now.

And she was right.

Konstantine beamed, his joy unmistakable. "*Sì, amore mio.*"

He bent forward and kissed her, sliding his arms around her.

"*Sì*, this will be for Elena."

DID YOU ENJOY BLOOD RAIN? LOUIE'S STORY CONTINUES in *First Light, Shadows in the Water #12.*

GET YOUR THREE FREE STORIES
TODAY

Thank you so much for reading *Blood Rain*. I hope you're enjoying Louie's story. If you'd like more, I have a free, exclusive Lou Thorne story for you. Meet Louie early in her hunting days, when she pursues Benito Martinelli, the son of her enemy. This was the man her father arrested—and the reason her parents were killed months later.

You can only read this story by signing up for my free newsletter. If you would like this story, you can get your copy by visiting www.korymshrum.com/lounewsletteroffer

I will also send you free stories from the other series that I write. If you've signed up for my newsletter already, no need to sign up again. You should have already received this story from me. Check your email and make sure it wasn't marked as spam! Can't find it? Email me at kory@korymshrum.com and I'll take care of it.

As to the newsletter itself, I send out 2-3 a month and host a monthly giveaway exclusive to my subscribers. The prizes are usually signed books or other freebies that I think you'll enjoy. I also share information about my current projects, and personal anecdotes (like pictures of my dog). If you want these free stories and access to the exclusive giveaways, you can sign up for the newsletter at www.korymshrum.com/lounewsletteroffer

If this is not your cup of tea (I love tea), you can follow me on social media in order to be notified of my new releases.

ACKNOWLEDGMENTS

Here we are with our *eleventh* Shadows in the Water book finished and done.

This is where we drop the curtain and share a round of applause.

First off, many thanks to my amazing production team. Hats off to The World's Best Editor: Toby Selwyn. A round of applause The Most Excellent Cover Designer: Christian Bentulan.

And we certainly can't forget my ever-enthusiastic critique group, The Four Horsemen of the Bookocalypse. Katie Pendleton, Angela Roquet, and Monica La Porta. Monica in particular does a great job correcting all the Italian and of making sure I understand Italy's food culture. *Grazie*!

And we can't wrap up these thank-yous without acknowledging my lovely street team. Thank you for reading the books in advance, reporting those lingering typos, and posting honest reviews. Your continued support makes the work worth it.

Everyone listed above is perfect and can do no wrong. Therefore, any remaining errors in the book are my own.

ALSO BY KORY M. SHRUM

Night Tide

The City / 2603 series

The City Below

The City Within

The City Outside

Other Fiction

Jack and the Fire Eater

Blade Born: A Borderlands Novel

Short Fiction

Thirst: new and collected stories

Nonfiction

Who Killed My Mother? a memoir

Learn more about Kory's work at: www.korymshrum.com

ABOUT THE AUTHOR

USA TODAY bestselling author Kory M. Shrum has published thirty books including the bestselling *Shadows in the Water* and *Dying for a Living* series.

In 2020 Kory began podcasting. In addition to her true crime podcast "Who Killed My Mother?" about her mother's tragic death, she has a second show called "A Well Cared For Human", which focuses on debunking self-care myths and offering strategies for improving mental health and overall well-being.

She also publishes poetry under the name K.B. Marie.

When not writing, podcasting, or indulging in her true calling as a stay-at-home dog mom, she can usually be found under thick blankets with snacks. The kettle is almost always on.

She lives in Michigan with her equally bookish wife, Kim, and their rescue pug, Charley. Learn more about Kory and her work at www.korymshrum.com

Made in the USA
Monee, IL
15 April 2024

56999260R00177